"Do you have any idea why the thieves would be interested only in our Confederate friend's remains?"

Annja frowned. "That's all they took?"

"They were only interested in the skeleton and the documentation pertaining to it that you and Professor Reinhardt assembled. Nothing else was touched, including items of considerable value that were in plain view in Dr. Reinhardt's office."

That put an entirely different spin on things. Breaking and entering to steal museum pieces worth millions was one thing; doing so just to make off with the recently recovered remains of a Confederate captain no one even knew existed was another.

Her thoughts turned immediately to the shadowed figure she'd encountered in the catacombs the night before.

There was more going on here than she'd realized.

Titles in this series:

ROGUE ANGEL

Alex Archer

CRADLE OF SOLITUDE

A GOLD EAGLE BOOK FROM

WORLDWIDE.®

TORONTO • NEW YORK • LONDON
AMSTERDAM • PARIS • SYDNEY • HAMBURG
STOCKHOLM • ATHENS • TOKYO • MILAN
MADRID • WARSAW • BUDAPEST • AUCKLAND

Recycling programs
for this product may
not exist in your area.

First edition November 2011

ISBN-13: 978-0-373-62152-1

CRADLE OF SOLITUDE

Special thanks and acknowledgment to
Joe Nassise for his contribution to this work.

The
LEGEND

...THE ENGLISH COMMANDER TOOK
JOAN'S SWORD AND RAISED IT HIGH.

The broadsword, plain and unadorned,
gleamed in the firelight. He put the tip against
the ground and his foot at the center of the blade.
The broadsword shattered, fragments falling
into the mud. The crowd surged forward,
peasant and soldier, and snatched the shards
from the trampled mud. The commander tossed
the hilt deep into the crowd.
Smoke almost obscured Joan, but she continued
praying till the end, until finally the flames climbed
her body and she sagged against the restraints.

Joan of Arc died that fateful day in France,
but her legend and sword are reborn....

1

Richmond, Virginia
April 2, 1865

The choir had just begun the "Hallelujah" chorus when the door to the church flew open with a bang. Confederate President Jefferson Davis, seated at the front of the church next to his wife, Varina, turned and watched as a man raced down the center aisle toward him.

That he had come from the front lines was obvious; his face and hands were covered with dirt and soot, while his uniform looked as if it hadn't been washed in a month. A bloodstained scrap of bandage encircled his head just below the hairline, but since it didn't seem to slow him, Davis guessed that the wound it covered was at least a few days old. Rank insignia on his uniform indicated the man was a captain, though Davis couldn't remember the man's name.

Reaching him, the soldier leaned against the end of the pew, took a moment to catch his breath and then stammered, "G-G-General Lee's line at Petersburg has broken, sir, and he intends to fall back and evacuate the city immediately."

Shocked murmurs erupted as those within earshot repeated what was said to those around them. Even the Episcopalian minister presiding over the day's worship services came down from his lofty perch on the pulpit to hear the news.

Davis ignored everyone but the messenger.

"How long can Lee hold them, Captain?"

The man shook his head. "Not long, sir. He bid me to urge you to hurry. He can give you a few hours, but expects that the enemy will be inside the city limits by nightfall."

Nightfall. That gave them five, maybe six hours at most. If they were going to get the government out of Richmond, never mind save what was left of the treasury, they had to get started immediately.

"Convey my regards to General Lee and tell him that we will execute our retreat plan. Godspeed, Captain."

As the messenger hurried from the church, Davis turned to his wife and made his apologies. There was no way he could sit through the service now, not with the evacuation of the entire city to plan and carry out in less than half a dozen hours. He caught the eye of his aide-de-camp and the two of them rose and rushed down the aisle.

Time was of the essence and Davis didn't intend to waste any of it.

Fifteen minutes later the president was ensconced with the vice president and several members of his cabinet in the living room of the house on the corner of Twelfth and K streets that served as both the executive mansion and his family residence. An evacuation plan had not been established, for neither Davis nor any of the other members of his administration had foreseen the fall of the city. The rest of the day would be spent trying to correct that oversight. The executive mansion held thousands of documents that might give the Union a leg up in their push to destroy the Confederacy and aides were immediately set to the task of burning as many of them as possible. The vast warehouses of stockpiled supplies also had to be dealt with, for to allow them to fall into Union hands and be used against the very soldiers they had been intended for was completely unacceptable. Orders were given to deal with the problem. Perishable foodstuffs would be given away free of charge until sundown to any who arrived at the warehouses to claim them. The casks of rum and other liquors would be smashed open and poured out in the streets, to keep the public from indulging in a drunken frenzy when they most needed to keep steady heads on their shoulders. But it was the order to burn the tobacco warehouses that pained Davis the most, for the crop inside them represented the future for so many of the citizens he had sworn to protect. Losing their harvest would be devastating.

Of course, it paled in comparison to losing their homes. But at least he would do what he could to see that as many of them escaped ahead of the Union Army as was possible.

Lee was just going to have to hold on.

The night loomed ahead of them, growing more threatening by the minute.

THE TRAIN WAS LATE.

Captain William Parker sat astride his horse near the end of the platform and stared worriedly down the tracks into the darkness. He could hear the Union guns in the distance, shelling Lee's lines, and he knew it wouldn't be long before the order was given for the retreat. The general could only hold out so long and he was already well beyond the time frame he'd given the president. Soon the front would fall, the Confederate troops would retreat through the city streets, and Richmond would fall into Union hands. When that happened, the chances of getting out of the city at all, never mind getting out with their cargo intact, would shrink considerably.

Where the hell is that train?

He turned and looked back at the squad of men he'd commandeered to help him carry out his mission, shaking his head at the sight. With every able-bodied soldier doing their damnedest to keep the Yanks from entering the city limits, he'd been forced to make do with a group of midshipmen off the *Patrick Henry,* the thirteen-hundred-ton side-wheel gunboat he'd converted into a floating school for the Navy. Some of the "men" in his command weren't more than twelve years old!

God help me. How am I supposed to guard the treasury with schoolboys?

Thankfully, the plan was simple enough. A single rail line still stood open between Richmond and Danville. With two trains at their disposal, President Davis and his staff would be on the first one out, with Parker and his special cargo following in the other. Once in Danville, they'd go their separate ways.

Parker had no illusions as to why he and his cargo—about seven hundred thousand dollars worth of gold ingots, gold coins, silver bricks and Mexican silver dollars—were on the second train. If things became difficult farther down the tracks, the unspoken hope was that the Union soldiers would be more interested in the treasure than in securing the president, thereby allowing Davis to evade capture and escape.

It was a good backup plan, made better by the fact that it actually had some hope of success, and Parker approved of it despite the risk to himself and those under his command. The Confederacy might be able to replace the treasury, but it wouldn't recover from the capture of its beloved president.

A glance at his pocket watch told him that it was past eleven. The fact that they'd made it this late in the night without being overrun by the enemy was another of General Lee's miracles. He'd dug in just outside the city and withstood charge after charge, buying them the time they needed, doggedly determined to keep the Yanks off the streets of the capital as long as possible. Lee's predicated deadline of nightfall had come and gone and still the Army of Northern Virginia held out. Parker didn't know how he did it; he was just thankful they had a man like Lee on their side.

But even Lee could not keep it up much longer.

A rumbling sound broke his reverie and he looked up to see the locomotive coming down the tracks toward them, smoke pouring from its stack. His feelings of relief quickly turned to concern, however, when the engine drew closer and he saw the condition of the train.

Getting here hadn't been easy, it seemed. Great dents marred the smooth curve of the boiler and the sides of the cab had been shot full of holes. The roof of the tender had been torn away entirely, most likely the result of a well-placed cannon shot, and the engineer manning the coal shovel had a bloody bandage wrapped around his head and covering one side of his face. The cars beyond hadn't fared much better.

The train had already slowed considerably by the

time it reached Parker and he watched it roll on and continue for a few more yards before coming to a stop with the hiss of brakes and a cloud of steam. No sooner had it done so than Army officers swarmed inside, checking it over. When the okay signal was given the boarding began, starting first with the president and his cabinet, followed by what was left of their staff.

Parker didn't have time to watch the parade, however, for the second train arrived on the heels of the first and he had work to do.

"Quickly now!" he shouted to the boys in his command and they snapped to, unloading the heavy chests from the wagons and carrying them aboard the train, stacking them against the rear wall of the car to which they'd been assigned.

Halfway through the job one of the midshipmen stumbled, dropping the sack he carried and spilling silver coins over the edge of the platform onto the tracks below.

Parker grabbed the boy as he readied himself to climb down and retrieve them.

"No time, son," Parker said. "Some lucky fool will no doubt pick them up, but it's not going to be you or me. Back to work now."

It took them just shy of an hour, but at last all of the cargo was loaded and the rest of the cars were filled with as many of the people fleeing the city as they could possibly pack into them. Parker gave up his seat to another passenger, finding a place on the roof of the car alongside his second in command, Lieutenant Jonathan Sykes, and two midshipmen whose names he couldn't dredge up from memory in his exhausted state.

No sooner had he settled himself onto the roof of the car than the train lurched into motion without warning, the usual whistle being dispensed with so as not to alert the enemy to their escape. The train moved slowly at first, sluggishly pulling away from the platform, and Parker found himself silently urging it on, as if his thoughts could somehow propel the train faster down the tracks.

Refugees lined either side of the tracks, moving forward through the darkness like the wandering tribes of Israel headed for the promised land. Parker was thankful it was too dark to see their faces, for his own despair and dismay were enough for him; he didn't need to witness anyone else's.

As they rolled across the bridge at the city limits, Sykes suddenly shouted, "Look!"

Parker followed his pointing finger back toward Richmond and saw an angry red glow lighting the sky. The thunder of distant explosions reached his ears as the glow grew brighter, spreading across the horizon.

Richmond was aflame.

"Damn Yanks have fired the city!" One of the midshipmen cursed.

Parker knew better, but he didn't bother correcting the young man. Morale was bad enough; the men in his command didn't need to know that the fire was the result of a direct order from the president, designed to ensure that nothing of value would be left for the Union troops to use against them. The warehouses along the waterfront had been full of powder and shot, too much to be moved swiftly, and rather than allowing it to fall into the hands of the enemy, Davis had ordered the entire lot to be set alight.

With the skyline glowing brightly behind him and the enemy's guns echoing in the distance, Parker set his gaze forward and settled in for the ride.

2

It was only one hundred and forty miles from Richmond to Danville but the slow-moving train, overburdened as it was with excess cargo and the need to constantly stop and repair the track in front of it, required the night and most of the day to get there. A light rain was falling as they pulled into the station, but Parker was so tired that he barely even noticed.

The president's party had come and gone by that time, but orders had been given and four wagons were waiting alongside the platform, guarded by a pair of infantrymen. They approached as Parker disembarked and one of the men handed him a folded piece of paper.

The note was from George Trenholm, secretary of the Treasury, ordering Parker to use any and all means necessary to evade the Union troops in the area and see his cargo safely to the old U.S. Mint in Charlotte, North Carolina. It also let Parker know that the Union cavalry had been spotted in the area and that he was to avoid contact wherever and whenever possible.

Parker laughed aloud upon seeing the final order.

What does he think I'm going to do? Stage an attack on General Sheridan's cavalry column with a handful of midshipmen and half a dozen muskets?

The very notion was absurd. Still, these were desperate times and Parker had little doubt there would be some in his position who might just be daring enough to do something like that. Sometimes a bold move at just the right moment...

He shied away from the thought, before he could be tempted. Glory be damned, he told himself. Get the treasury to Charlotte. That's the goal.

But Charlotte was a long way off and the chances of meeting the Union cavalry on the main road seemed pretty high. Sticking to the lesser known byways and backcountry roads would decrease his chances of running into the enemy but it would also slow him down.

Opt for speed and take the main road, praying they didn't run into anything they couldn't handle, or take the slower, surer route and chance arriving too late to do any good with the money they had in their care?

It was a difficult choice and one that needed some thought.

Concerned that a wagon train full of bulging money sacks and wooden chests stamped with the words *Richmond Loan and Trust* would be too tempting a target, Parker sent his men out to scavenge for containers they might use to hide the contents of their true cargo. It took well over two hours to make the switch, but when they were finished the treasure was hidden in barrels and crates that had once held sugar, flour, tea and other consumables. With the lids hammered tight, there was nothing to tell the casual observer that the financial future of the Confederation was contained within.

By the time the wagons were loaded and the men ready to head out, Parker had made his decision.

The money they carried was needed to keep the regiments in the field equipped with enough food, powder and shot to continue operating, never mind being able to pay the men for their service. They'd take the fast road and hope they arrived in time to do some good with the cargo entrusted to them.

They were in decent spirits when they left Danville behind, despite the steady rain. Parker, Sykes and one of the midshipmen, Daniels, were in the lead wagon, while the other men were split evenly among the rest. They kept a tight formation and managed to make decent progress for the first hour, covering nearly ten miles, but then the weather took a turn for the worse. What had started as a light drizzle turned into a downpour, soaking the men to the bone and turning the road into little more than a muddy track. It became difficult to see that the horses pulling each wagon were tied to the back of the one before them, ensuring that none of them fell behind and got lost.

They barely managed another mile during their second hour on the road and Parker was starting to consider where they might find a place to hole up for the rest of the night when they were confronted by several figures who suddenly loomed out of the rain ahead as they rounded a bend in the road.

"Whoa!" Parker cried, and pulled up quickly on the reins, stopping them a few dozen yards apart.

At this distance it was hard to see anything for certain, but Parker thought there were at least a dozen men in the party ahead them. Three or four on horseback, it seemed, and another ten or so on foot.

They weren't significantly outnumbered, which

was good, but given the level of experience of the men under his command, even that wouldn't be too much of a blessing.

He glanced at Sykes. The other man held his musket lightly, the muzzle pointed forward. Not enough to be overtly threatening, but ready to be used if things went south.

Sykes must have sensed his attention, for he turned his head and gave Parker a slight nod, letting him know he was ready for whatever was to come.

He was a good man, Parker thought.

Before Parker could do anything, however, one of the riders ahead kicked his horse into motion. Parker let him close half the distance between them and then shouted, "That's far enough. Identify yourself or my men will open fire!"

The rider pulled his horse up short.

"Easy, Captain," the man called out. "Didn't mean to startle you."

Parker knew the voice, but sheer surprise kept him from responding right away, and while he struggled to find his voice the other man unveiled the lantern in his free hand, letting the light fall upon him.

Even through the downpour Parker recognized the face of their benefactor, secretary of the Treasury, George Trenholm.

Still, Parker was cautious. "Be ready for anything," he told Sykes as he handed over the reigns. "If this looks like a trap, get the wagons out of here as best you're able."

Sykes never took his eyes off the men ahead of them. "You can count on me, sir."

Parker climbed down from the wagon and walked forward to where Secretary Trenholm was waiting for him. As he drew closer the other man dismounted, as well, which helped put Parker at ease.

Trenholm extended his hand and the two men shook.

"Good to see you, Captain. I was starting to think we'd missed you."

"The rain, sir. You know how it gets."

Parker didn't know much about Secretary Trenholm's history, but it seemed a safe bet that the man had never had to lead a wagon train through a torrential downpour. Trenholm came from money, and old money at that.

But war has a way of leveling social classes, Parker knew, and he found it mildly ironic that the two of them were to meet here, in the midst of a muddy track that could barely be called a road, the rain beating down on both their heads with equal abandon.

Oblivious to his subordinate's thoughts, Trenholm went on. "There's been a change of plans, Captain. I'm to escort you to an important meeting where you will receive your new orders. If you would come with me…"

Parker frowned. "My men, sir?"

"About a hundred yards up the road there's a place where they can get off the main thoroughfare and wait for your return. I'll leave several of my own men to stand guard with them. On a night like tonight, I doubt they'll run into any difficulties."

Trenholm was probably right, but that didn't make Parker feel any better about leaving his men in the middle of nowhere, particularly given their level of inexperience. Still, an order was an order.

"Yes, sir. Give me a moment to explain the situation."

He returned to Sykes and let him know what was going on. The young lieutenant wasn't thrilled with the situation, either, but there was very little that they could do about it. Parker ordered him to keep his eyes open and wait for his return.

One of Trenholm's men loaned him a horse and five minutes later they were under way. Trenholm led him a mile or so through the woods on a narrow track that was little better than a game trail really, until they came to a clearing. Parker could see that several campaign tents had been erected there and men in Confederate uniforms were moving about.

Trenholm took him to a larger tent set slightly off from the others and asked him to wait inside.

"Someone will be along shortly to give you further instructions."

Ever the dutiful soldier, Parker complied.

He found the tent was sparsely furnished, with just a pair of camp chairs on either side of a makeshift table made from a few scraps of wood and a blanket-covered cot off to one side. It was warm inside, thanks to a camp stove that was burning in the far corner, and Parker soon found himself literally steaming as the heat sucked the moisture out of his clothes.

He didn't mind. Being out of the rain, even if only for a few minutes, was a welcome relief.

When, after fifteen minutes, no one had yet arrived to deliver his new orders, he dragged one of the camp chairs closer to the stove and sat down.

I'll take a few minutes of rest, that's all, he thought.

He must have dozed off, however, for he came awake with a start when he heard someone enter the tent behind him. He leaped to his feet and spun about.

He didn't know who he expected to see waiting there for him, but President Jefferson Davis himself was not on his list of possibilities.

So surprised was he that for several long moments all he could do was stand and stare. The president didn't seem to notice.

"Thank you for coming so quickly, Captain," he said as he laid the books and papers he was carrying on the desk and hung his coat on the back of the other chair before dragging it closer to the stove. "Please, sit down."

Parker nodded, then found his voice at last as he waited for Davis to sit down before doing so himself. "Thank you, Mr. President."

"Don't thank me yet," Davis said, his expression darkening at some private thought. "Not until you've heard why I've called you here, at any rate."

An aide came in bearing two glasses of brandy on a tray. He gave one to the president, then offered the other to Parker.

Drink in hand, President Davis turned to him and said, "I have a very special assignment for you, Captain."

3

Paris, France
Present day

Annja came out of the dojo's locker room drying her long hair with the towel she kept in her gym bag for just that purpose. She was startled to find a man waiting outside the door for her. He was of medium build, with a short, dark beard, and was dressed in a nicely fitted suit of a deep chocolate brown.

He stepped forward as she approached.

"Excuse me. Miss Creed?"

He had a strong French accent.

"Yes?" she replied.

She searched her memory, but she was pretty sure she didn't know him. Having strangers approach her was nothing new. People often recognized her from *Chasing History's Monsters,* the cable television show she cohosted, but something told her this guy wasn't a fan looking for a quick autograph.

"Please forgive the interruption. I am Commissaire Laroche, of the Police Nationale."

Annja knew the Police Nationale was the main civil law enforcement agency in France. Commissaire was a commissioned officer rank, sort of analogous to a senior detective in the United States. In other words, this guy was a heavy hitter in the local police community. Annja was alarmed. She'd stayed out of trouble while on vacation and hadn't done anything to elicit interest from the police.

This time around, at least.

Seeing he had her attention, Laroche continued. "I'm looking for some assistance with a—how do you say… peculiar? yes?—situation. Your name was given to me by Monsieur Garrison at the embassy."

That, at least, was a name she recognized. She'd met Billy Garrison at a press junket she attended on behalf of the show the last time she'd been in Paris. He was on the ambassador's staff and had taken her to dinner a few nights later, but there hadn't been any spark and she'd declined his offer for a second date.

Being dateless was preferable to listening to Billy ramble on about French politics for hours again. Thanks, but no thanks.

"May I see some identification, Commissaire?"

He bowed slightly, an outdated but courtly gesture. "Of course, Miss Creed. And please, call me Henri."

He handed over a leather case that contained his badge and ID. She glanced at it, confirmed that the man in the picture and the one standing in front of her were one and the same, then handed it back.

"Thank you. One can't be too careful these days…."

"Of course, of course," he replied, waving off her apology.

"So how is Billy?" she asked, more to gauge the inspector's reaction to him than anything else.

He didn't disappoint. "Monsieur Garrison is as long-winded as usual," he replied, giving her a tight smile.

Yep, that was Billy.

"So what's this peculiar situation that you need help with, Henri?" she asked.

Laroche hesitated, glancing over her shoulder as he did so. "Perhaps we might take this outside?" he asked.

When she followed his gaze and found the rest of the dojo's students watching their discussion, Annja readily agreed.

She accompanied him out the door into the bright spring sunshine and fell into step beside him as he walked slowly up the street, explaining as he went.

"For the past several weeks construction teams have been working on the southern line of the Metro, widening the existing tunnels to make room for the new branch that will be added to the system in May."

Annja was aware of the project, for the construction workers with their bright orange reflective vests were a familiar sight on the trains in and out of the area.

Laroche went on. "Late yesterday afternoon the floor gave way beneath a work crew in one of the newly expanded tunnels. Thankfully, only two of the men sustained injuries and in both cases they were minor ones. When the dust cleared the crew discovered that they had fallen into a previously unknown second tunnel, running parallel beneath the first. Further exploration revealed several antechambers just beyond, each one filled with stacks of human bones."

Annja could scarcely believe what she was hearing. A previously undiscovered section of the catacombs? Her heart skipped a beat at the thought.

Prior to the creation of the catacombs in the mid-1700s, the dead of Paris were buried in small cemeteries alongside local churches. But as the city grew, the cemeteries ran out of space. Mass interments became common, often without caskets, and over time this led to the contamination of ground water as the bodies decomposed in the earth.

To deal with the problem, city officials moved to outlaw all burials within the city limits from that point forward. Existing graves were exhumed and the remains were relocated to a series of abandoned limestone quarries that were, at that time, on the outskirts of town. The process of disinterring the bones from their original resting places was carried out with reverence for the dead as well as consideration for the living. The quarry space was blessed, the long trains of carts moving the bones were accompanied by priests and the activity was always conducted at night. No attempt was made to identify or separate the individual bodies, but each set of bones was marked with a plaque indicating the cemetery from which they originated and the year they were moved. By 1860, when the relocation was completed, some five to six million skeletons had been moved to the catacombs.

Eventually, the city expanded and what had once been outside the city limits now lay hidden beneath its streets. Annja knew only a small section of the massive tunnel network was accessible to the public. That left close to two hundred miles of tunnels and caverns extending like a spider's web beneath the city that only a handful of people had ever seen.

"Most of the men on the crew had seen the catacombs at one point or another in their careers so the rooms full of bones were not at all surprising to them,"

Laroche said. "However, the discovery of a fully intact skeleton, partially buried beneath a pile of those older bones, was."

Annja considered that for a moment. "Sounds like a job for the police rather than an archaeologist," she said.

"Ordinarily, I'd agree with you," Laroche replied, "but this particular discovery turned out to be a bit more complex than first thought."

They paused, waited for the light to change, then crossed, continuing walking along the other side of the street.

"When the crime scene unit arrived, it didn't take them long to determine that the job would be better off in the hands of a forensic anthropologist. While arrangements were being made to bring one in, word of the find was also sent to the American Embassy."

Annja was surprised. "The embassy? So your mysterious skeleton is that of an American?"

"In a manner of speaking."

That's like saying you're kind of pregnant, she thought, but when she pressed him on it Laroche wouldn't explain any further.

"I'd rather not prejudice your opinion," he said as they turned left onto another thoroughfare. Caught up in the puzzle he was laying out before her, Annja barely noticed where they where headed.

"What's my opinion got to do with any of this?" she asked.

Laroche smiled. "Because of the nature of the find, it was agreed that a representative from the United States should be present when the skeleton is excavated. Mr. Garrison suggested that you would be ideally suited for the task."

"Is that so?"

Laroche grinned devilishly. "*Oui*. In fact, it sounded like he said something about you preferring the company of the dead over that of the living, but perhaps I misheard him."

He is so going to pay for that one, Annja thought, before realizing that in order to carry out her threat, she'd have to see him again.

Perhaps he wasn't as dim-witted as she'd taken him to be.

Putting the thought aside for the time being, she focused on the opportunity being offered to her. "So are you asking me to get my hands dirty or will this be strictly observational in nature?"

"You can get as dirty as you like, Miss Creed."

"Am I being brought on as an official consultant?" she asked.

Reading between the lines, Laroche said, "The embassy has agreed to cover your costs and to provide a reasonable fee for your time. Monsieur Garrison would not discuss the specific details with me, but stated he would be happy to take your call so he could provide you with the specifics."

So Billy *wasn't* so dim-witted, after all, she thought.

"Well, when do you want to get started?" Annja asked, chuckling to herself.

Laroche slowed, and then stopped. "As a matter of fact, I was hoping you would be free right now."

Startled, Annja glanced around, only then realizing that they were standing in front of a Metro station. A pair of sawhorses stood in front of the entrance, holding a sign noting in French that the station was currently closed for repairs.

This time Annja laughed aloud. "You certainly

know how to show a girl a good time, Henri!" she said. "You've piqued my curiosity and given me an intriguing puzzle to boot. How could I say no?"

"Excellent!" Laroche said.

They descended the stairs and entered the station proper, where Laroche used his badge to get them past the police officer stationed there.

Once past the turnstiles, Annja followed Laroche onto the subway platform and over to the far end, where a selection of equipment was stored under a tarp. The detective removed two lanterns from beneath the cover, turned them both on and passed one to Annja. Then he led her off the platform and onto the track.

The air was cool in the tunnel and Annja was glad she'd had the foresight to grab a sweatshirt when she'd left her hotel that morning. At the moment the change in the temperature felt refreshing after the heat of the bright sun above, but it wouldn't be long before the chill seeped into her bones if they spent any length of time down below.

She was starting to suspect they would.

As if hearing her thoughts, Laroche spoke. "The entrance to the catacombs is several hundred yards ahead. I'm sorry, but there is no alternative but to walk."

Annja smiled at his apologetic tone. "Walking's something an arcaeologist gets used to very quickly. It's no problem at all."

They kept to the center of the track, where the pathway was reasonably clear of debris and the chance of one of them turning an ankle was reduced. Not that the chances of doing so were all that great in the first place; the subways in Paris were far cleaner than those back home in Brooklyn.

Annja had spent much of her professional life clam-

bering around inside crumbling ruins and forgotten old
tunnels, so the weight of all that earth above their heads
didn't bother her in the slightest. The same couldn't be
said about her companion, however. No sooner had they
started down the tunnel than the conversation dried up
and his repeated glances at the roof over their heads
let her know just how uncomfortable he was. Figuring
he'd say something if it got to be too much, Annja kept
her thoughts to herself and simply walked along in his
wake.

They'd been underground for about fifteen minutes
when a faint glow could be seen coming from around
a bend in the tunnel ahead of them. The light grew
brighter as they approached, until, rounding the curve
in the tunnel, Annja could see that it was coming from
a set of portable arc lights that had been erected on
stands near a hole in the tunnel floor. Several people
were milling about, but didn't appear to actually be
doing much of anything.

Waiting for the boss to return, Annja thought.

It turned out she was right. As soon as the group
caught sight of the two of them approaching, they settled down and waited to be told what to do.

"Please wait here for a moment," Laroche said, and
then stepped over to confer with his people. After listening to an update from one of his subordinates, the
detective issued a flurry of orders, sending his people
scurrying off in a variety of directions on several different tasks. Doing so seemed to help him forget the
weight of all that earth above and it was a steadier man
who rejoined her a few moments later.

"I'm told that Professor Reinhardt from the Museum
of Natural History is already waiting for us below. As
the official representative from my country, he will be

in charge of the project, though any actions that impact the remains directly must be approved through you. Will there be a problem with that?"

Annja shook her head. Bernard Reinhardt was an old friend. She'd worked with him on several projects and tried to find time to say hello whenever she was in Paris. His conduct in the field was impeccable; she couldn't have asked for a better partner.

"Let's get to it," she said.

Stepping over to the ladder that extended out of the hole in the tunnel floor, Laroche swung himself onto its rungs and started downward.

Annja gave him a moment, and then followed.

4

Lights had been strung along the ceiling of the tunnel and in their glare Annja could easily see the differences between this tunnel and the one above. It was narrower, for one, with walls of hewn limestone rather than concrete, and with a ceiling that was a good two feet lower than the previous passageway. Where they had been able to walk two abreast with room to spare in the tunnel above, down here they were forced to move single file down the narrow corridor. It was also quiet. Gone were the faint sounds of distant trains rumbling through the walls; the limestone surrounding them seemed to swallow up even the slightest echo, devouring it before it could move more than a few inches from its source.

The most striking difference, however, was the sense of age that filled the rough-hewn walls around them. This tunnel had been around for a long time, that much was obvious, and Annja found herself wondering just what it had seen and been witness to over the years.

"This way," Laroche said as he led her down the tunnel. They'd only walked a dozen or so yards before the opening to a chamber loomed on their left. The string of lights led inside and Laroche and Annja followed them.

Entering the room, Annja stopped short, her eyes widening at what she saw.

The entire chamber was fashioned of bones.

Human bones.

Tibias and femurs by the thousands were stacked neatly side by side, interspersed regularly with rows of skulls, their empty eye sockets staring at her as if in accusation. Here and there the skulls had been arranged in artistic patterns, a cross being the most common. There were no intact skeletons, the goal of the arrangement clearly having been to make the best use of the space available, and Annja could only assume that the rib cages, spines and other bones that would have made up the rest of each skeleton had been used to fill in the spaces behind the larger bones. Most of the stacks rose to a height of about 5 feet and from what she could see they were a few yards deep in some places. To her left was a plaque noting the year the bones had been interred as well as the cemetery from which they had come.

Clearly they had entered the original catacombs.

"Annja!" an exuberant voice cried, pulling her away from her study of the skulls before her. She turned to find her colleague, Professor Bernard Reinhardt, emerging from the chamber just beyond, his hand extended in welcome. The smile on his face was outmatched only by the size of his handlebar mustache, which stretched a good inch past his cheeks on either side.

Reinhardt was a large, portly man in his early sixties, though he had the exuberant energy of a man half his size and age. He'd been known to work right through the night and into the next day while on an important dig, putting most of the graduate students who worked with him to shame. In the narrow confines of the underground passageway he appeared twice as big as usual and Annja found herself having to stifle the urge to back away as he thundered toward her. He was dressed in a thick flannel shirt, jeans and solid pair of hiking boots, a far cry from the three-piece suit, complete with pocket watch and chain, that he liked to wear while at the museum.

Annja had met him several years before while in Paris for a symposium during which he'd delivered a presentation on the Saxon conquest of Normandy. She'd been so impressed with his quick mind and engaging delivery that she'd introduced herself after his talk. Despite the obvious difference in their ages and educational backgrounds, their shared love of European history had turned them into colleagues with genuine respect for each other's specialties.

"Hello, Bernard," she said, ignoring his outstretched hand and giving him a quick hug, which earned her a hearty embrace.

"It is so good to see you, Annja," he said, releasing her. "Have they told you why you are here?"

"Just that they've discovered something of interest to both your government and mine," she replied.

Bernard grinned. "Well, then, if they didn't spoil the surprise, I'm not going to, either. This way, my dear."

He turned and led her through several other chambers, each one similar to the last. The stacks of bones seemed to go on and on; everywhere she looked, the walls were covered with them. Not that Annja was surprised. She'd heard it estimated that there were more than six million skeletons interred down here in the dark.

That's a lot of ghosts, she thought.

Ahead of her, Bernard came to a halt at the entrance to a side chamber.

"Is this it?" she asked.

He nodded, then extended a hand, as if to say, *After you*.

Her lantern held high, Annja entered the chamber.

The room was small, no larger than ten square feet, she estimated, and so it didn't take her long to pick out what she'd been brought there to see.

The skeleton was seated with its back against the wall of the antechamber, its legs stretched out before it. A cavalry saber was gripped in one hand, in the other, a Colt revolver. At first glance both weapons appeared to be in excellent condition. So, too, was the uniform the skeleton wore—wool trousers and a light shirt, both partially covered by a long frock coat that hung to midthigh. The three bars that designated the rank of captain had been sewn onto the coat's collar. A kepi hat was still perched atop the skull where it rested against the back wall.

The dirt and dust that had settled on the remains of the clothing made it difficult to determine the exact color of the uniform, but there was no mistaking the brass emblem of a wreath pinned to the front of the hat. The arms of the wreath rose on either side, surrounding the three letters nestled between them.

CSA.

As she stared at the emblem in surprise, Annja finally understood what Laroche had meant. They weren't questioning that the remains belonged to an American. Not at all. They were questioning his status because the America he'd belonged to no longer existed.

The Confederate States of America.

5

Annja walked over to the skeleton and settled into a crouch before it, her gaze moving slowly and carefully, taking in the details. Behind her, she heard Bernard step into the room.

"Fascinating, isn't it?" he said, his voice hushed, as if in reverence for the dead man before them. "To think he's been down here for a hundred and fifty years, just waiting for someone to come along and find him."

Annja nodded. She was amazed that anyone had done so, frankly. The chances of the construction team finding the adjacent tunnel, never mind following the right series of chambers to wind up here, several hundred yards from the entrance, were astronomical.

"Any idea who he was?" she asked, looking back at her colleague.

Bernard shook his head. "Not a clue. But that's why we're here, my dear, to solve the mystery."

And a mystery it was. Annja couldn't think of a simple reason why a Confederate soldier, a captain no less, would have been wandering around down here in the catacombs miles from any known entrance. Had he simply gotten lost? Stumbled around in the dark, unable to find his way back out, until eventually he'd succumbed to a lack of food or, more likely, water?

If that was the case, what was he doing with a cutlass and pistol in hand? Just who, or what, had he been defending himself against?

An interesting puzzle, to say the least.

And just the kind of thing that Annja lived for.

She reached into the bag at her side and pulled out her digital camera. She rarely went anywhere without it and it was times like this when she was thankful she'd adopted the habit. Eventually, she knew, they were going to have to remove the skeleton from the catacombs and take it back to Bernard's laboratory for proper examination, but there were a lot of things they needed to do before that and documenting the site as they'd found it was the first priority. The position of items in relation to others and the context in which they were found were just as important to an archaeologist as the items themselves. The photographs would help them establish a record of where each item was in relation to all the others, allowing them to reconstruct the site down to the finest detail if necessary as their investigation progressed.

She started by taking several wide-angle shots, panning her way around the room until she had covered it all. They would be able to make a panorama-style shot from the photographs showing the entire room and even use them to create a three-dimensional computer model.

When she was finished with that task, she focused on the skeleton itself. She took several shots to establish its position against the wall, then moved in for close-ups. She'd taken about a dozen pictures and was about to call it quits when the light from the flash bounced off the uniform the skeleton wore and highlighted something she hadn't previously noticed.

Bernard must have seen her sudden tension.

"What have you got, Annja?" he asked as she leaned in closer to get a better look.

"Not sure yet," she murmured, her gaze on the skeleton in front of her.

As the flesh beneath it had decayed, the uniform coat had folded down upon itself, hiding small stretches of fabric between the folds. The light from the flash had thrown back an oddly shaped shadow from one of them, suggesting that there was something else there. Annja withdrew a pen from her pocket and gently lifted the edge of the folded material, revealing what lay beneath.

The blackened edges of a bullet hole stared back at her.

Gently, Annja used her pen to lift the coat's edge away from the shirt beneath. The dark stain that covered the yellowed linen shirt beneath answered one question that had been nagging at her.

The soldier, whoever he was, hadn't wandered down here, gotten lost and eventually died of thirst, as she'd first hypothesized.

He'd been shot in the chest.

And from the looks of it, he'd died pretty quickly thereafter.

This hadn't been an accident; it was murder.

Bernard crouched beside her and she showed him what she found.

"See the rounded edges of the bullet hole?" she asked, pointing with the end of the pen. "And the way the fabric is still intact all around it, rather than stretched or torn?"

Bernard nodded. "The musket ball was moving so fast that it didn't have time to do much damage to the material as it passed through. Must have been close range, then."

"Just what I was thinking, as well."

She sat back on her haunches and stared at the dead man in front of her. "He wasn't here by accident. We're too far away from any easily accessible entrance for that to be the case. He came here deliberately, perhaps to meet someone…"

"And whoever it was gunned him down where he stood," Bernard finished for her.

"It's no longer an interesting archaeological puzzle," Annja said as she climbed to her feet. "Now it's a homicide investigation."

The police, however, wanted nothing to do with such an old murder. After a few quick calls back to headquarters, Laroche approached and informed Annja and Bernard that they were still in charge of the investigation, that their skills were going to be more valuable in terms of identifying the victim and perhaps even his murderer than anything the police could bring to bear on the problem.

Homicide or not, it was their problem to solve.

Several technicians from the museum arrived, summoned earlier by Bernard when he'd realized what it was they were dealing with. The technicians had a portable specimen case with them, essentially a long, flat box that looked like the case for an electric keyboard, and carried several toolkits of different shapes and sizes. Annja stepped out of the way to give them room to work in the narrow confines of the antechamber.

One of the technicians withdrew a video camera from the case he carried and, switching on the high-powered light attached to it, began to pan his way around the entire room in unwitting mimicry of what she had done earlier with the still camera.

When he was finished, he nodded at one of the other team members, who opened another case and began assembling an odd-looking device from the parts inside.

Annja was expecting the skeletal removal to be a long, drawn-out process of removing each bone piece by piece and then placing them into the specimen case, so she was surprised when the man she was watching picked up the device he'd been assembling and moved over to stand next to the skeleton. The device looked like a fire extinguisher, though the canister was blue rather than red, and the operator wore it hanging from his shoulder on a strap. The other end of the hose running out of the top of the cylinder was attached to a gunlike device in his right hand. He turned and aimed the gun at the skeleton.

"Hey! Wait a min—"

She didn't get any further. The technician squeezed the trigger and began spraying a fine white mist over their mystery man. The mist settled on the skeleton for a moment and then ballooned up into a white foamlike substance that hardened in seconds. Less than five minutes later the entire skeleton was wrapped in a cocoon of hardened foam.

Annja turned to Bernard and asked, "What, exactly, is that stuff?"

The older man smiled. "Do you like it? It's a new tool my staff and I have come up with in order to transport delicate artifacts."

He stepped over to the skeleton. "The foam is genetically engineered and completely biodegradable. Flash a UV light on it and it fades away to literally nothing.

But in the meantime——" he reached down and rapped on the foam with his knuckles "——knock, knock, it's as hard as steel."

Something that hard must weigh a ton, Annja thought.

"How are you going to move it?"

Bernard eyed the cocooned skeleton with something like genuine affection. "That's the beautiful part. It's light as a feather."

It was, too. With one technician at the feet and another at the head, the skeleton was gently lifted off the ground and placed inside the specimen box with barely an effort.

"Will wonders never cease?"

She was impressed. That foam could have saved her hundreds of hours of effort on earlier digs.

"How long have you been using it?"

Bernard's expression went sheepish and he mumbled something under his breath.

"I'm sorry, I didn't catch that," Annja said.

"That was our, um, first field test."

If he hadn't been on the other side of the specimen case, she would have throttled him where he stood. As it was she had to settle for giving him her best glare and vowing to make him pay for using one of her digs as his guinea pig.

They closed up the specimen case and, with one person on either end, carefully lifted it up and carried it out of the room. It wasn't heavy, but the close confines of the tunnel made it awkward and they took turns carrying it back out to where the catacombs intersected the Metro line. Bernard spent a few minutes talking with Laroche before returning to Annja's side.

"Help will be here shortly," he told her.

Ten minutes later a pair of Metro workers arrived, pushing a small handcart along the subway tracks. The newcomers showed one of the museum techs how to operate the cart, the specimen box was loaded on it and, as a group, they set off on the last leg of the walk back to the surface.

As they emerged from the steps leading to the underground, they found a small crowd had gathered around the station entrance, attracted by the museum van that was parked haphazardly on the curb. A few people pointed in her direction and more than one began taking pictures with their cell phones.

As she glanced away, Annja thought, *These are not the droids you are looking for. Move along.* The memory brought a smile to her face.

Bernard must have noticed, for he asked, "What's so funny?"

Trying to explain *Star Wars* humor to a French archaeologist was an exercise in futility so she just shook her head. Thankfully, Bernard let it go, as he was needed to help get the specimen case properly situated into the rack designed to hold it inside the van. Annja glanced once more at the crowd nearby, wondered just what it was that had drawn them and then climbed into the front seat to wait for the others to finish.

A DARK-HAIRED MAN in his mid-forties, dressed in blue jeans and a hooded sweatshirt, glanced at the picture he'd just taken with his cell phone from across the street. He grunted in satisfaction. It wasn't the best image, but it was good enough. The woman's companion, Professor Bernard Reinhardt, was well known to them, but she was a mystery. The photo would help them identify her and from there they could assess just what kind of threat she posed to their plans.

Satisfied, he sent the image as part of a text message, dropped his phone into his pocket and started walking down the street.

He hadn't gone more than a few blocks before the phone rang in response.

"Michaels," he said, answering it.

The voice on the other end was younger, full of cockiness. "Next time give me something difficult, will ya? Her name's Annja Creed. She entered France on the fourteenth with an American passport."

American? Interesting, Michaels thought.

"What's she doing in Paris?"

"She's the host of a cable television show that features monsters, myths and legends entitled, appropriately enough, *Chasing History's Monsters*."

Myths and legends. Michaels didn't like the sound of that. Their contact in the police department had tipped them off that Reinhardt had been called in to examine something discovered during the excavation of the new Metro line. That had brought Michaels down there this morning. His organization had protected certain secrets for generations and any new find, particularly in this area, raised the possibility that some of those secrets might be exposed. He couldn't allow that to happen.

He hadn't been concerned at first. They received tips like this at least a handful of times per month and the majority of them led to nothing. Normally he would have sent one of his men to check it out, but he'd been in the area when the call had come in and had decided to deal with it personally. If nothing else, it gave him a chance to stretch his legs and enjoy the change in the weather.

But then he'd seen the crowd that had gathered and watched as the crew removed a large specimen case from the tunnels below and his disinterest changed to concern. A fateful meeting had taken place in this area more than a hundred years before and it wouldn't bode well for certain people if the facts of that meeting came to light. It was his job to prevent that from happening.

The presence of the American television host certainly had the potential for complicating matters.

"Is she here representing the network?" he asked the man on the other end of the phone.

There was a pause. "I'm not sure yet."

Michaels didn't like uncertainties; they tended to create problems later on down the line. His silence must have adequately conveyed his displeasure, for the other man quickly amended his statement.

"I'm working on it, though. I should have an answer shortly."

"Good. And her relationship with Reinhardt?"

"I'll have that for you shortly, as well."

"Next time, call me when you actually know something."

Ending the call, Michaels slipped the phone back in his pocket and continued down the street to where a black Mercedes waited for him at the curb. As the driver started to get out to open the door for him, Michaels waved him off, climbed in the backseat on his own and then instructed the other man to take him back to the office.

Without a word the driver slid the big car into traffic smoothly and headed off. As they cruised past the van from the museum, Michaels could see the Creed woman sitting in the front seat, seemingly lost in thought while waiting for the rest of the team to finish loading the equipment in the back.

It would be a shame to have to mess up that pretty face, he thought as they drove away.

6

After unloading the specimen case from the van, Dr. Reinhardt had his students carry it downstairs to one of the basement labs. There, he and Annja lost no time getting to work.

They transferred the foam-wrapped skeleton to the top of the long examination table in the center of the lab. Because the skeleton had been in a seated position when it was encased in the foam, they placed a board behind its back for support. Next it was photographed and filmed, just as it had been down in the tunnels. The images would later be combined with the earlier ones to help establish the chain of control over the artifact throughout the examination process. For now, though, Annja took over filming with the video camera as Bernard plugged in a portable UV lamp and prepared to remove the protective foam from the skeleton.

"Ready?" he asked, his fingers poised over the lamp's power switch.

Annja nodded. She knew she didn't need to remind

him how angry she'd be if the foam had damaged the bones in any way.

She thought about the captain. That's how she was thinking of him now. She didn't know who he was yet, but she hoped to uncover his identity in the process of their investigation. She wanted to put a name and maybe even a face to the remains. In the meantime, the title would remind everyone that this had once been a living, breathing person and therefore deserved their respect.

Bernard hit the switch on the lamp and it began humming slightly.

For a few minutes the sound was the only outward evidence that the device was even working. The light it emitted was not visible to the human eye, but eventually the foam began to bubble and break down. It reminded Annja of the head atop a soft drink after being dispensed from a soda fountain.

As the foam broke down, Bernard gently lowered the inclined backboard, inch by inch, until the skeleton rested flat on the examination table, the bones still arranged mostly in the same position in which they'd been discovered.

That's pretty damn slick, Annja admitted to herself.

Bernard was obviously thinking the same thing, for he threw a huge grin in her direction. It was as if the foam had never existed.

Very carefully, they began separating the bones from the clothing. Each one was carefully measured and then photographed from multiple angles before being placed on another lab table for Bernard to examine more carefully. While he did that, Annja turned her attention to the clothing.

She started with the heavy jacket that had been worn over the uniform. Known as a regimental sack coat, it had a stand-up collar and six CSA buttons running down the front. It was made of wool and had held up pretty well in the cool atmosphere and low humidity of the catacombs. She had no doubt it had once been dyed gray, but the vegetable dye that was used in those days tended to break down quickly and the coat looked more brown than gray at this point.

The blood from the chest wound that had killed their subject had stained the inside of the coat and sealed the lip of the interior pocket closed. When she carefully pried it open, she discovered an envelope inside.

Annja felt her heart starting to beat faster.

Picking up a pair of rubber-tipped tweezers from the selection of tools on the table beside her, she gently inched the envelope out and placed it on a nearby light box where she could examine it in more detail.

"I've got something here, Bernard," she said, and waited for her partner to join her before continuing.

They took multiple photographs to document the specimen. Then, with Bernard's help, Annja carefully opened the envelope and withdrew the single sheet of paper it contained.

The paper was yellow and brittle with age. Worried that even the slightest pressure might cause an unwanted tear, Annja took her time, unfolding each section using the tweezers. When she had the page lying flat on the light board, she laid a piece of clear laminate over the top, much like the cover on a microscope slide. The laminate would allow her to view the paper clearly, without worrying about accidentally damaging the surface of the letter itself. She breathed a sigh of relief once it was in place.

With the protective cover in place, Annja clamped it

down on each corner and then flipped the switch that activated the light board.

When illuminated from below, the ink appeared in sharp contrast to the faded surface of the paper, making it easier to see.

It was a letter.

Annja skimmed through the text, her eyes widening with each line. Upon reaching the signature she gasped in surprise. She heard Bernard whisper, *"Mon Dieu,"* mere seconds later.

The letter identified the bearer as Captain William Parker, Confederate Navy, and assured the recipient that not only did the captain have the letter writer's complete confidence but that he was also empowered to act on his behalf with respect to an agreement involving mutual support and satisfaction.

The letter wasn't addressed to anyone in particular and Annja puzzled over that for a moment until she realized that it had apparently been intended to be hand-delivered to its recipient. That was unfortunate, because knowing who the recipient was might have allowed them to trace things back in the other direction and gain some insight on what Parker, if that was indeed who it was, had been doing in the catacombs.

There was no doubt about where the letter had originated, however, for it had been signed in a thin, spidery script.

Jefferson Davis
President
Confederate States of America

Bernard broke the stunned silence first.

"What was a naval captain bearing a letter of introduction from the president of the Confederate States of America doing in the Paris catacombs?"

Annja shook her head. "I haven't got a clue, but I promise you this—we're going to find out!" she said excitedly.

She got up from the examination table and headed over to where she'd set up her laptop computer on a nearby desk. Firing up the web browser, she went to Google and typed *Captain William Parker, Confederate Navy* into the search bar.

The search produced more than a million hits.

The first one on the list was a short biography from the Naval Historical Center created by the U.S. Department of the Navy. She read parts of it aloud to Bernard, who was using a magnifying glass to examine the letter in more detail.

"Born in New York in 1826…graduated from the Naval Academy and served aboard the *Yorktown* off the coast of Africa…promoted to lieutenant in 1855."

She jumped ahead a few lines, focusing in on his wartime service.

"Abandoned the North for the South in 1861 by joining the Confederate Navy. Commanded the gunboat *Beaufort* during the battle of Roanoke Island in 1862 and also saw action at Hampton Roads and Drewry's Bluff that same year. In October of 1863 he was promoted to captain and took command of the Confederate Naval Academy, situated aboard the steamboat *Patrick Henry* in Richmond."

So far, nothing really unusual, Annja thought. As commander of the Naval Academy, Parker might have had some interaction with the members of the president's cabinet. But there was nothing that indicated he would have moved in the same social or political circles as the president himself.

Annja kept reading.

"After the war he served as captain of a Pacific mail steamship, was president of Maryland Agricultural College for a time, and even took a post as minister to Korea. He died in Washington in 1896.

"He's best known for his role in guarding the Confederate treasury during the evacuation of Richmond following Lee's defeat at Chancellorsville and rumors still persist about his involvement in the disappearance of the treasure."

"What do you mean disappearance?" Bernard asked.

Annja was already typing *Lost Confederate Treasure* into Google. This time there were about three hundred thousand hits and she quickly skimmed through several articles to get a sense of the story.

"Apparently Captain Parker was given the difficult job of getting what was left of the Confederate treasury out of Richmond ahead of the invading Union troops. Like President Davis and his cabinet, the treasury made it out of the city aboard one of the last few trains headed for Danville. Once in Danville, the treasure was loaded onto a wagon train, which then set out under Parker's command, headed for the old U.S. Mint in Charleston. Apparently it never made it. The treasury, all seven hundred thousand dollars of it, disappeared en route."

Bernard frowned. "Treasure or no treasure, it would seem we're no further along than we were before finding the letter because there's no way that man—" he pointed over at the skeleton "—can be Captain Parker if what you're saying is correct."

Annja agreed. The letter must have been stolen or given to someone else, an aide perhaps, in order to prevent Parker from falling into just the kind of situation that had killed their subject.

Unless...

She stared at the floor, thinking it through.

When she didn't say anything for a few minutes, Bernard gently shook her arm.

"What is it?" he asked.

She shrugged. "It's nothing, really—a hunch, just a long shot...."

But Bernard knew that look and wouldn't let her off without an explanation. "Out with it. What are you thinking?"

"All right. This is totally off the wall, I know," she said, "but what if you're wrong? What if that really is Captain Parker?"

Her colleague's frown grew deeper. "But how is that possible? Given what you just read to me, I'd say he had a rather public face after the war."

That was true, but something about the idea nagged at her and she wasn't ready yet to let it go.

"I don't know," she told him. "Maybe he was charged with carrying out some kind of secret negotiation for the president and someone else took his place. Decoys were often used. When the war ended, and Parker didn't come back, the impostor had to keep impersonating him to keep the secret from getting out."

Bernard laughed at the idea even as he walked back to his station, and after a moment, Annja couldn't help but laugh along with him.

It sounded crazy, even to her. After all, the simplest explanation to any problem was often the correct one, to paraphrase the principle behind Occam's Razor. In this case, it was far simpler to believe the letter was either

a forgery or, if it *was* authentic, that it had been stolen from Parker at some point near the end of the war.

And yet...

It would be a much more interesting story if my theory was right, she thought.

Crazy or not, there was one thing she could do to
begin getting at the truth, at least.

Pulling her cell phone out of her pocket, she hit the
speed dial and waited for the phone to be answered
thirty-six hundred miles away in New York City.

"Doug Morrell's office."

"Hi, Doug, it's Annja."

Doug Morrell was her producer on *Chasing History's
Monsters*. He was younger than Annja, more than a bit
self-involved and had little to no actual knowledge of
historical events prior to the previous decade, but had
somehow managed to land his current position regardless of that fact. It probably had to do with his uncanny
knack for capitalizing on historical issues and turning
them into the kind of television fodder fans of the show
ate like candy.

He could be highly annoying, but he had also covered her back on more than one occasion. In an odd
way, Annja counted him as one of her friends.

"Who do we know at the Smithsonian?" she asked
him.

"What's this *we* stuff? Apparently you don't know
anyone. Otherwise, you wouldn't be calling me."

Annja had a lot of contacts at the Smithsonian but
she'd called on so many people for favors over the years,
and knew she'd probably need more in the future, so
she wanted to use the show's contacts if at all possible.
Besides, this discovery was of historical significance

and had nothing to do with the unusual adventures she was constantly being drawn into.

"I meant *we* as in we the show, not as in you and me," she told Doug.

"Of course you did. But since you, meaning you, yourself and, well, just you don't know anyone at the Smithsonian and, miracle upon miracles, I do, this would seem to be an ideal time for me to extract some payment for all the phenomenal episodes I've been forced to squelch thanks to your lack of interest and participation."

He can't be serious, she thought.

She needed him to focus, and that meant she had to nip this in the bud right away.

"Trust me, Doug," she said, "no one would have bought the amphibious chupacabra episode. Those injuries were from jellyfish stings, plain and simple."

"That's funny. I seem to remember your area of expertise was Renaissance history, not marine wildlife. Or at least it was, last time I checked."

"It doesn't take an expert to know that was a stupid idea, Doug."

"Right. Next you'll be telling me that you don't like the ghost shark idea, either."

She didn't have to respond to that one; her silence said it all.

"Oh," Doug replied, indignant. "So that's how it's going to be, is it?"

Apparently he'd woken up on the wrong side of the bed that morning. Sighing, Annja said, "Look, Doug, we both know that—"

The dial tone pulsed in her ear.

She pulled the phone away, shook it and listened again.

He'd hung up on her!

"Why that little...jerk!"

Ignoring Bernard's chuckles from the other side of the room, Annja hit the redial button.

"Doug Morrell's office."

"You hung up on me!"

"See that? I knew there was a reason we paid you to host the show. You're remarkably observant."

Honey not vinegar, Annja, honey not vinegar, she told herself.

She tried a different approach.

"I'm sorry, Doug. I'd be happy to discuss the ghost shark episode with you when I get back to the States," she told him, ignoring the fresh round of chuckling that erupted from the other side of the room.

"I want a favor."

"What?"

"I'd be happy to put you in touch with my contact at the Smithsonian, but it's going to cost you a favor."

I know I'm going to regret this, she thought. She sighed. "What is it?"

"Oh, no. I don't mean right now. Just sometime in the future. You'll owe me a favor, that's all. Deal?"

"Owe you a favor? Are you out of your mind?"

"It was good talking with you, Annja. Enjoy the rest of your vacation and I'll—"

"Fine," she said, biting off her anger along with the end of the word. She knew she shouldn't have laughed at the chupacabra thing but owing Doug a favor? No good could possibly come of this.

"What do we need the Smithsonian to do for us?" Doug asked.

Gritting her teeth, she said, "I need to have a letter authenticated."

"Why didn't you just call them up and ask yourself? It shouldn't take more than a few months."

Annja was shaking her head. "It's not that simple, Doug. I'm helping the French police with an investigation in the catacombs—"

"Whaaat? The catacombs? You're running an investigation in the catacombs and you didn't tell me? I'll send a crew over immediately."

"It's not like that, Doug. There's nothing here of interest to the show. The authorities stumbled on the skeleton of a man in a Civil War uniform and—"

He interrupted her again. "Wait, I thought the catacombs were full of skeletons. What difference does it make that they found one in a French uniform?"

"The American Civil War, Doug, not the French. The French didn't have a civil war."

How he managed to run a show about historical subjects with such a limited view of world history constantly astounded her, but he took her correction in stride, seemingly without a second thought.

"American, okay, got it. Union or Confederate uniform?"

"Confederate. But that's really beside the point."

He didn't seem to hear her. "This is good, Annja, real good. We can turn this into a world-class episode, just leave it to me."

Knowing Doug, he'd find a way to suggest that the Paris catacombs were full of Civil War zombies, getting ready for the second rise of the South. Leaving it to him was the last thing she intended to do.

"Doug, we're not doing an episode on this. I just need the letter authenticated."

"Who's it from?"

"The letter?"

"Yes, of course the letter. Try to keep up, Annja."

I swear, one of these days I'm going to run him through with my sword, she thought.

"Jefferson Davis."

"Confederate President Jefferson Davis?"

Maybe he did know something about history, after all. Either that or he was quick with Wikipedia.

"The one and the same."

There was silence for a moment.

"Annja?"

"Yes, Doug?"

"Let me be sure I've got this straight. You discovered a skeleton, dressed in the uniform of a Confederate soldier, carrying a letter from President Davis, in the midst of the Paris catacombs and you don't think there's anything of interest there for the show?"

Annja had to admit he had a good point.

In the end, Doug agreed he would use whatever cachet the show had to get someone at the Smithsonian to examine the letter as quickly as possible. In return, she agreed to send over a copy of the video footage they'd taken to date so that it could be cleaned up and potentially used in an episode about discovering the skeleton at a later date.

Once that was settled, they agreed to check in with each other if anything significant developed and ended the call.

Not thirty seconds after getting off the phone, Annja realized that she probably could have just called up the embassy and asked Billy Garrison to get it done for her, given that she was officially working on a government matter, anyway.

But that would, of course, require talking to him and he'd have wanted to get together to discuss the situation in more detail, say, over dinner and drinks, and she'd have felt obligated to do so in order to get the letter properly authenticated and…no. Doug was the better option.

Owing Doug a favor couldn't be all that bad, could it?

After a moment, she decided that, yes, it could be all that bad. Doug was the guy who had once asked her to pretend to be dead for a few weeks to milk the sales of the commemorative DVD set he'd put out when she'd been incorrectly reported dead.

Dutifully ignoring Bernard's chuckles, Annja got back to work.

7

After examining the sack coat, Annja turned her attention to the pistol and sword Parker had been holding when he'd died.

The gun was a single action revolver, which she recognized as a Colt 1851 Navy Revolver from the engraving of a naval battle on the cylinder. The gun had been popular at the time of the Civil War. Her research told her that famous Navy Revolver users included Wild Bill Hickok, "Doc" Holliday and General Robert E. Lee.

Drawing back the hammer, she discovered that three of the six chambers still held percussion caps, indicating that they were loaded and ready to fire.

Apparently Parker's enemy hadn't been the only one who'd gotten a shot off at the fateful meeting, she thought.

She emptied the revolver, carefully storing the percussion caps, bullets and powder in separate vials, eliminating the chance of an accident while she examined the weapon.

When she was finished with the revolver she turned

her attention to the sword. Since she'd miraculously inherited Joan of Arc's famous sword, bladed weapons had become a passion for Annja and she immediately recognized this one as a Shelby cavalry sabre, named after General Joseph O. Shelby, leader of the Iron Brigade. When the Confederacy fell, Shelby, one of the few Confederate generals who had never been defeated in combat by Union troops, took his entire command to Mexico rather than surrender. The cavalry sword he'd carried throughout the war, a common enough model produced by the Ames sword company, was renamed in his honor after the war.

The blade was about forty inches in length and bore the CSA, or Confederate States of America, inscription, as did the brass guard. The grip was leather, wrapped with twisted brass wire. The entire weapon seemed to be in excellent shape and Annja gave it a few experimental swings through the air to get the sense of it. It was well-balanced, though shorter and lighter than the weapon she was used to using.

Putting the weapon back down on the examination table, she moved over to the rest of Parker's clothing.

He'd been wearing leather cavalry boots rather than the usual leather brogans, but Annja wasn't surprised by this, as Confederate footwear had been notoriously bad. The boots were in fairly good shape, but didn't tell her anything new about their owner. The same was true for the regulation trousers that she examined next.

The shirt was a bit more interesting, if only because it held the evidence of the gunshot that had ended Parker's life. There was a bullet hole in the front of the shirt, just to the left of the sternum, but no corresponding hole on the back. This meant the bullet hadn't passed completely through his body, as she might have expected at such close range, but had remained lodged somewhere inside his chest. It was a good reminder that modern weapons were far more powerful than those of a hundred years ago and she told herself to keep that in mind as she examined the evidence of Parker's demise.

Annja wished they had the bullet to examine, as it might have been able to tell them something about the gun that had been used. That could have narrowed their avenues of inquiry a bit, but she'd been unable to find it among Parker's remains.

It's probably on the floor of the antechamber. Maybe I'll go back and try to find it later, she thought.

Annja was about to put the shirt aside when she noticed an odd double stitch along one of the seams. She ran her fingers over the cloth at that point and felt something there, just beneath the surface.

It was small, no more than an inch long and less than a quarter-inch thick, and it hadn't gotten there by accident. Whatever it was, someone had taken a bit of trouble to hide it inside the seam of the shirt.

"I think I've got something," Annja said, and when Bernard came back over to her station as he had done before, she showed him what she had found. They both agreed that it merited further investigation. They photographed the shirt from a variety of angles, wanting to preserve a record of its condition before they altered it in any way, and then they x-rayed it, as well. The latter was inconclusive, however; it showed the object and confirmed its rectangular shape, but it didn't provide any information as to what it might be.

They were going to have to take a look for themselves.

Scalpel in hand, Annja carefully cut each of the threads that held the seam closed and then, using the

flat of the blade, she lifted the edge of the cloth, revealing what was hidden inside—a folded piece of paper.
Annja held the pocket of cloth open with the scalpel
while Bernard used a pair of tweezers to tease the paper
free of its hiding place and move it onto its own examination plate.

With the aid of a low-power magnifying glass Annja
could see that two edges of the paper were evenly cut,
while the others were ragged, indicating it had been
torn from a larger source.

A few words had been written on the small slip of
paper in a hurried scrawl. Using the magnifying glass,
Annja read them aloud.

"Berceau de solitude."

Annja didn't need Bernard to translate. She knew the
words were *Cradle of Solitude,* but she hoped he might
have some insight on what it meant, because she didn't
have a clue.

"Only place I know by that name is a monastery in
the Pyrenees," he told her.

"A monastery? Can you think of any reason it might
be connected to our mysterious friend here?" she asked.

"Not particularly. If memory serves, it started out
as a convent in the early 1500s, was abandoned about
a hundred years later and then was bought by a sect of
Benedictine monks just before the French Revolution.
They've been running the place ever since."

Benedictine monks. She couldn't think of any obvious connection between the religious order and the
Confederacy, but it wasn't her area of expertise. Still,
there had to be a connection, for no one went through
the kind of trouble Parker had to hide a piece of paper
if it wasn't important.

The monastery was the key to this mystery.

She was sure of it.

"Is it far from here?"

Bernard shrugged. "Four, maybe four and a half hours by car. There's a train that runs in that direction, as well, but you'd have to find transportation up the mountain. Not much sense in going, though."

"And why's that?"

"It's closed to the public. Outside visitors have to be approved in advance by the abbot and the process takes several months. I spent some time there a few years ago examining one of the books they have in their library and I remember the process being an absolute nightmare to get through."

"So you've met the abbot?"

"The abbot , hmmm. Abbot Deschanel. Yes, I have. A charming man, actually."

"Would he remember you?"

"I should think so," Bernard told her. "We spent several evenings discussing a variety of topics over a glass of wine or two and I..." He paused, finally putting two and two together. "Oh, no."

Annja smiled at him sweetly. "What?"

"You want me to call over there and try to get you in to see the abbott without going through the standard process."

"You'd do that for me?" she replied, letting her eyes go wide and feigning innocent surprise.

Bernard laughed. "I'm supposed to believe that the idea never even occurred to you, right?"

"You can believe what you want. But now that you've brought it up I think it's an excellent idea."

"It's been more than a hundred years, Annja. What do you expect to find?"

She shrugged. "I don't have any idea. But I'm sure

something will occur to me once I'm there. There has to be a reason that Parker went through all the trouble of hiding the name of the monastery inside the seam of his shirt. That doesn't just happen by accident."

Bernard considered that statement. "You think he knew he was going to run into trouble," he said slowly, thinking it through, "and he took precautions in case he did?"

"I do. And I think somewhere in that monastery is the answer to just what kind of trouble he was expecting. If we know that, we might be able to figure out just what he was doing here in France in the first place. Isn't that the point of all this?"

She knew she was stretching things a bit. The authorities hadn't been all that clear on exactly what they wanted her and Bernard to do. Identify the body if at all possible, sure, but given the state of the skeleton they probably didn't expect them to have all that much success. Turning the skeleton over to the museum had pretty much achieved what the police had most likely wanted to achieve, which was passing the buck on to someone else. Now that the skeleton wasn't in the catacombs and potentially slowing down the construction of the Metro tunnel, the details really weren't all that significant to the police.

But they were to Annja. Now that she was involved, she was determined to find out all she could about Captain Parker's fate, if indeed the skeleton really was his.

She thought it was. Regardless of how outlandish the idea sounded when said aloud, at this point she was all but convinced that she was right. She wasn't sure why she felt that way, as the evidence was scant at best, but something deep inside rang true at the thought. That meant tracking down what had actually happened to him might possibly lead them to the missing Confederate treasure, as well.

And *that* was definitely a prize worth pursuing.

In order to do that, she had to get inside the monastery.

"So you'll do it?" she asked.

Bernard, however, wasn't convinced. "I'll give it some thought," he said.

Deciding she wasn't going to get any more out of him at this juncture, Annja let the matter rest for the time being. She'd hit him up again before leaving that afternoon once he'd had a chance to think it over.

In the meantime, she had a lot of work to do.

8

About the time that Annja was examining the sword, Blaine Michaels, a direct descendant of the man who had fired the shot that had taken Captain Parker's life, received a phone call at home from the same computer technician he'd spoken to earlier that afternoon.

The information he received was more complete this time around, outlining what had happened in the tunnels earlier that morning.

"You're certain that they said the skeleton came from inside the catacombs and not the Metro tunnel itself?"

"Yes, sir."

Michaels grunted, most decidedly not thrilled with those circumstances.

"And the Creed woman?"

"Because the skeleton was dressed in the uniform of a U.S. soldier, the police contacted the embassy and asked to have a representative present. Apparently the Creed woman was suggested by someone on the ambassador's staff and was brought in to represent their interests."

He didn't bother to correct the misinformation in his subordinate's report; he had better things to do with his time than explain the difference between the Confederate States and the United States. It was the fact that they had discovered the body at all that had him on edge.

He didn't exactly know why. After all, the body had been down there in the dark for more than a hundred years. There was nothing that could tie his family or the organization as a whole to the crime, if it could even be called a crime at this point, and there was little enough to be done even if they could.

Relax, he told himself.

But no matter how hard he tried, he couldn't. After struggling against it for some time, he got up and made his way to his study. Locking the door behind him, he moved over to the safe, knelt in front of it and dialed the combination lock. Opening the door, he reached deep into the back, past the stacks of cash and bearer bonds, and took out his great-grandfather's journal.

The old man had recorded the events of the night in question in considerable detail, just as he'd been taught to do. As the current head of the society, Blaine had done the same thing himself many times, making note of the steps he'd taken and the motivations behind them so that the one who followed in his footsteps—his son, most likely—would understand how those actions fit into the society's long-term plans.

He wasn't troubled by what had happened that day, at least with regard to the actions the society had taken. Anyone who crossed them would meet a similar fate. No, what was troubling were the goals they'd failed to meet—namely, determining where the traitor had hidden the treasure promised to them. His great-grandfather had been unable to force the information from the traitor before killing him and all of their searches to date had ended with nothing to show for them.

Blaine Michaels had been haunted all his life by his great-grandfather's failure. Those in the society had long memories and there had been considerable opposition to his rise to power as the group's current leader, but he'd been determined to win back the position of power his great-grandfather had forfeited in the face of his failure.

More importantly, he was determined not to let history repeat itself.

And that, he realized, was the source of his unease.

He couldn't seem to shake the feeling that there was something they had missed that night, something that might have provided the clue they needed to figure out just where the treasure had been hidden.

Blaine knew that the original meeting had quickly devolved into an argument, which in turn led to violence. A running gun battle through the catacombs had ended with both men wounded, the traitor mortally so. Time had been of the essence in getting his great-grandfather to safety. Afterward, there was confusion about where, exactly, the traitor's body had been left behind and the searches that followed had been unable to locate it in the hundreds of miles of twisting tunnels beneath the Paris streets. Eventually, his great-grandfather had been forced to step down from the position of leadership and the incident had been swept under the rug as a total failure.

But now, it seemed, there was a chance to correct the errors of the past. If the body held information that might lead them to the missing treasure, then he couldn't afford to pass up the chance to find it.

Decisive action. Yes, that's exactly what the situation needed.

Satisfied he'd come to the right conclusion, he reached for the phone.

DECIDING TO CALL IT a night, Annja and Bernard gathered all the notes and photographs they'd produced during the day, transferred them to Bernard's office down the hall and then locked the lab behind them. "Tomorrow morning, then?" Bernard asked.

"Sounds good," Annja replied. "And give some more thought to getting me in to see the abbot, will you?"

Bernard smiled. "Your persistence is what makes you such a good archaeologist," he said, and then, before she could object to his playful teasing, he added, "but yes, I will. You have my word."

Satisfied, she rode the elevator up to the ground floor. The museum had closed for the day and the halls were empty and silent around her. She paused for a moment at the entrance to a hall devoted to Egyptian artifacts, breathing in all the history that surrounded her, and was struck with the odd sense of being at home.

Yeah, and if you don't get out and have a life one of these days, you'll end up a stuffed mummy just like those in there, she thought wryly.

She'd been working straight through since leaving the dojo earlier that morning and only had a few more nights left to enjoy Paris, so it was time to get out and see the sights.

No sooner had she decided to take a break, however, than she found her thoughts returning to the whereabouts of the missing bullet. The gunshot wound had almost certainly killed Captain Parker and it should have been there with his remains. Not having the bullet irked her; it was like finishing a puzzle only to find out that you're missing one last little piece. It was a tiny detail, she knew, but an important one, and she was just detail-oriented enough to want to put it to rest.

You've spent all day on this, she thought, what's another hour or so?

The spent bullet was probably lying on the floor of the chamber near the wall against which Parker's skeleton had been resting. It shouldn't be all that hard to find.

Go on, take a quick look. If you find it, great, and if not, at least you'll know you gave it a shot, she thought.

Decision made, she caught a cab over to the Metro station they'd used to gain access to the catacombs earlier that day. The trains were still being rerouted around the station due to the construction and so her footsteps echoed off the walls as she descended the steps.

A uniformed police officer was waiting for her at the turnstiles, alerted to her presence by the noise of her footsteps. Obviously bored with the duty he'd been assigned, he told her the station was closed and only looked up at her when she thrust the pass under his nose that she'd been given by Laroche.

"You'll be wanting to go into the tunnels, then?" he asked.

"Yes, I shouldn't be long."

"But it's after dark."

Annja didn't see how that was relevant. She was going underground, where it was always dark. What difference did it make that the sun had gone down?

Rather than get into it with him, though, she simply said, "Yes, it is," and smiled sweetly at him, hoping her charm would get him to open the gate.

What she really wanted to do was to laugh at his

superstitious attitude, for the things she'd faced since acquiring her sword made the idea of roaming around in the tunnels beneath the Paris city streets seem like child's play, but she knew that doing so would kill any chance she had of getting through the gate.

Thankfully, her official pass seemed to be enough. He gave her a look that clearly said he thought she had a few screws loose upstairs but he didn't say anything as he unlatched the gate and let her in.

She jogged through the station and down to the same platform where Laroche had taken her. Arming herself with a lantern just as they had earlier in the day, she climbed down onto the tracks and set off toward the break in the tunnel that marked the entrance to the catacombs.

More sawhorses had been set out at the site since she'd been there earlier, their blinking orange lights bouncing down the tunnel and letting her know she was getting close. She followed the glow like a trail of bread crumbs until she reached the spot where the workers had broken through into the older passageway inside the catacombs.

She was relieved to see the ladder she'd used earlier was still in place and she quickly descended into the lower tunnel. At the bottom of the ladder she paused, glancing back up the way she had come. For a moment she thought she'd heard something, but the sound didn't repeat itself.

Probably just a rat, she thought, and shuddered.

She brushed it off and continued on her way.

The cemented tunnel had given way at the bottom of the ladder to the smooth limestone of the catacombs themselves. The antechamber where they had found Parker's remains was just ahead and she found herself hurrying the last few dozen feet to its entrance, eagerness spreading through her veins like a drug. As she entered the room the thousands of skulls stared back at her, eerie in their eternal silence, but her attention was solely focused on what she'd come here to find and she barely noticed.

She moved over to the spot where the skeleton had been found and got down on her hands and knees. Resting the flashlight on the floor so that its beam filtered across the area she intended to search, she began hunting for the missing bullet. When she'd gone over the entire area in one direction, she went back again in the other, crisscrossing her initial efforts so she could be assured that she hadn't missed a spot.

When that failed to turn up what she was looking for, she moved her attention over to the wall against which Captain Parker's remains had rested. Perhaps the shot that had killed him had actually passed through his body completely, even though they hadn't found evidence of an exit wound. It was something that wasn't completely outrageous if it had happened at close range. Perhaps the bullet had embedded itself in the wall instead of falling to the floor when the body decayed.

Searching the wall, however, proved to be much harder than the floor. Comprised as it was of hundreds of human skulls, there were too many nooks and crannies and shadowed surfaces that could be hiding the impact point of the bullet. With just the beam of her flashlight to illuminate the wall's surface, there was no way she was going to find something that small amid all the stacked human bones.

Better to come back in the daytime with a team of grad students and a full bank of lights, she told herself, and decided to really call it quits for the night. The beam of her flashlight swept across the floor as she turned away and out of the corner of her eye she caught the glint of something reflecting back at her.

She turned in that direction and carefully made her way forward, shining the beam of her flashlight ahead of her, searching for whatever it was. When she reached the wall she slowly spun in a circle, still searching, knowing that whatever it was had to be here somewhere.

It couldn't just get up and walk out on its own.

There!

It was a heavy gold signet ring set with a dark colored stone. It was lying on the floor near the wall directly across from where they had found Parker's remains and it was partially obscured by the collapse of several loose bones, which explained why she and the rest of Bernard's team had missed it.

She kept the flashlight beam trained on it as she walked over, not wanting to lose sight of it, and then bent to pick it up.

She turned as she straightened up, ring in hand, and she caught sight of the dark form standing behind her. He was so close and it was so unexpected that she flinched back in surprise.

The move saved her.

The fist that came hurtling out of the darkness struck her on the edge of the jaw rather than in the center of her throat, where it would have crushed her larynx. Instead, the force of the blow picked her up and flung her backward, tossing her against the carefully piled bones lining the wall behind her. The whole mess came tumbling down around her in a hard rain, bones bouncing off her head and shoulders in an unyielding waterfall that threatened to knock her unconscious.

She knew if that happened it was all over, so she

fought back against the grayness threatening her sight and struggled to extricate herself from the jumbled pile of human bones.

The scrape of a shoe against the stone floor let her know her attacker was moving toward her. She had seconds at best, but the fall had knocked the wind out of her and the blow to the head had her thoughts ringing like a church bell in a steeple, messing with her concentration.

Get up! her mind screamed at her, but it was like swimming against the current, her body not quite obeying the commands her mind was giving.

In the darkness she sensed rather than saw a dark shape bending over her and the sudden spike of adrenaline that poured into her system wiped away the haze.

Her right hand folded around the hilt of a sword that hadn't been there seconds before as she willed it into existence from the otherwhere. She swung out with a savage yell like that of a falcon on the hunt. The sword slashed, almost with a mind of its own, and she felt it slice through the flesh of the man's arm.

Blood splashed across her face and whoever it was howled in pain and drew back, giving Annja the time and space she needed to scramble to her feet. She kicked away the bones of some forgotten French citizens as she did so, wanting solid ground beneath her already shaky feet for the fight to come.

Ambushing a woman in the dark was one thing but fighting that same woman, now angry and armed with a sword she knew how to use with a finesse born of hours of practice, was something else. Rather than move in and press his advantage, her attacker turned and ran, his footfalls echoing off the stone around them.

Annja took off after him.

He only had a few seconds head start, and so she should have been able to catch up to him quickly, but her head was still pounding and the lack of a light source quickly had her steps faltering and slowing to a stop after only a few dozen yards. Getting lost in the dark was not something she wanted to experience, no matter how badly she wanted to know who it was that had followed her down here or why they'd attacked. Wandering for hours through pitch-dark tunnels until she fell down an unseen chasm or died of thirst was not on her list of happy endings.

In the distance, her attacker's footfalls faded away to silence.

She took a moment to catch her breath and gather her thoughts. She realized, with no little surprise, that her left hand was still clenched tightly around the ring that she'd picked up off the floor.

Thank goodness for small favors, she thought.

Not wanting to lose it after all this, she slipped it into her pocket to look at later. With her hand against the wall to use as a guide, she made her way carefully back down the tunnel until she could see the thin beam of light from her flashlight spilling out of the entrance of the antechamber.

She stepped into the room, retrieved her flashlight and decided that she'd had enough excitement for one day. Sword still in hand, she cautiously retraced her steps back up to the subway tunnel and from there to the station itself. She kept on the lookout for any sign of her attacker, but didn't see or hear anyone along the way. Before entering the station she released her sword back into the otherwhere, for coming out of a dark tunnel carrying a sword in hand didn't seem like the safest way to reacquaint herself with the police officer on duty.

As it turned out, she needn't have worried. The guard was nowhere in sight.

That's not a good sign, she thought uneasily.

He wouldn't have left on his own without being relieved; at least, she couldn't imagine him doing that knowing full well that she was in the tunnels. That meant that something had happened to him.

He probably ran into the same bastard that I did.

If that was the case, he could be lying somewhere unconscious, perhaps even seriously injured. She couldn't leave without looking for him.

It didn't take very long. She found the police officer lying against the far side of the ticket booth, a thick trickle of blood leaking from the swollen lump on the side of his head. His breathing was steady enough, she was relieved to discover. Annja used his radio to make an Officer Down call to headquarters. When they asked her to identify herself, she broke the connection. The officer was starting to stir so she got up, and walked off without a backward glance. It wasn't the most Good Samaritan–like thing to do, but all she wanted was to return to her hotel and take a hot bath to ease the aches and pains out of her muscles. She wouldn't get that if she had to spend the next three hours downtown answering questions.

Back at her hotel, she had room service send up hot chocolate and some croissants. While she waited, she took the ring from the pocket of her jeans, cleaned it off and held it up to the light for a good look.

It was a man's signet ring, just as she'd thought. The stone set in its face was a deep crimson in color that seemed to absorb the light rather than reflect it. It had been gently cut, with a beveled face and eight short sides. The gold itself was unadorned. She suspected it was Parker's, but it could also have belonged to whomever he had been meeting there. There was no way of telling at this point. She slipped the ring into a little glassine envelope and then tucked it inside one of the zippered pockets of her backpack.

Her snack arrived, so she signed the check, locked the door behind her and devoured the food. Then she headed into the bathroom where she had drawn a bath. She stripped off her clothes and climbed into the water for some relaxation. She'd been going nonstop ever since she'd left for the dojo that morning and her body was telling her to take it easy or else. The hot water soothed her tired limbs the same way the hot chocolate had her throat.

When she was clean and relaxed, she climbed into bed and was asleep in what felt like seconds.

9

Given the type of activity that went on at the Museum of Natural History on a daily basis, as well as the price-less nature of some of the artifacts that were cleaned and restored within its walls, the lab there had a highly sophisticated alarm system designed to prevent unauthorized entrance to the facility. The alarm was the pride of the museum's director, for he had spent nearly two years on the research and testing that went into selecting the product they had finally decided to install. It was, the manufacturer said, the best of the best and perfect for protecting a facility such as this.

The three men who entered the lab at half past two that morning went through it like butter.

The fact that they had the sixteen-digit code that was needed to render the alarm system inoperable made things a bit easier.

Once inside the lab, one of the men moved to the drawer containing Captain Parker's remains. He didn't hesitate, didn't pull out any of the other drawers looking for the right one, but went immediately to his intended target, like a man who knew precisely what it was he was looking for and where it could be found. He opened the canvas duffel bag he was carrying and started placing the captain's remains into the sack.

As he was doing so, his two companions were carefully scouring the lab for any trace that the long-missing Confederate soldier's remains had ever graced the building with its presence. Papers, thumb drives, video cards—if it could possibly contain any information about the discovery of the dead man's remains it was picked up and dropped into a sack identical to the first. Within ten minutes the three men had searched the entire lab and removed everything that might possibly contain any information relative to the discovery of Captain Parker's body. When they were finished the leader gave a quick nod to the other two and what had once been a carefully organized search-and-retrieval mission turned into a free-for-all as they set about ruthlessly destroying everything they could get their hands on. Computer monitors were thrown to the floor and then stomped under foot. Desks were overturned and the contents of their drawers scattered throughout the room. High-tech spectrometry equipment costing hundreds of thousands of dollars was covered with foam from the wall-mounted fire extinguishers and then smashed with what was left of the desk chairs.

It became like a game to them, seeing who could cause the most destruction in the shortest amount of time. It wasn't long before the room was practically unrecognizable.

Finally, their energy spent and their job complete, the three men left the same way they came in, with no one the wiser.

10

When Annja arrived at the museum early the next morning, she was met with a scene of confusion. Several law enforcement vehicles were parked outside the entrance and when she tried to use the temporary pass Bernard had given her to gain access, she was politely informed by a uniformed officer that she would have to wait.

"It's okay, I'm expected," she told him.

The officer wasn't impressed, and told her that they had a "situation" on their hands, and that all unnecessary personnel were to wait in the lobby.

The officer's emphasis on the word *unnecessary* irked her enough that she let her irritation show. "Wait for what, exactly?" she asked.

"Wait for someone to come get you," was the reply.

"Can you at least call down and let Dr. Reinhardt know I'm here waiting?"

"No. Sorry."

Yeah, I'll just bet you are, she thought.

It seemed that something was terribly wrong. There

was no way she was just going to stand and wait; she'd be here all day. If the officer wouldn't call down to the lab, she'd just have to do it herself. She pulled out her cell phone and called Bernard's office.

The phone rang several times and then went to voice mail.

She hung up without leaving a message and tried again. "Come on, Bernard," she coaxed beneath her breath as she waited for him to answer.

No luck.

Annja was trying to figure out what to do next when she caught sight of Commissaire Laroche crossing the lobby behind the police line.

"Commissaire!" she called. "Henri!"

He turned at the sound of his first name, recognized her and made his way across the room.

"What can I do for you, Miss Creed?"

Annja smiled, trying to ease the tension she could see on his face. Something must have happened to one of the museum's pieces, she thought.

"I'm sure you have your hands full with whatever this all is," she began, waving her hand to indicate the police officers milling about, "but I'm due to continue work on the Metro skeleton with Bernard and the officer on duty won't let me past the police tape."

Henri stared at her for a long moment, his expression inscrutable.

"You haven't heard, have you?"

Her stomach clenched as anxiety shot through her. "Bernard? Is he…?"

"Professor Reinhardt is fine, Miss Creed," Laroche said gently, putting a hand on her arm as he realized the distress his offhand comment had caused her. "My apologies. I didn't mean to alarm you."

"Well, if it's not Bernard, then what… It's Captain Parker, isn't it?"

His brow furrowed in puzzlement. "Captain Parker?"

Annja remembered that they hadn't informed anyone of their suspicions yet. "The skeleton from the Metro."

Henri's eyes widened. "You've identified the body already?"

They had as far as she was concerned, but she knew that they didn't have enough conclusive evidence to prove it yet so she explained that all they had at the moment were a few suspicions and that they were using the name as a matter of convenience only.

"It seemed more respectful than referring to him as 'the skeleton' all the time. I think we're getting closer, though, and I can show you what we've done so far if you'd like."

"I see. That's too bad—you had my hopes up for a moment there. You see, proving your theory is going to be much more difficult now, as the museum was burglarized during the night and the thieves made off with the skeleton."

Annja couldn't believe what she was hearing. Why would someone steal the skeleton?

Laroche's next comment made her heart sink.

"Professor's Reinhardt's office was ransacked, as well."

Annja grimaced. "Our notes and photographs?"

The commissaire shook his head. "Gone, as well, I'm afraid."

At least they still had the Davis letter in their possession. Bernard had insisted on locking it away in the museum's vault for safekeeping the minute he'd recognized the letter's potential value. If the U.S. government didn't exercise their right to claim it, there were more than two dozen universities and museums he could think of off the top of his head that would pay handsomely to add it to their collections, his own included. He hadn't been inclined to take any chances with it. And thank heaven for that.

Laroche was looking at her expectantly, making her realize that she must have missed his question while thinking about the letter.

"I'm sorry. What was that again?"

"I asked if you had any idea why the thieves would be interested only in our Confederate friend's remains?"

Annja frowned. "That's all they took?"

The museum was full of priceless artifacts worth far more than the missing Confederate remains. A fair number of excellent pieces were stored just down the hall from Bernard's office. Once past the security system and inside the museum, it would have been a simple matter to force the locks on those storerooms and walk off with dozens of priceless artifacts. She had assumed that the thieves had hit Bernard's office and lab as part of a larger sweep for items of value.

"They were only interested in the skeleton and the documentation pertaining to it that you and Professor Reinhardt assembled. Nothing else was taken, including items of considerable value that were in plain view in Dr. Reinhardt's office."

That put an entirely different spin on things. Breaking and entering to steal museum pieces worth millions was one thing; doing so just to make off with the recently recovered remains of a Confederate captain no one even knew was there was another, she thought.

Her thoughts turned immediately to the shadowed figure she'd encountered in the catacombs the night before.

There was far more going on here than she'd realized.

Laroche was still waiting for her to answer his question so she put on her game face and told him that she didn't have any idea. She didn't like keeping information from him, but she also didn't feel that she had any choice. Someone must have revealed the skeleton's presence to the thieves and until she knew who that someone was, she wasn't taking any chances with the information she had gained. Right now everyone was suspect, including the commissaire. After all, she barely knew him. It was clear that Laroche didn't quite believe her, but he didn't push the issue and that was good enough for her. Since she was an integral part of the team that had been responsible for the skeleton's retrieval and examination, he let those on duty know that she was free to come and go as she needed. He then escorted her through the police barrier and over to the elevator leading to the lower floors where Bernard's laboratory was located.

"If you think of anything that might be helpful, please give me a call," he told her as she got inside the elevator car.

Annja assured him that she would. And at some point, if she decided it was the right thing to do, she would.

The scene was no less erratic on the lower floor than the one above. Police officers stood in small groups of twos and threes while crime scene technicians moved through the various rooms, carrying out their usual duties. She spotted Bernard standing off to one side, a pained look on his face and a cup of coffee in his hand. He must have felt her attention on him for he looked up, caught her gaze and then nodded his head in the direction of a nearby staff room.

Annja met him there a moment later, away from the scrutiny of the others in the hall.

"Is it true that they got everything?" she asked.

Bernard nodded glumly. "I'm afraid so."

It wasn't what she wanted to hear, but no more than she'd expected. "At least we still have the Davis letter."

Bernard didn't say anything.

"You did put the letter in the vault, right?"

"I was going to do so, but it was late and I thought the safe in my office would be adequate for one night."

Damn it! There went their only possible proof that not only were the remains those of William Parker but that he had been there on an official mission for the president of the Confederate States.

This was not turning out to be a good day.

Annja could see that Bernard was feeling guilty over his part in the process, and right then she was having a hard time forgiving him.

He used that moment to break what little good news he did have.

"I took the liberty of calling Abbot Deschanel late last night," he said quietly.

"And?"

"He's agreed to see you. Apparently mention of Captain Parker piqued his curiosity."

"Well, at least there's that."

Bernard didn't appear thrilled with the idea, however.

"This has become very serious business, Annja. It's obvious that someone out there knows more about what's going on than we do. If they went to the trouble of breaking into the museum to disrupt our investigation, there's no telling what they're willing to do."

Again, she thought about the man she'd encountered in the tunnels. Who was he? What did he want?

Without mentioning any of that to Bernard, she reassured him that she would be careful.

Not fully satisfied, but knowing he couldn't do anything about it, Bernard shrugged and continued speaking.

"Abbot Deschanel expects you later this afternoon," he said, handing over some handwritten directions outlining the route to the monastery and a pair of car keys. "You can use one of the vehicles from the museum motor pool, as well. I had it arranged when I came in this morning, before I discovered this mess."

Annja gave him a quick hug, surprising him, and herself.

"We've still got a chance to break this wide open, Bernard," she said as excitement over what was to come stole over her. "The monastery holds the answer to all this, I know it does!"

With a four-hour drive ahead of her, Annja didn't waste any more time. She said her goodbyes to Bernard, thanked him again for the directions and the vehicle and then got out of there before the police decided that they wanted to question her.

11

It was a beautiful day for driving. The sun was shining in a bright blue sky, and for a time Annja forgot about the morning's events and simply enjoyed the scenery. The farther she got from Paris, the more the landscape changed. The rolling green hills gradually gave way to the foothills of the mountains and by the time she reached the final hour of her drive she was winding her way through narrow mountain passes and verdant pine valleys. As she neared her destination, her thoughts turned to the meeting ahead of her. She decided the best plan of action was to simply lay it all out there for the abbot, letting him know what had happened so far. Whoever had broken into the museum had gotten the scrap of paper with the monastery name on it, along with the rest of their discoveries. They might not be able to put the puzzle pieces together as swiftly as she and Bernard had, but there wasn't any reason to believe that they couldn't do it. That meant the thieves could very well be on their way to the monastery at any time. The abbot deserved to know if the people under his care were in danger and she had no intention of keeping that information from him.

She glanced out the window, taking in a nearby river as she drove on past, and then, as she came around a bend in the road, she got a glimpse of the monastery for the first time.

It sat on the edge of a high promontory, like a castle guarding the mountain approach. In fact, it looked sort of like a castle, fashioned of stone that shone in the bright sunshine, with high crenellated towers and several balconies that jutted out from the protective walls.

More twists and turns in the road kept the monastery from view, until about fifteen minutes later when she found the way forward blocked by a locked set of wrought-iron gates. They were twice her height and barred entrance to the property. A small bell hung off to one side and with no better idea of how to get the attention of those she had come to see, she drove up next to the bell, grasped the rope and gave it a solid yank.

The bell rang crisp and clear. Several minutes passed, long enough that Annja was thinking about giving it another pull, when the front door of a small shack on the other side of the gates that she hadn't noticed before opened and a man dressed in the brown robes and sandals of a Benedictine monk stepped out. He came down the walk and stood on the other side of the gate from her, a questioning expression on his face.

When he didn't say anything after a moment, Annja volunteered through the gate, "I have an appointment to see the abbott."

The monk raised his eyebrows and then mimed seeing some ID, still without saying anything.

The monk was under a vow of silence, she realized. Annja dug her driver's license out of her backpack and then got out of the car so she could hand it over to him. He glanced at it, compared the picture on it to her face and then triggered a switch that opened the gates electronically. He handed her a photocopy of a hand-drawn map to follow.

She drove through the gates and continued onward through the trees for a few hundred yards until she emerged into an open space, a parking area roped off on her right with the bulk of the monastery rising up on her left.

She parked the car and got out, surveying the massive structure in front of her. She'd expected something small, innocuous, not this sprawling behemoth of a monastery that seemed to occupy every square inch of the promontory on which it was built.

Some kind of warning must have passed from the guard shack to the monastery itself, for another brown-robed monk was waiting for her on the front steps.

He watched her without saying anything as she got out of the car and approached along the walk. It was only when she actually reached the top of the steps that he let a smile settle on his face and stepped forward with his hand out.

"Good morning, Miss Creed. I'm Brother Samuel."

Annja shook the offered hand, a relieved smile on her face. For a minute there she'd thought he, too, was under a vow of silence. "Pleased to meet you," she told him.

"The abbot has asked me to escort you to his office in the chapterhouse."

He turned and entered the complex, Annja at his heels. Just inside the front door was a long central hall with offices on either side. Typical office sounds reached her ears even through the closed doors—the ringing of phones, the clack of computer keyboards, muffled voices, even the sound of a kettle whistling away somewhere.

They passed through a set of double doors at the end of the hall and found themselves outside once more in the cloister, a large square area of ground open to the sky and surrounded by covered walkways on each side split repeatedly by arched openings known as arcades. The soaring heights of the cathedral rose up over the walkway directly opposite them and Annja was struck with the desire to wander through the interior and see what the centuries-old church looked like. Brother Samuel, however, turned right and Annja had to hurry along to catch up with him.

He noticed her interest in the church, and began pointing out some of the details around her. "This part of the claustral complex contains several of the most highly trafficked areas—the cathedral, the administrative offices, the chapterhouse and, of course, the living quarters."

They came to the end of the walkways and he pointed out across the grounds to another set of buildings. "Over there we have the kitchens, the storehouses, the infirmary and the guest quarters."

He turned left this time, so that they were headed toward the cathedral once more, but they had only gone a few yards before they found themselves standing at a plain, unadorned door.

The monk knocked and then led her inside.

The room she entered was a simple office that contained only a desk, two chairs and a kneeler for prayer. A cross hung on the wall behind the desk, over the head of the wizened old man seated at the desk.

Smiling, he rose and extended his hand. "Good afternoon, Miss Creed. I'm Abbot Deschanel. It's a pleasure to make your acquaintance."

"Thank you. And thank you for seeing me on such short notice."

"Happy to help. Tell me, how is Professor Reinhardt?"

"As impetuous as ever," she replied, correctly sensing that Abbott Deschanel was looking for confirmation that she did, indeed, know Bernard Reinhardt personally. She couldn't imagine what anyone would gain by faking such a relationship, but that didn't mean someone wouldn't try to do it, she supposed. Bernard came across in casual meetings as a steady-as-a-rock type of personality. It was only once you'd worked with him a bit that you began to realize just how impulsive he really was. The business with the spray-on packing foam was just one example.

Her answer must have satisfied the abbot, for he gestured for her to take the seat before his desk as he sank back into his own.

"So how can I help you?"

"Well, it's a bit of a complicated story actually," she began, and then laid it all out for him. How the section of the catacombs had been discovered and what the Metro workers had found lying within. How she and Professor Reinhardt had been asked to manage the excavation and what they had found once they had moved the body to the museum. How she'd been confronted in the tunnels and how the remains had been stolen from the museum the night before.

"Sewn into Captain Parker's shirt was a small scrap of paper. Written on it was the name of this place, Berceau de solitude."

The abbot sat watching her without any change of expression.

"And so I thought, maybe, I mean it's been a long time, more than a hundreds years, I know, but still…"

Get to the point. You're rambling, she told herself.

She took a deep breath. "I thought maybe you'd have some record of him coming here," she finished in a rush.

A small smile slipped over the abbot's steady facade.

"Well," he said, "that's quite a story. Quite a story."

I can feel a "but" coming on, Annja thought.

"But I'm not sure I understand. We're just a poor community of brother monks. Why would a man like that have come here, of all places?"

Abbot Deschanel's tone was light, the question a relatively innocuous one, but Annja felt goose bumps rising on her arms nonetheless.

He knows something.

Trying to keep the eagerness out of her voice, she replied. "I honestly don't know. I was hoping you could tell me."

"If I had such information, and I'm not saying I do—I'm just speaking hypothetically at this point—what would you do with it?"

Annja suddenly felt as if she were standing on a precipice. Something about the way the abbot held himself, the slightest change of tension in his frame, betrayed the importance of her answer.

Say the wrong thing now and you can kiss your answers goodbye.

She'd told him the truth about everything so far, and that seemed the wisest course of action.

"I had the body of a man I believe to be Captain Parker back in the laboratory at the museum. He was the victim of a gunshot wound, his remains previously lost in the depths of the Paris catacombs until their discovery yesterday. And yet a man claiming to be the very same Captain Parker survived the war, held public office and eventually died peacefully in his sleep at the age of seventy. Clearly one of them was not who he claimed to be. I'd like to solve that mystery."

He watched her carefully for a moment, as if weighing the truth of her words. Apparently her motives must have met his approval for he said, "You are right, Miss Creed. Captain Parker did indeed come here. The abbot at the time, Brother Markum, was actually a distant cousin on his mother's side, you see."

Annja felt a surge of excitement.

"According to Brother Markum's account, Captain Parker was agitated, perhaps even fearful for his life, and he gave my predecessor specific instructions to watch over a piece of his property until someone came to retrieve it in his name."

Annja was leaning forward in her chair, full of questions, but Deschanel raised a hand and held her off, at least for a moment.

"There is no indication in Brother Markum's account as to the specific nature of Parker's mission or the source of his fear. Just that he was clearly afraid and that he felt it likely that he might not be back to retrieve the object himself. But I don't know any more than that and, unfortunately, Brother Markum is no longer around for us to ask him ourselves."

After a century and a half I certainly hope not, Annja thought.

"Do you have any idea what the object was that Captain Parker placed into the abbot's safekeeping?"

Annja was thinking it might be another letter, or

maybe a journal. A journal would be ideal, as it might describe in more detail what was going on.

But Abbot Deschanel's answer surprised her.

"It was a wooden box. About the size of a microwave."

A box?

"Do you, by chance, still have the box?"

Then, at last, Deschanel showed some of her own excitement.

"I do," he said, his grin spreading from ear to ear. "And because you have come asking for Captain Parker's legacy in his name, you've allowed us to fulfill our vow to him. This is a blessed day indeed!"

He rose, saying, "I'll just be a moment," and slipped out the door, leaving Annja waiting anxiously for his return.

It took less than ten minutes. When Deschanel came back through the door, he was carrying a small chest. It was about the size of an old-fashioned bread box and was covered with a thick patina of dirt and dust, as if it had been stored in the back of a closet for some time.

It's probably been sitting in the same place for the past hundred years, Annja thought.

He set it down on top of his desk and gestured for her to open it.

This is it. This is what you came here for.

She could feel her pulse racing, could hear her heart pounding in her ears as she realized that the box in front of her might hold the answers to several questions. What had Parker been doing in Paris? Why the letter of introduction from President Davis? What, exactly, had happened to the missing Confederate treasure?

With hands that only slightly trembled, Annja opened the chest.

Inside was a small lacquered box the size of a jewelry case.

She recognized it immediately.

It was a Japanese puzzle box.

"May I?" she asked.

The abbot nodded. "Be my guest," he said.

Reaching inside, she drew out the puzzle box and set it down next to the crate. As she did so the slip of paper that had been stuck to the bottom of the box came loose and drifted to the floor.

Picking it up, Annja saw that it was a short note in an unfamiliar hand.

Sykes,

Time is of the essence so I must be brief. The FotS want more than Davis is willing to grant and the negotiations have turned ugly. I fear for my life. This box contains everything you need to locate the specie stolen from the wagon train. I trust you will see that it reaches the right hands if I do not return.

Faithfully,
Will

She'd been right! Thanks to her research earlier that morning, she knew that Parker's second in command had been a man named Jonathan Sykes, so there seemed little doubt now that the remains did, indeed, belong to the Confederate captain as she'd suspected.

It was the contents of the rest of the note that really caught her attention, however.

Specie, she knew, was a term used to describe money in the form of coins, usually gold or silver, that provided the backing for paper money issued by the government. Parker had to be referring to the money from the treasury. The wagon train he'd driven out of Danville had been ambushed by brigands; his official report had listed the gold as stolen.

If the note was to be believed, then Parker clearly knew exactly where the treasure was, which made the official report a bold-faced lie.

She didn't have to think about it very long to come up with a handful of reasons for his doing so, either. Perhaps he'd been ordered to fake the treasury's disappearance. Perhaps he'd taken it upon himself to protect it during the hectic days at the end of the war. Or maybe he'd simply taken advantage of the opportunity to secure a future for himself and his family for when the war was over.

Any way it happened, the answer to a historic mystery was about to be solved.

All she had to do was open the puzzle box.

She thought about what she knew about puzzle boxes. Originating in the Hakone region of Japan in the late eighteenth century, puzzle boxes, or disentanglement boxes as they were sometimes known, were exquisitely crafted works of art that could only be opened by following a certain sequence of movements. Some were made up of multiple sliding pieces that, when moved, unlocked other pieces, which in turn released a side panel of the box, and so on, until the top was finally released, allowing the box to be fully opened. Others required putting pressure on certain locations in a specific sequence, which then released various panels that eventually unlocked the box. An individual box might require as few as two or as many as sixty-six moves to open it.

The trick, she knew, was finding the right starting point.

She picked up the box and examined it carefully. It was made of a highly polished hardwood—linden or perhaps cherry—and was lacquered to a fine finish. A mosaic of different colored squares covered the top, but the sides were free of decoration of any kind. Nor did it show even the slightest hint of any seams.

For all practical purposes, it looked like a solid block of wood.

Annja knew better, though.

She examined the mosaic, looking for a pattern that might provide a hint as to where to begin. When that failed, she began to press the colored squares in a variety of common patterns. Four corners. A cross in the center. Crisscrossing the middle.

Nothing.

She glanced up at the abbot, who was watching her curiously.

"It's a puzzle box," she said, answering his unspoken question. "In order to open it, you have to follow a certain sequence of motions."

He nodded sagely. "And how to do you know that you are on the right path?" he asked.

"You don't."

"Ah, so the box mirrors life, no?"

She supposed that it did, though that didn't help her get it open.

Parker hadn't left any instructions telling Sykes how to open the box, so she knew that the key had to be something they both would have understood. Maybe a prearranged symbol or word? Maybe something that Sykes would associate with Parker, something that he would think of right away?

She ran through the obvious list of ideas—names of their wives or children, birth dates, their current ranks in the Navy. None of them worked.

She looked at the layout of the colored tiles on the lid again. The checkerboard was fourteen squares wide by eight squares high. The fifth and tenth vertical row were slightly darker than the others, subtly dividing the mosaic into three even sections four squares across by eight squares deep.

Three even sections.

Her thought from a few minutes earlier came back to her.

It had to be something Sykes would immediately think of, something that was important to both of them.

Three even sections.

Could it be that easy?

Reaching out with one finger, she pressed firmly on the squares in the first section and traced the letter *C*.

A sharp click sounded.

"Did you hear that?" the abbot asked, excitement in his voice.

She had. It meant she was on the right track.

She did the same thing in the center section, but this time traced an *S* rather than a *C*.

Another click.

Grinning now, she moved her hand to the final section and traced the letter *A*.

CSA. The Confederate States of America.

Something near and dear to both of them.

The square in the exact center of the mosaic slid aside with a sharp snap, revealing a depression beneath.

It was just large enough to fit the average person's finger.

Intrigued now, the abbot reached out a hand, intending to press the location, but Annja pulled the box out of his reach.

"Wait," she said. "It could be booby-trapped."

She'd run into more than a few of those in her years as an archaeologist and wouldn't have put it past the box maker to build a trigger into an obvious location like this one.

It would be a good way to lose a finger.

She snagged a pencil off the abbott's desk and used the eraser end to poke the center of the depression.

Nothing happened.

She tried again.

Still nothing.

"Perhaps the pencil isn't wide enough?" the abbot suggested.

She tried a third time, but with two pencils held together rather than one.

The box just sat there, silently gloating at them.

After everything she'd been through so far, there was no way was she going to let a stupid wooden box beat her.

She bent over, closer to the table, and stared at the depression in the lid. From that angle it was clear that rather than being smooth, as she'd originally suspected, it was beveled in a simple pattern.

It looked familiar somehow.

She stared at it for a long moment, trying to give it shape and form, to understand what the object that would fit into it might look like.

Suddenly she got it.

"Yes!" she cried, startling the abbott. Getting up from the table she went over to her backpack and dug in the pocket for the envelope containing the ring she'd found during her sojourn into the catacombs the night before.

Parker's ring.

With the break in at the museum, she hadn't had the chance to properly catalog and store it. In fact, she'd almost forgotten she still had it.

Taking it out of the glassine envelope she'd stored it in, Annja held the ring up to the light and examined the stone. It appeared to have the same basic shape as the depression in the box. And it was the right size, too.

Annja would bet anything that both Parker and Sykes wore identical rings!

She stepped up to the table and without hesitation pressed the stone atop the ring into the depression in the lid of the puzzle box.

A sudden clicking and whirring erupted from the box, like the sound a windup toy makes when it has been released. Panels across the surface of the box popped open, twisted and turned with the help of mechanical gears buried deep inside the contraption, and these in turn opened others. It took a good three minutes for the box to stop rearranging itself on the table in front of them, and by the time it was finished Annja could see a definite crease where the top separated from the rest.

When she was reasonably confident that the box wasn't going to start rearranging itself again, she reached out and separated the two pieces.

Inside, in a velvet-lined chamber, another envelope rested much like the one she'd taken from the pocket of Parker's sack coat.

Just to be safe, she poked that with a pencil as well before reaching in and picking it up.

Inside was a single sheet of stationery.

In the cellars of the wine god
>   Lies a key without a lock
>   That will lead you to the place
>   Where the two mouths meet
There you'll find the Lady
>   Left alone and in distress
>   You must secure her when you're able
>   And take Ewell's Rifle from her crest
Take the rifle to the place of Lee's greatest failure
>   Where the Peacock freely roamed
>   Find the spot where my doppelgänger rests
eternal
>   Deep beneath the loam
Disturb him in his slumber
>   Wake him from his rest
>   To find that which you are seeking
>   Use the key to unlock the chest

Another puzzle. Annja was seriously starting to dislike this guy.

"Not what you were expecting?" the abbot asked. Grimacing, Annja replied, "No, not quite. I'd been hoping for the answer but this is just another piece of the puzzle."

"But one more than you had before, no?"

The abbot was right; it was one more piece of information than she'd had before. For that she should be thankful.

"Yes," she said, smiling at him. "You're right. And I'd do well to remember it."

She thanked him for his time and asked if it would be all right if she kept the letter.

"Please, take the box, as well. It is yours now—my duty as caretaker has been fulfilled."

They put the puzzle box back inside the chest it had been stored in and wiped down the chest with a towel the abbot fetched from another room. Once she could carry it without getting her clothes covered with dust, she shook hands with the abbot, picked up the box and followed the monk he'd summoned to lead her back to the front door.

As she got in her car, Annja was full of excitement over what she'd learned. The trip had been well worth the drive. With the information she now had, she could conclude that Parker had been in Paris to carry out some kind of secret negotiation on behalf of President Davis. Not only that, but she could also make a pretty good case that the money from the Confederate treasury hadn't been stolen by brigands at all, but had actually been rerouted by Parker himself to assist with the mission assigned to him. It was the kind of discovery that could make someone a superstar in the field of archaeology practically overnight and Annja wasn't at all displeased by the idea. People recognized her on the street thanks to her hosting gig on *Chasing History's Monsters,* but she'd much rather gain the respect of her academic peers than the adoration of the viewing audience any day of the week.

Then again, if she found the treasure itself, she could have both!

She was so distracted by thoughts of the future that she nearly ran into a group of six monks walking behind her car as she backed out of the parking space. Thankfully, they were paying more attention than she was and were able to skip out of the way quickly enough.

Embarrassed, she gave a little wave of apology, drove back to the gate and headed down the mountain.

She'd been driving for about ten minutes when something started nagging at her. Something about the monks she'd nearly run over. It was right there, on the edge of her awareness. She reached for it...only to have it slip away.

The feeling left her for a moment and she'd convinced herself that it was just a result of her lingering sense of embarrassment for having almost run them over, when the sense that something was terribly wrong overcame her again. The image of her sword flashed before her eyes, as if urging her to make the connection. She concentrated, trying to make the feeling come further into focus. Something about the monks...

She had it!

The scene unfurled before her again on the movie screen of her mind—the monk skipping back away from her car as she got too close, the hem of his dark brown robe riding up over his feet, revealing the pair of dark black boots he wore beneath.

All of the monks she'd seen inside the monastery had been wearing hand-woven sandals.

She slammed on the brakes, skidding to a stop. Fortunately, there was no one behind her. As soon as the car had stopped moving forward, she spun the wheel and stomped on the gas pedal, practically sending her little borrowed car into convulsions as the tires spun and she took off back in the direction she'd just come from.

A terrible feeling unfurled in her gut, a sense that some invisible line had been crossed and that she was already too late to stop whatever it was from happening. She quickly found herself urging the car to go faster as she raced up the mountain road at dangerous speeds.

12

Annja rounded the final curve and the sprawling towers of the monastery came into view, the brick blooming in the sunshine. For a moment she thought she'd been mistaken, that her concerns had all been for nothing, but then she saw the smoke billowing out of one of the upper-story windows and knew that she'd been horribly, terribly right.

She drove through the still-open gates, skidded to a stop in the middle of the circular drive and was up and out of the car before the engine had even stopped idling. As she rushed up the steps she willed her sword into existence. Its familiar weight was a reassuring presence as her hand closed around its hilt.

One glance was all it took to know that the man in front of her was dead. The bullet hole in his forehead stood out starkly against his pale flesh, but did little to hide his features and it was easy for her to recognize him as Brother Samuel.

Someone was going to pay for this, she vowed.

She slipped inside the door and stood in the hallway

Samuel had led her through a short time earlier. The office doors on either side of the hall were standing open but as she made her way down its length, cautiously glancing inside each room as she passed, she found that all the rooms were empty.

The door at the far end of the corridor was closed but not latched, so she used the fingers of one hand to ease it open slightly. From where she stood Annja could see part of the cloister and a stretch of the covered walkway that ran perpendicular to her position. The body of another monk lay sprawled across the stone pavement, a dark stain spreading beneath him.

A gunshot rang out, breaking the oppressive silence that lay over the place like a funeral shroud, and Annja jumped at the sound. It was very close. Just beyond the door, in fact, in the section of the cloister she couldn't yet see.

She gave a push with her hand and sent the door gliding open on well-oiled hinges, revealing the scene in the open space of the cloister just beyond.

A monk in the now-familiar brown robe and sandals was dragging himself on his stomach across the green grass, leaving a trail of bright red blood in his wake from the bullet wound in his leg. Behind him stalked another, similarly dressed individual, but this one was wearing combat boots instead of sandals and carried a 9 mm automatic pistol in his hand. Even as Annja watched, the second man sighted along the length of his arm and shot the wounded monk in the other leg.

Blood sprayed.

The monk screamed in pain.

The intruder threw back his head and laughed.

That was enough for Annja. Without a second thought for her own welfare, she sprinted from the doorway, leaped through the nearest arcade and charged the gunman.

The monk on the ground saw her first, his eyes growing wide at the sight of her charging forward, sword held high, and the fear in his face alerted his tormentor that there was something wrong. The other man twisted around, the muzzle of his gun coming up as he tried to line up a shot even before he knew what his target would be.

Annja wasn't taking any chances. The first swing of her sword slashed his arm just below the elbow, his gun flying free as his arm hung uselessly. Annja used her momentum to spin around and her second strike caught the intruder at the collarbone and drove diagonally down through his neck.

He was dead before he even had the chance to make a sound.

Unfortunately, so, too, was his victim. As Annja knelt down to help the injured monk she found him staring up at her with unseeing eyes. The second bullet must have found the femoral artery, for there was a rapidly expanding pool of blood in the grass around his legs that hadn't been there moments before.

She reached out and closed the dead monk's eyes, vowing as she did so not to let any more of his brethren suffer the same fate.

Noise from one side caught her attention. She turned to see several men emerge from the door to the chapterhouse on the far side of the cloister, dragging the abbott between them. To her dismay, one of them looked up and saw her crouched there over the body.

"Hey!" he shouted.

Annja didn't hang around to hear what he said next. A glance at the entrance to the church a few feet away showed the massive oak doors propped open with what looked to be stacks of hymnals and Annja slipped inside, saying a silent thank-you to whatever enterprising monk had decided a little fresh air might do the old worship center some good as she did.

She stood still for a moment, letting her eyes adjust to the dimness and trying to get her bearings. The cathedral, she knew, was shaped like a cross lying on its side. The main section of the church ran east to west and the door she'd entered through put her halfway along the length of the nave. The presbytery containing the altar, as well as the north and south transepts that formed the crossbeam of the cross, were to her right.

She had no doubt the gunmen would follow her, so she quickly ran across the center aisle of the church and hid among the pews of the north transept. From there she could keep an eye on the door and still have room to maneuver if need be. She released her sword into the otherwhere, not wanting to have to worry about it sticking up and giving her away.

Annja had just knelt behind the corner of a pew when three men entered the cathedral through the same doors she had used, guns in hand. The leader glanced around, then sent each of his men along the outer edge of the church while he advanced down the center aisle.

Since the intruders were still dressed in the brown habits they had used to infiltrate the complex, she couldn't tell anything about them. There were no identifying marks on their clothing, nor did she recognize any of the men, from what little she'd seen of their faces. With what she'd discovered so far, which was practically nothing, she was going to be little use in helping the authorities catch those in charge of masterminding the massacre.

The leader of the gunmen shouted to the others in French, directing them to move in on the far end of the church.

That, of course, would bring them right down on her position. She needed to get out of there and find a way to take one of the gunmen captive. If she could do that, she could get the information she needed about who they were and what they were after. She would then figure out what to do from there.

Annja turned and scurried down the length of the row, staying in a crouch to keep her head from showing above the backs of the pews. Her intent was to sneak around behind the advancing gunmen and use the opportunity to slip back out the door she'd entered.

Unfortunately, fate had other ideas.

She reached the end of the row and stuck her head around the corner, only to discover one of the gunmen coming from the opposite direction, intent on sneaking up on her in a similar fashion.

They saw each other at the exact same moment, but Annja was a split second faster in her response. She swept her hand out and to the side, pinning her opponent's gun hand against the back of the pew. At the same time she thrust her other hand forward, summoning her sword in the process, intent on running her opponent through.

Some instinct must have saved him at the last second for he twisted to the side and the sword thrust that was intended to skewer him in the chest merely pierced his abdominal area instead. He screamed in pain and reflexively pulled the trigger of his firearm, sending several shots flying down the length of the pew.

While keeping the pressure on the man's wrist, Annja drew back her sword-bearing arm and, with an adrenaline-fueled thrust, drove the hilt into his chin. The force caused his eyes to roll back in his head and sent him into unconsciousness.

Her opponent might be out of the fight, but the damage had been done. When she poked her head up to get a sense of where the rest of the intruders were, bullets thundered into the wood of the pews around her and she felt a sting of pain as a long sliver of hardwood was blown free and slashed across the side of her cheek. Her quick look had shown her several dark forms making their way down either side of the nave in an effort to box her in.

She couldn't stay put.

Not if she wanted to live.

She scrambled over the unconscious body of her opponent and then crab-walked down the length of the pew to the other end. From there she looked out over the presbytery, hunting for a way out.

She had a good view of the altar, as well as the rest of the presbytery space behind it. Chapels lined the rounded rear wall, small alcoves with a statue of some saint or another and a kneeler, sometimes two kneelers, in them. Nothing that looked at all promising as an escape route.

She was about to start looking elsewhere when she saw it.

Between the sixth and the seventh chapels, roughly straight back from the altar as seen from the front of the church, was a door.

It was deftly designed, the undecorated surface of the door blending in with the rest of the dark wood that made up the rear wall, and if the light hadn't reflected off the narrow metal of the sunken handle she might never have seen it.

Where it led, she had no idea.

But anywhere's preferable to here at the moment, she thought.

Of course, getting there was going to be a bit of a challenge. She would have to expose herself to gunfire from several sources as she dashed up the platform, past the altar and over to the door. If she got there and found the door locked she would be in real trouble.

Of course, if she stayed and did nothing, she'd only be making things easy for them. It wouldn't take them long to surround her and, when they did, it would be like fish in a barrel.

She had no other options.

Annja mapped out the route in her mind, doing what she could to prepare herself for what was to come, and then counted it down in her head.

One...

Two...

On three, she lunged to her feet and ran.

Her sudden movement must have taken her pursuers by surprise, for she made it up the platform and halfway to the altar before she heard a shout from the somewhere behind her and the gunfire started once more.

The cacophony was deafening, as the acoustics of the cathedral sent the echoes of each gunshot bounding around the interior, filling the space with thunderous applause of a murderous kind. As she flung herself behind the thick protection of the rectangular marble altar in the center of the platform, several bullets whistled past close enough for her to feel the heat of their passage.

No sooner had she reached the safety of the altar than she was scrambling and charging forward again, except this time she had the bulk of the altar between her and her attackers. A hail of bullets slammed into the marble while she scrambled on hands and knees over to the door she'd seen from the other side of the room.

She grabbed the door's handle and pulled it open, revealing a set of spiral steps leading upward.

Choir loft, she thought, though there was no way of knowing for sure. Wherever they led, she'd deal with it. Right now she just wanted to get out of the line of fire!

As if to punctuate her argument, bullets slammed into the door beside her.

Annja dashed up the stairs.

She'd guessed correctly and emerged into the choir loft. What she hadn't known was that the loft was accessible from the opposite end of the church through the use of two wide walkways and a staircase at the front of the church. As she came up level with the choir loft, several shots ricocheted off the staircase around her, fired by the gunmen running down the walkways in her direction.

With nowhere else to go, Annja continued up the winding staircase, hoping against hope that somewhere above her was a way out.

She emerged into the cupola of the bell tower, an octagonal-shaped room with large arches open to the elements on each side. Beneath her, the staircase rang with the sound of booted feet and the thrumming of the railing under her hands let her know that the gunmen were in hot pursuit. She had only seconds to act before they caught up with her.

With the gunman on her heels and nowhere else to go, Annja took the only course of action available to her. She rushed across the room, clambered through one of the open arches and stepped out onto the roof.

A gunshot rang out as she did so, the bullet slamming into the edge of the archway by her left hand, but she knew better than to look back.

The roof stretched out ahead of her, but she could already see several other intruders climbing onto it from the access ladders on the other wing and were she to head in that direction she'd quickly find herself trapped between two groups of gunmen.

A glance in the other direction showed her the edge of the rooftop only a few yards away, overlooking a long drop to the thundering river below.

Footsteps on the ladder told her she had only seconds to make up her mind.

She turned and ran.

The gunmen continued shooting at her, perhaps divining her intent, but she ignored them as best she could, thrusting downward with her legs, pushing for every ounce of speed she could get.

It was going to be close....

As bullets filled the air around her, Annja raced toward the edge of the rooftop and flung herself out into space.

13

The fall was a good couple of hundred feet and Annja knew that in order to survive it she was going to have to control how she entered the water. Crisp and clean was the order of the day. If she was even the slightest bit off center, she'd bounce off the surface just as if it were fashioned of six feet of solid cement.

Her arms and legs pinwheeled for a moment and then gravity took over, hauling her downward. The fall might feel like it was taking forever, but Annja knew she had only a few seconds in which to prepare herself for the impact at the bottom. She brought the image of her sword to mind and did her best to emulate its long, sleek form with her own body, tucking her arms flat against her sides and squeezing her legs together tightly, her toes pointed. From somewhere in the distance came a shout and the echo of a gunshot, but she didn't have time to think about either right now. She tucked her chin against her chest and hoped for the best.

The collision, when it came, was everything she expected it to be, a bone-jarring crash into the surface of the water followed by a swift plunge toward the bottom. She had no idea how deep the water was and found herself praying that she didn't run out of room before she bled off all that downward momentum she'd picked up from the drop.

Thankfully, the river was deep and she felt herself slowing down before she struck the bottom. This presented her with a new set of difficulties, however, for no sooner had her downward momentum slowed that she felt the tug of the current trying to pull her along in its wake. Realizing the danger she was in, she began clawing her way toward the surface, driving herself upward with powerful kicks of her long legs.

But for every foot she rose upward, the river carried her two feet sideways and it wasn't long before she began to feel herself tiring. Her lungs protested her treatment of them, as well, demanding fresh oxygen, but to open her mouth at this depth meant a sure death by drowning, so she clamped her mouth shut and fought for the surface as hard as she could.

The churning water kept her from being able to feel the natural buoyancy of her body and kept her from trying to open her eyes underwater, worried as she was about all the natural debris rushing along in the current with her.

Was she struggling so hard because she was headed for the bottom rather than climbing toward the surface? How could she tell?

The thought nearly paralyzed her, the fear it evoked overwhelming in its intensity. The animal side of her brain began screaming at her, telling her she was going in the wrong direction and that she was going to die if she didn't do something about it *now,* and it took all of her concentration to force that monster back into the mental closet it had suddenly lurched out of. She fought to think clearly, rationally, but her burning lungs were demanding she take another breath and she felt her lips peeling back as her body disobeyed the commands her brain was giving it...

Annja broke through to the surface of the water with a tremendous gasp, surprised to feel the cool mountain air filling her lungs like a miracle from above. Her relief was short-lived, however, for the rush of the water swept over her head and forced her back underwater seconds later.

This time, though, she was prepared for it, her fear now firmly in check, and so she was able to swiftly fight her way back to the surface and keep her head above water as she sought a way out of the predicament her wild jump had gotten her into.

Looking around, she discovered that she was being swept downstream even faster than she'd thought. She was already quite far from where she'd entered the water and even as she looked back the way she had come she was carried around a bend in the river and the monastery was lost from view. Perhaps even more disconcerting, however, was her realization that the water itself was shockingly cold, so much so that staying in it for too long was not an option.

If I don't do something, I'm either going to freeze to death or get swept all the way to the English Channel.

The right bank was closer, so with grim determination she turned toward it and began swimming perpendicular to the current, trying to make her way across. Thankfully, the river was reasonably free of jutting rocks and she didn't have to worry about being slammed against them as she was swept along.

It was hard going, the current fighting her for every

inch of progress and the cold leeching the energy from her limbs, but she didn't have any choice but to continue pushing forward. Bit by bit, the shore drew closer, until at last she felt the river bottom beneath the soles of her shoes. After another ten minutes of grueling effort she broke free of the current and emerged into shallower depths at the river's edge.

She dragged herself out of the water and up onto the shore, rolling onto her back and doing what she could to catch her breath after the ordeal she'd just been through. She didn't lay there long, though, for once out of the water the coolness of the mountain air cut through her wet clothes like an Arctic wind and she quickly found herself shivering on the riverbank despite the afternoon sun above.

Annja knew that if she didn't get out of her wet clothing soon she'd be in serious danger of hypothermia, especially once the sun went down.

I've got to get moving, she thought.

She climbed to her feet, only to have a bolt of pain shoot up her left ankle. It hurt enough that she promptly sat back down and gave it a look. She could move it in a slow circle, so she knew it wasn't broken, and with her shoe on it didn't seem to be overly swollen, but it was definitely tender to the touch and was already turning a deep shade of bluish black.

I must have twisted it when I hit the water, she thought.

She could see the road through the trees about a dozen yards away and knew she had to head in that direction. She was miles away from even the smallest town and didn't remember passing a single house or homestead during the final part of her drive. The chances of a random motorist headed in the direction she was going were pretty slim, which meant she was going to have to make her way back up the mountain to the monastery on foot.

At least there she could find some dry clothes, check to see if there were any survivors and even call for help, if no one had done so already.

All she had to do was walk a couple of miles, uphill, on a sprained ankle.

14

Annja's pace was even slower than she thought it would be. Her injured ankle bore her weight, but just barely, and she was forced to limp along at a pace made all the more frustrating by the fact that she knew there were people at the facility above who needed her help.

She spent the entire journey in a state of tension, listening for the sound of an engine, worried that the attackers would find her alone on the road after leaving the monastery above. She was constantly checking the undergrowth on either side of the road, picking out potential hiding places that she could reach quickly and with a minimum of fuss should the sound of an approaching vehicle reach her ears, but in the end she didn't need any of them; not a single vehicle passed her going in either direction.

That meant the attackers had probably done what they had come to do and had left the monastery behind while she was still trying to save herself from the river's current.

That wasn't a good sign.

Step by step, teeth gritted against the pain, she made her way up to the monastery gates as quickly as she could.

The gates stood wide open, which wasn't a good sign. As she hobbled through them, she caught sight of a brown-robed figure lying unmoving in the grass between the gates and the small guardhouse nearby. The dark stain that covered the front of his robe didn't bode well for his chances, but she had to check to be sure before moving on. If he was only injured and she left him behind...

As she drew close enough to see his face, she recognized the silent monk who had let her into the complex earlier. From the looks of it, he'd been shot with a short burst from an automatic weapon. Kneeling down next to him, she checked for a pulse but, as she'd expected, didn't find one. His eyes were open, staring at the sky above, and so she brushed her hand over them, and then got back to her feet.

Her car was still in the parking area, but the driver's window had been smashed and the line of bullet holes stitched across the hood let her know that she wouldn't be taking it anywhere in the near future. Since it wasn't her car, she didn't feel all that torn up about the damage; it wasn't the first vehicle wrecked by those she'd been forced to confront since taking up the sword. No, what made her want to scream in anger and frustration was the fact that they'd gotten the chest, and therefore the puzzle box that it contained. When she'd returned to the complex and rushed back into the monastery, she'd left the chest on the rear seat of the car, easy pickings for anyone looking for it.

Stupid, stupid, stupid!

Of course, hindsight was twenty-twenty. There was

nothing to do now but soldier on and see what she could make out of the mess.

There were two more bodies on the front steps to the main building and another just inside the door. Each of them had been gunned down in similar fashion. Farther inside she found more of the same. It appeared that the intruders, whoever they had been, had wanted to be certain there wasn't anyone left to serve as a witness to what had happened here.

She kept up her search for survivors all the way to the cathedral, but she didn't find a single one by the time she reached her destination.

Inside, she found the abbott lying on the floor in front of the altar, a bullet through the skull. Four of the fingers on his left hand were broken and horribly twisted, letting her know that there'd been a serious effort to get him to tell them something. Whether he'd divulged what they wanted or not was uncertain, for they could have executed him after he'd given up the information or when they'd decided that they didn't have any more time to waste.

In the end, it hadn't really mattered, she thought. They'd gotten what they'd come for, anyway—thanks to her carelessness.

Standing there, looking down at the body of the man who only hours before had helped her uncover a key clue to the mystery unfurling before her, Annja felt a rage begin to build inside her. She vowed that she'd bring the perpetrators to justice, no matter what.

She searched the rest of the complex, but didn't find a single survivor. The monks living there had been slaughtered to a man.

No witnesses, she thought bitterly.

She did, however, find a phone on the abbott's desk. It

was the only one she'd seen so far in the entire monastery, so she was thankful that the intruders hadn't torn it loose from the wall. It was an oversight that could have come back to haunt them, had any of the monks been quick enough to capitalize on it, and Annja was pleased to see it. It meant the enemy, whoever they were, made mistakes.

Mistakes could be exploited.

She punched in 1-1-2, the general emergency number throughout all of France, and explained to the operator that there had been a violent attack on the monks at the monastery. She identified herself when asked and stated that they could contact the American Embassy for confirmation of who she was so that they would know this was not a crank call of any kind. Given the nearest town was almost an hour away, and she didn't remember seeing any kind of emergency response services when she'd driven through, Annja knew she had a long wait ahead of her.

Now that she had taken care of the most pressing issues, she realized that her teeth were chattering and that she was shivering violently. Her clothing was still wet despite the long walk and the chill mountain air hadn't helped any. She suspected she might be slipping into hypothermia and knew she had to do something about it quickly.

But a search of the abbot's quarters turned up nothing but boxers, socks and the long brown robes she'd been seeing on every monk she encountered. The same held true of the rest of the rooms she looked into at the other end of the hall.

The idea of meeting the authorities dressed like Friar Tuck didn't appeal to her at all, but what choice did she have? She selected a robe that looked to be the closest fit, stripped out of her wet clothing and used a towel from a nearby bathroom to dry herself as best she could. Resigning herself to the inevitable, she pulled the robe on over her head. To her surprise, the fabric was much softer than she'd expected, and warm, as well. She might be stuck looking like an extra from *Monty Python and the Holy Grail,* but at least she'd be comfortable while doing so.

Only half an hour had gone by when the sound of a helicopter's rotors caught her attention. She glanced out the window, saw it approaching in the distance and went out to meet it.

The aircraft came in over the trees, nose forward, so Annja didn't get a good look at the aircraft until the pilot spun it around and lined up for landing. That's when the insignia, a stylized dragon in midflight, became visible on the black fuselage.

Annja knew that logo.

It belonged to Dragontech Security Services, one of the many companies owned by her sometime-ally, sometime-nemesis Garin Braden.

"All-the-time pain-in-the-ass Garin Braden is more like it," she said.

The helicopter landed on the grass beside the parking area. The door opened almost immediately and a squad of armed gunmen disembarked, moving with the kind of crisp efficiency that marked them as former military personnel. They fanned out in a half circle, the assault rifles in their hands pointing beyond her at the windows of the monastery.

Behind them came Garin Braden.

She'd met Garin at the same time she'd acquired her sword, the one that had once belonged to Joan of Arc. Whatever power had been imparted to the sword at the moment of Joan's death had also affected Garin and his former mentor, Roux. Both of them had been her failed protectors. Both of them had been there to witness Joan's execution. Both of them had subsequently discovered that they no longer aged as other men did, that unless they were killed by injury or violence, it seemed they would most likely live forever.

Over the years they'd gone from being squire and master to equal competitors to deadly enemies. Only the arrival of Annja, and the reforming of the sword that had been broken, had brought them grudgingly back together again.

At first, Garin had been convinced that the sword controlled his destiny, that by possessing it Annja could threaten his very existence. He'd schemed to take it from her on more than one occasion, but thus far without success. Lately his overt activities toward that end had seemed to have been put on hold, but she was still wary around him.

Even knowing he often didn't have her best interests at heart, Annja found it hard to simply dismiss Garin Braden. The fact that he was terribly handsome, with his black hair and immaculately trimmed goatee, didn't help. He was also one of those larger than life personalities and being in his presence made her forget some of what she'd experienced with him. She constantly had to remind herself that he had a devil's heart to go with his devilishly good looks.

Even that didn't dampen her attraction to him, however.

He had a habit of turning up unexpectedly but just what the hell was he doing here?

Annja waited for him at the base of the front steps as he strode across the lawn. He was dressed beautifully, as always, in a suit that was tailored to show off his muscular frame. It was only as he drew closer that she remembered she was barefoot and naked beneath the monk's robe. She wanted to sink right into the stone beneath her feet.

"Hello, I'm looking for… Annja, is that you?"

She used irritation to try and hide her embarrassment. "What are you doing here, Garin? Did you get lost on your way home?"

He ignored her jibe, focusing instead on what she was wearing.

"I must say you look ravishing in mud brown, Annja. And the way it accents your curves—"

"Cut the crap. What are you doing here? What do you want?"

A pained expression crossed his face. "Must I always want something?"

She didn't hesitate. "Yes."

"Well, you have me there," he replied, grinning.

Annja tried not to think about how that grin made her feel.

Garin surveyed the scene behind her, taking in bodies just inside the open door. When he looked at her again his expression had gone serious. "Any survivors?"

"I haven't checked the entire grounds, but inside, no."

He nodded, acknowledging her remark, and then waved to one of his men, summoning him over. They had a brief conversation outside of Annja's earshot and then the first man was joined by two others as they fanned out to search the grounds.

"Come on," Garin said. "We've got to get you out of here."

Annja snorted. "I'm not going anywhere with you,

Garin. The authorities will be here soon. Do you just expect me to leave all these bodies behind because you say so?"

The only person who knew where she was going was Bernard and she had no reason to believe the two men even knew each other. The more she thought about it, the more Garin's sudden appearance wasn't making any sense.

Garin's joking manner abruptly disappeared. "Yes, that's exactly what I expect. Every minute you stay puts you in more danger. We need to leave."

"I told you, I'm not leaving. I called this in. I have a responsibility to be here when the authorities arrive."

"That's exactly what they are counting on!" He clenched his fists in frustration. "Do you think I came out here just to see you looking like a reject from the local Renaissance faire?"

Garin's insistence, and his single-mindedness, had her worried.

"What's going on? What aren't you telling me, Garin?"

"For heaven's sake, woman, we don't have time for that—"

"You'll make time," she cut in, "or I'm not going with you. Now out with it."

But rather than say anything more himself, he pulled a digital recorder out of his pocket and hit the play button.

"The Creed woman apparently survived the fall from the roof. She needs to be eliminated before she speaks to the police. Get back up there and get rid of her before she becomes more of a nuisance."

Annja didn't recognize the voice, but it was clear that whoever he was, he had intimate knowledge of what had happened at the monastery.

Garin wasn't kidding around.

"How did you get that?" she asked.

"I'd be happy to explain everything, but right now I think it's better if we got out of here, don't you?"

As Annja opened her mouth to answer, the sound of a racing engine reached their ears. They turned to see a dark model Mercedes bounce through the iron gates less than three hundred yards away and rush toward them. Even as they watched, the front passenger window rolled down and a man's head and shoulders appeared.

In his hands was an automatic weapon.

"Run!" Garin shouted as the bullets began to fly.

15

Annja didn't need any further encouragement. She turned and ran for the helicopter...only to fall flat on her face as the hem of the robe got tangled in her feet and spilled her to the ground.

The sound of gunfire joined the growl of the car engine, both of which were suddenly drowned out in the rhythmic beat of the helicopter rotors as the pilot saw what was going on and prepared to get his aircraft out of there.

Annja glanced back to see the Mercedes change direction and head right for her.

She scrambled to her feet.

Bullets whip-cracked through the air as Annja frantically glanced around looking for some protective cover, but there was none to be found. She could make a run for the helicopter over open ground or she could turn around and head back inside the monastery, hope to find a different way out before the gunmen caught up to her.

She was wavering between the two actions when the choice was decided for her.

A hand with a grip like steel grabbed her arm.

"Come on!" Garin shouted, half carrying her along beside him as he ran for the chopper.

This time Annja used her hands to hike up the hem of the robe, not wanting to trip on it again. There wasn't anything she could do about the gravel slicing into the bottoms of her feet, though, so she just ignored it. She'd been through worse and it was a damn sight better than getting a bullet in the head.

Garin's security team had finally gotten into the act, sending a blistering hail of gunfire at the Mercedes as they raced forward to plant themselves between the enemy and their employer, protecting him as they had been trained to do.

The open door of the helicopter loomed ahead of them.

Garin's longer stride put him out ahead of Annja by a few feet, so he reached the helicopter before she did. He jumped inside the open doorway and then turned to face her, ready to lend a hand.

She was looking right at him when the bullet took him high in the right side of his chest, tossing him backward into the darkness inside the helicopter.

"Garin!" she screamed.

She covered the last few feet and then leaped inside the helicopter as bullets slammed into the metal fuselage around her. She barely had time to grab hold of a nearby seat before the pilot took them up, arcing away from the gunfire as quickly as he could.

Annja spent an anxious minute holding on for dear life as the pilot leveled out and then she scrambled over to where Garin was lying against the opposite bulkhead.

She ripped open his suit coat, desperately afraid of what she'd find. Whatever mysticism gave Garin his extended lifespan also helped him heal more quickly than the average individual, but a sucking chest wound was serious even for him.

The black face of a bulletproof vest stared back at her.

"Thank God," she said.

"Can't keep your hands off me, huh?"

Annja glanced up to find Garin watching her with an amused look on his face.

"You bastard!" she said, backing up to give him some room. "I thought you were shot."

He coughed, grimaced and said, "I was. That's how I ended up on the floor, remember?" He pulled himself up into a nearby chair, then indicated Annja should put on one of the headsets hanging off the nearby bulkhead as he reached to do the same.

She did as instructed and she heard him telling the pilot to head for his Frankfurt house.

"What about your men?" she asked.

"They'll be fine. They'll neutralize the threat and then disperse as necessary. Don't worry, they know what they are doing."

The flight lasted about half an hour. Annja was too worn out to say much and Garin kept his thoughts to himself, which was fine with her. She was still surprised at his sudden appearance and previous experience had her wondering what else he was keeping from her.

As was typical of both Garin and Roux, the "house" could more accurately be labeled a mansion, with two large wings extending off the main building. The pilot set them down on a helipad atop the roof without issue.

Once inside, Garin led Annja to a private suite in

the west wing of the house and suggested that she meet
him in the den after showering and changing into more
practical clothes.

She was all too happy to oblige.

The suite was beautifully decorated, with a luxurious
king-size bed and a sunken tub that one could probably
swim in. She eyed it enviously for a moment and then
decided that a hot shower might be more practical.

She looked around for the clothes Garin had mentioned and found an array of styles and sizes in the
wardrobe and the walk-in closet. She stared at all of
them for a moment, wondering just who they belonged
to. The styles were all quite current, so it couldn't have
been one of Garin's lovers from ages past. Perhaps he
just kept a well-stocked wardrobe of women's clothing
available for whenever one of his companions might
need it?

She wouldn't put it past him.

Annja sought out the most practical outfit she could,
which wasn't easy given most of the clothing was designed to be skintight or extremely revealing. In one of
the drawers, however, she found a pair of cargo pants
and paired them with a black T-shirt.

She took a hot shower, scrubbing the last of the river
grime from her body, and then dressed in the clothes
she'd found. They fit her as if they had been custom tailored. That made her speculate that perhaps they actually had been, which took her down all kinds of roads
she didn't want to think about. She found socks in the
wardrobe drawers and saw more shoes than she'd ever
seen anywhere outside of a shoe store in the closet, including a pair of hiking boots that looked like they'd
fit reasonably well. She decided to pad around shoeless
for the moment.

Feeling pretty much back to her usual self, she wandered out of the bedroom suite and went in search of Garin.

She found him in the den, dressed casually in jeans and a loose-fitting shirt.

Annja didn't bother with pleasantries. She'd been patient; now it was time to get to the bottom of things.

"What were you doing at Berceau de solitude?"

Garin stared at her.

Misinterpreting his silence, she said, "The monastery, Garin, the monastery."

His reply was in perfect French. "I understood you perfectly, Annja. I was simply distracted by the notion that I think you looked better in that brown robe of yours."

Typical Garin.

In the same language, she replied. "And that's just about what I'd expect from a bore like yourself. Shall we do this all night?"

Garin laughed, a deep baritone that filled the room with his pleasure.

"Always the feisty one," he said, switching back to English. He held up his hands, palms out. "I surrender, Annja. You win. Please, sit down. We have a lot to talk about."

She did as he asked, taking a seat on the couch opposite where he sat and curled her legs up underneath her. The room was furnished in post-modern minimalist, it seemed—all black and chrome functionality with little that wasn't absolutely needed. The couch, however, proved to be surprisingly comfortable.

Garin gave her a frank look for a long moment and then answered her original question. "I was at the Cradle of Solitude because of you, Annja."

She raised her eyebrows but didn't say anything, waiting for him to expand on his remark.

"As I'm sure you realize, information is power and much of Dragontech's success comes from the fact that we have greater access to more detailed information than our competitors."

Or your enemies, she thought.

"We monitor a wide variety of communication channels through several different processes, looking for certain words or phrases that can give us a leg up in our business dealings. After you came along and claimed the sword, your name was one of the terms I asked our monitors to watch for. As the emergency response lines are one of the frequencies we monitor, when you gave your name to the 1-1-2 operator this afternoon, the call was flagged and sent to my attention."

So that's how he always seems to keep tabs on me, she thought.

"No sooner had word of your call been relayed to me than we intercepted another transmission, this one from a cell phone tower in Paris, which also mentioned you by name. That was a tape of that call I played for you earlier."

Annja suddenly had an image of Garin sitting amid a bank of computer monitors, listening to signals bounced down from satellites all around the world. Shades of Big Brother. It was just a bit creepy to think that a man with Garin Braden's resources was intentionally keeping regular watch over her.

Garin went on. "I tried to reach you by cell phone to warn you of the problem, but was unable to do so. As my team and I were already here in Frankfurt, I made the decision to attempt to warn you in person. It would seem I arrived just in time."

His story had the ring of truth to it. He hadn't been able to reach her on her cell because by then it was lying at the bottom of the river somewhere; she'd had it in her pocket when she made the leap off the roof. The distance from Frankfurt to the monastery was about half an hour air time, which would have put his arrival in the right time frame for him to have intercepted and then reacted to her emergency call.

Given what they'd been through in the past, it wasn't a big surprise that she hadn't trusted him right off the bat. In the early days, he'd tried to kill her on more than one occasion. Lately, though, he seemed to have come to peace with the fact that she wasn't going to surrender the sword to his control willingly and had gone from being a threat to an occasional ally and, dare she say it, even a friend.

One thing was for certain, no one could ever say her life wasn't complicated.

"What, exactly, are you caught up in this time, Annja?" he asked.

Deciding to take him into her confidence, she told him everything that had happened to her since leaving the dojo the morning before.

He listened silently until she got around to describing the note Parker had left for Sykes, then interrupted.

"The FotS? You're certain that's what it said?"

She was. She no longer had the letter, but her recall of anything she'd read was quite good and she was certain she had it down word for word.

"That's interesting. I wonder…?"

Before she could ask what it was he was wondering about, he pulled his cell phone out of his pocket and hit the speed dial key.

"Griggs? Dig up whatever we have on the Friends of the South and bring it to me, please."

He closed the phone and gave her his attention once more. "Go on."

She finished out the rest of the tale, describing the letter the puzzle box had contained and her belief that it led to the missing Confederate treasure.

In for a penny, in for a pound, she thought. She'd trusted him this far so letting him know her ultimate objective—recovery of the treasure—wasn't all that big a risk. Besides, Garin knew her pretty well and would sense that there was a bigger motive behind it all than just identifying the remains.

His next comment showed that was true.

"You don't care about the value of the treasure itself, do you?" he asked. "You just want to solve the mystery."

She nodded. Finding the actual treasure would be nice, no doubt about it, as her bank account was looking more than a bit dismal, but for her, the real accomplishment would be discovering exactly what had happened after the treasure had supposedly been "stolen" on that night in 1865. That was the prize she was after.

The door behind them opened and a medium-size black man with a shaved head and a soul patch on his chin stepped inside. His name was Matthew Griggs and he was some kind of senior operative with Dragontech Security. Annja had first met him in the aftermath of the Indian tsunami, when he'd flown in by helicopter to rescue her and the rest of her dig workers.

"Ms. Creed," he said in that lilting island accent of his, a smile on his face.

She smiled back at him. "Nice to see you, Griggs."

Griggs crossed the room and handed a manila folder

to Garin, who thanked him and began leafing through its thin contents as Griggs left them alone once more.

Annja itched to know what was in the file, but there was no way she was going to give Garin the upper hand by asking. She'd known him long enough to understand that he was constantly turning everything into a competition, vying for dominance with every issue no matter how big or small. He knew she'd want to know what was in the file. He would purposely keep it from her until she asked. But if she asked, she lost face in his eyes, which only reinforced his already monumental ego. Of course, making her play the game at all was considered a win for him as well in his eyes, so it was a losing proposition for her either way.

Instead, she sat back and waited patiently for Garin to finish reviewing the documents in front of him. Several minutes passed. Finally, perhaps realizing that he wasn't going to get any kind of rise out of Annja, Garin closed the folder and spoke up.

"You might not care about the treasure but it's clear that someone else does."

There wasn't any doubt about that. Whoever they were, they were clearly willing to kill over it, as well.

"Sounds like you're going to need some help," Garin said.

She had to admit that was true. She *was* going to need some help. The question was whether Garin Braden was the best person to provide it.

"What did you have in mind?" she asked.

He didn't hesitate.

"Sixty-forty split on the treasure, with the larger portion going to me as I'll be putting up all the financing and security for the search."

Annja immediately shook her head. That would give

him control over the find and there was no way she was going to allow that. He'd auction it off to the highest bidder and the lost Confederate treasury would disappear into some private collector's vault, never to be seen again. As far as she was concerned, the treasure was a part of history and deserved to be shared by all. The finder's fee they'd receive from the government would be more than enough compensation.

She made a counteroffer. "Fifty-one, forty-nine split. I retain control of the expedition and make all decisions regarding whether it goes forward or not. You provide funding and materials, which will be paid back out of my portion of the find if we're successful."

Garin opened his mouth to say something, but Annja cut him off.

"Without what's up here," she said, tapping her forehead in the process, "you're dead in the water."

To her surprise, he grinned. "Done!" he said, and stuck out his hand to shake on it. While doing so, Annja couldn't help but wonder if she'd outnegotiated him or just fallen victim to some trap she hadn't seen coming.

It was not a pleasant feeling.

Garin set the file he'd been examining on the coffee table between them, but didn't offer any comments on its contents. Instead, he asked, "What happened to the note Parker left behind with the puzzle box?"

"They were stolen when the gunmen first attacked the monastery."

Garin didn't like hearing that. "So we *are* dead in the water until we identify the attackers and retrieve the messages?" he asked.

"I didn't say that. Give me something to write on." He got up, walked into the next room and returned with a pen and pad of paper in hand. Taking them, Annja quickly reconstructed both the letter that had accompanied the puzzle box, as well as the rather cryptic instructions the box itself had contained, from memory. When she was finished, she passed them over.

He glanced at the note to Sykes briefly and then turned his attention to the riddle. After studying it for several minutes he said, "Seems easy enough. All we have to do is find where Parker's doppelgänger is buried and we'll have the treasure, right?"

"Wrong. It's never that simple."

"So enlighten me."

She waved a hand at the pad in general. "Messages like these were never as straightforward as they seemed. Content was important, yes, but it was often what wasn't being said that was the real key.

"Four paragraphs, four different clues. Most people would do what you just did—jump to the final clue with the idea that if they can solve that, they can solve the puzzle overall. But that's incorrect."

"So you've said," Garin replied dryly.

Ignoring him, Annja continued. "Perhaps *incomplete* would be a better word than *incorrect*. The fourth clue will eventually have to be solved so the effort to do so wouldn't be entirely wasted. But if you look at the wording of each paragraph, you can see that they have to be solved in a specific order."

Pointing at each of the individual paragraphs in turn, she said, "Each clue is dependent on the one before it. You can't find the Lady without the key. You can't find the doppelgänger's resting place without the rifle. You can't find the treasure without the resting place."

Garin nodded to show he understood.

"In this case, it seems to be even more important than usual, because each clue requires you to bring a physical object to the next location. Arrive at the final location without them and the treasure will still elude you."

He glanced at the paper. "So we start at the top, 'in the cellars of the wine god.'"

"Right. What's the first thing that comes to mind when you hear that phrase—'wine god'?"

"Bacchus."

It wasn't the answer Annja was looking for, but it was a correct one nonetheless. Bacchus had been the Roman god of wine and the madness or euphoria it produced. It was from his name the English word *bacchanal* originated.

Should have seen that one coming, she thought. Garin loves wine, women and luxury, so naturally he'd think along those lines.

"Right part of the world but wrong culture," she told him.

"Well, Dionysius, then," came his swift reply.

"Correct. So how does someone named Dionysius fit into the story of the missing Confederate treasury?"

Garin scowled. "I don't have a clue," he said. "You're the one with all the answers. Why don't you tell me?"

Now there was the Garin she was used to. Impatient and not one to take kindly to remarks on his intelligence, oblique as they might be.

"When trying to find information on Captain Parker, I came across several sites that listed some of the common theories regarding the location of the treasure," Annja said. "As you might guess, the Union Army was particularly interested in locating it. Seize the treasury and you basically eliminate the South's means of waging war, because no money meant no supply and no pay for the soldiers.

"It was generally thought at the time that Parker and his men had hidden the treasure on the grounds of a plantation owned by Dionysius Chennault, an elderly planter and Methodist minister."

Garin grinned. "So the cellars of the wine god are most likely…"

"…the wine cellars of the Chennault plantation," Annja finished for him.

Garin got up from the couch, suddenly energized. "Excellent! We'll start there first thing in the morning."

"You might want to leave a little more time than that," Annja said. "After all, the plantation is in Washington, Georgia."

16

After Annja had gone to sleep, Garin sat in the living room alone, considering the turn of events that had brought him to this point.

He was not a man who believed in coincidence, not after all he'd seen in the centuries since that fateful day under the hot sun when an innocent woman had been consumed in the flames before him. Fate's bloody fingerprints were all over his memories of that event and many others since. The fact that he was still alive and well, hundreds of years after his body should have returned to the dust from whence it came, reminded him that there were forces at work in the world that he just did not understand. He'd come to believe that while some things were just the luck of the draw, others happened for a reason.

He thought about the events of that afternoon. He'd been monitoring Annja's movements for some time; it was just common sense for him to keep track of her, given that the sword she carried was in some way responsible for his continued existence. He'd never planned to be in a position to help her if she ran into difficulty; in fact, if he'd had more time to think about it, he probably wouldn't have helped. She was constantly courting danger and he was usually content to sit back and watch. But when the word of the current situation had reached him, something in his gut had prompted him to take action.

The results, as they were, only confirmed his sense that the Fates had reached down once more and interfered in his life.

He glanced at the file he held in his lap. His pretense of reviewing the material in front of Annja was just that, a sham. He was intimately aware of the contents of most of his files, for the same mysticism that had kept him alive for so many years had also blessed him with a remarkable memory, and this particular file had been reviewed and added to multiple times over the years. The Friends of the South was simply a front for a small but ruthless organization, and several times during the past two centuries Garin had found his interests and goals in direct opposition to theirs. He'd worked hard, then and now, to be certain that they did not gain the upper hand with regard to such situations.

He hadn't thought about them much in the past several months, other matters having occupied his attention, and then Annja showed up out of nowhere, in need of assistance and running from the machinations of his old enemy. Coincidence be damned; that was the hand of fate if ever it had shown itself.

Garin got up and fixed himself a glass of brandy, swirling the liquid in the glass as he considered the opportunities available to him.

As he'd told her earlier, he fully intended to help Annja recover the long-lost Confederate treasure. She thought he had a strictly monetary interest in the adventure, but that was the least of his concerns. He'd accumulated a vast treasure of his own over the years. After all, it wasn't all that difficult when you had literally centuries in which to do it. Even if they found the treasure intact, it would only be worth a tiny fraction of what he already controlled. The value was certainly not enough to even be worth the effort, really. Sure, there might be some value in offering it intact on the black market to the private collector's circuit, but the work involved in doing so made it hardly worth the effort.

No, the true value in helping Annja rested in other areas. First, she'd feel some sense of obligation to him as a result, thanks to her do-gooder general nature. That alone made it worthwhile; he could manipulate that at a later time to his advantage, he was sure. Having her beholden to him was a strategic opportunity he just couldn't pass up.

Never mind it would drive her nuts thinking about it and that would prove to be a source of amusement for him in the future, he had no doubt. Second, beating the Order at its own game was an opportunity that didn't come around all that often. While Garin was loath to admit it, the Order had gotten the better of him the last time they had clashed and he fully intended to balance the books by making things as difficult as possible for them now. The current head of the Order was not the crafty adversary his ancestor had been, preferring blunt-force tactics over the chesslike precision that had been exhibited in the past, and Garin had no doubt that he was by far the intellectual superior.

17

Blaine Michaels stared at the one-hundred-and-forty-year-old missive and, after two hours of close scrutiny, had to finally admit that he didn't have a clue as to what it was trying to tell him. The legal pad beside him was full of the notes that he'd taken as he'd tried to work through the puzzle, but he was enough of a realist to know that it all amounted to nothing useful. He just wasn't wired to think this way.

He understood that William Parker's instructions were designed to lead the recipient to the location of the missing gold, with each stanza being a separate clue, but that was as far as he could go. He had no idea who the wine god was, never mind the Peacock. And how was a key supposed to lead you anywhere? It just didn't make any sense.

The day had not gone as well as he had hoped. After spending much of the morning reviewing the material his team had stolen from Professor Reinhardt's office at the museum, he'd correctly deduced that the only real lead was the scrap of paper naming the monastery. He'd expected to find much more and was frustrated that he didn't understand how or why the monastery fit into the situation. Things had continued their downward slide when his team ran into that damned Creed woman at the monastery a few hours later. What was supposed to be a simple smash and grab like the one at the museum had turned into a bloodbath. She'd actually attacked several of his men with a sword of all things! His men had managed to corner her on the rooftop, but she'd gotten away by jumping off the edge into the river below.

He'd thought that was the last of her, but then he'd received word that she'd placed a call to emergency services, summoning the police to the scene of the crime, and he'd been forced to order a group of his men back to the monastery in an effort to take her out for good.

Somehow, she'd managed to kill them and escape a second time.

That damned woman has more lives than anyone deserves, he thought.

Just what and how much she actually knew was still unclear, but that no longer mattered. She'd put herself squarely in his sights by interfering in his business. No one did that and got away with it. He was going to have to take care of her—and the sooner, the better.

Right now, though, he needed to make some decisions regarding the missive on the desk in front of him. As much as he hated to admit it, he knew he was going to find someone to decipher Parker's directions to the gold.

The question was who?

Ironically, he realized, the best option was probably Annja Creed herself. After all, she'd been the one to unearth the connection to the Cradle of Solitude and, if his guess was correct, she had convinced the abbot to hand over the puzzle box. Clearly she knew what she was doing. But the fact that she'd already taken up arms against him precluded him from making use of her services. It would be seen as a weakness in the eyes of his colleagues and he had no intention of giving them any ammunition that might enable them to mount a campaign to remove him from his position as leader of the Order.

No, Creed was unacceptable.

He'd have to go with his second choice, which, in the long run, was probably better than constantly sparring against that annoying woman, anyway.

Michaels reached for the phone, intending to order one of his crews out to do the job, but then he hesitated. Given the days events, he could foresee it ending in disaster and he couldn't afford another one.

He thought about one of his father's favorite sayings. "When you want something done right, you've got to do it yourself," he muttered.

It seemed that now might be a good time to listen to dear old Dad.

He rose from his desk and moved into his bedroom, where he quickly changed into dark jeans and a black sweater, attire more suited for the evening's activities. He pulled on a pair of dark rubber-soled boots.

When he was satisfied with his appearance, he picked up the phone and called downstairs to the head of his security team. He gave instructions that two of the three men who had handled the museum job the night before were to meet him out front in five minutes. As they were simply added muscle to be certain the job went off the way he intended it to, he didn't care which two were sent, which simplified things.

Taking the elevator to the lower level, Michaels retrieved an SUV from the garage and drove around front and picked up the two men. They were dressed in dark clothing and the telltale bulge of their shoulder holsters could be seen beneath their jackets. That reminded him to arm himself, as well, so he removed the automatic pistol from the glove box and laid it on the passenger seat beside him, where it would be readily accessible when he got out of the vehicle.

The drive was passed in silence; the two men in the backseat knew better than to strike up a conversation with the boss unless addressed directly. They cruised twice through the neighborhood, coming from different directions each time, getting a feel for the territory.

Their target lived in a community of freestanding town houses, each with its own small yard. Most of them had small fences running across the front of the lot, but they were so low that they could be easily stepped over and wouldn't cause a problem when it came time to make their move.

On their third pass they found a parking spot a few doors down from their target and pulled in to wait.

The street was quiet.

It was still early, so lights burned in several of the nearby town houses, but Michaels wasn't concerned. In this day and age, most people knew to keep their heads down and to stay out of business that didn't concern them.

He gave it fifteen minutes, noting the traffic patterns and watching the parked vehicles nearby to be certain they didn't contain witnesses. When he felt it was safe to make a move, he turned to the others.

"Our target lives in the town house on the end. If he's not home, we'll settle in and wait. We need him intact, so no violence unless I give the word. Questions?"

Both men shook their heads.

"All right, then, let's go."

The interior light had already been dismantled, so there was no telltale glow to call attention to them as they slipped out of the vehicle. They jumped over the low fence that fronted the property, and immediately disappeared around the back of the building.

Michaels quickly located the back door of their target's town house and gestured toward it. One of his companions stepped up and punched out the glass next to the doorknob, then reached in and unlocked the door.

Ten seconds later the three men were moving through the darkened house, searching for their quarry.

They found him in the study upstairs, watching old *Star Trek* reruns on the television. He started when he saw them enter the room, then recovered his wits enough to reach for the cell phone lying on the table nearby, but the gun Blaine pulled out and pointed at his head quickly disabused him of the notion.

"If you don't mind, Professor, we'd like the pleasure of your company for a few days."

Reinhardt had no choice but to agree.

18

Annja spent the night in Garin's spare bedroom, emerging from the suite to find him standing before the television in the living room, watching a newscast. He heard her come in and said over his shoulder without turning, "The events at Berceau de solitude have made the news."

The details were sketchy. Armed gunmen had invaded the monastery, killing fourteen residents. Some of the monks must have fought back, it was theorized, because two of the gunmen were found dead on the front lawn beside the burned-out hulk of their vehicle. A female caller had phoned in the tragedy and had then disappeared from the scene. The police were keeping her identity to themselves.

Annja could see Commissaire Laroche's hand in the fact that the media didn't have her name yet, but she knew it wouldn't stay that way for long. They were just too good at their jobs. And the commissaire's goodwill would only last so long. He wouldn't be happy that she'd left the scene of the crime but at least she had a good excuse for that. After all, people had been trying to kill her!

Still, she knew she'd better get in touch with him and explain what had happened.

"Can I use your phone?" she asked.

Garin pointed to a table on the other side of the room, where a slim telephone receiver rested. She was mentally rehearsing what she would say to the inspector as she crossed the room when the announcer's voice on the television behind her caught her attention.

"In other news, Professor Bernard Reinhardt of the Museum of Natural—"

Click. Garin changed the channel.

Annja spun around. "Wait! Go back!"

Garin shrugged, then flipped the television channel back to the news. The announcer was still talking.

"A neighbor stated that she saw Professor Reinhardt being forced into a dark-colored van by three men in their mid-to-late thirties, and when he tried to call for help, he was struck in the face by one of his abductors. Police are asking anyone with information that might help them locate the professor or his abductors to call the hotline. We turn now to our foreign correspondent…"

Garin flipped through several other newscasts. Reinhardt's abduction was mentioned more than once, but there was no more information on any of the other broadcasts. Nor had any made the connection between the break-in at the museum, the attack on the monastery and the professor's kidnapping.

It wasn't lost on Annja and she was furious with herself for not seeing it coming. A simple phone call last night might have saved Bernard from the entire ordeal.

Apparently sensing what she was feeling, Garin said, "It's not your fault."

"Of course it is. I should have called him when we arrived last night, no matter what the hour."

"Don't be ridiculous, Annja. You had no way of knowing they would target Reinhardt next. They got what they were after. Logically that should have been it."

Annja realized he was right. That should have been it.

So why did they need Bernard if they had the clues to find the treasure?

The answer, when it came to her, was obvious. They had the instructions from Captain Parker, but they didn't know what to do with them. They must have kidnapped Bernard in order to get him to work it out for them.

When she said as much to Garin, he agreed.

"So now what?" he asked.

"Now we find out who did this, rescue Bernard and make them pay for what they've done."

Garin regarded her soberly. "And just how do you expect to do that? We don't even know where to begin."

"There's got to be something. They didn't just appear out of thin air."

But even as she said it, she knew that, for all intents and purposes, that was, indeed, precisely what they had done. She had no idea who was behind the activity or why. Nor did she have any real clue where to start. She supposed the police report from the museum break-in might contain some information, but getting her hands on that…

It seemed hopeless.

"The best bet is to beat them to the treasure."

Annja stared at Garin. "Is that all you can think about? Your share of the treasure?"

To give him credit, Garin was actually offended by the statement, which was Annja's first clue that he was actually trying to be helpful.

"Don't give me that crap. I'm trying to help you rescue your friend. I don't give a rat's ass what happens to him, personally."

No surprise there, Annja thought.

But something about his very truthfulness made her want to hear him out.

"Sorry," she said, albeit grudgingly. "How will going after the treasure help Bernard?"

"If we're correct that the professor was taken to help them recover it, then they'll keep him alive until they do so and that means he's not in immediate danger."

"I'm sure he'd be thrilled at how blithely you're dismissing the danger of his situation."

"I'm not dismissing anything. I'm simply saying that running off half-cocked isn't going to help him."

"Okay, fine. Point taken."

"They want the treasure," he went on. "That's the point of all this. That's also our bargaining chip. They're not going to just let him go when they're through with him. You know that as well as I do. That would be stupid. Since they haven't done anything that fits that description so far, I think it would be a stretch to think they'd start doing so now."

"Agreed, but you still haven't answered my question."

"I'm getting to that. If the treasure is what they want, then the treasure is our most important bargaining chip. If we control the treasure, we can call the shots. Including forcing them to let the professor go."

"We have to beat them to the treasure," Annja finished for him.

"Right."

It made sense. As much as she hated to admit it.

Find the treasure, then use it to bargain for Bernard's life. It seemed like their only option.

Before they did anything, she knew she still had to get in touch with the police inspector.

She grabbed Garin's phone and made a call to Laroche's office. The operator wasn't able to locate Laroche, so Annja left a message telling him she was all right and that he could call her back or she would be in to speak with him later that day.

When she hung up, Annja found Garin watching her. He inclined his head in the direction of the phone.

"Do you think that was wise?" he asked.

"I don't know about wise, but it was certainly necessary. My wet clothes are still at the monastery, as is the car that Bernard loaned to me. Never mind that I identified myself on the emergency call. Not getting in touch would make it seem like I was complicit in some way."

Garin wasn't entirely convinced, but agreed to go along with what she thought best for the time being.

It didn't take long for Laroche to call back. He wasn't happy that she had left the scene and was far more brusque than usual in dealing with her. They made arrangements for Annja to come in for an interview later that day.

Two hours later Annja presented herself to the desk sergeant at police headquarters, Garin at her side. She was directed to wait off to one side of the crowded lobby for the inspector to come down to get her.

Thankfully, he didn't take long.

Laroche came out of the elevator a few minutes later and moved directly to her side.

"Miss Creed," he said, by way of greeting.

I'm getting the official treatment, she thought.

"Commissaire."

The inspector turned to face Garin. "I am Commissaire Laroche. And you are...?"

"Neil Anderson," Garin said.

Annja had to stifle a laugh.

"A pleasure. If you wouldn't mind waiting out here, we'll only be—"

"Sorry. I do mind," Garin said.

The inspector frowned. "This is a police matter, Mr. Anderson."

Garin smiled and Annja was instantly reminded of a wolf sizing up its prey. "Of course it is," he told Laroche. "Which is precisely why I'm here, representing Miss Creed."

"I see. Very well, then, if you would both follow me," Laroche said, frowning.

The police officer turned to lead them to the interview room, and as Garin's gaze caught Annja's he winked.

She had to hand it to him. He'd given the impression that he was there as her legal representative, ready and able to protect her rights, without actually saying he was an attorney. He'd used familiar phraseology and let Laroche hear what it was he expected to hear. Very smooth and very dangerous, she reminded herself.

Inside the interview room was a table and two chairs. Laroche took one and motioned for Annja to take the other. Garin, apparently, was going to have to stand.

Bet that's meant to annoy the solicitors, Annja thought. Bet it annoys Garin, too.

The inspector didn't waste any time.

"Please tell me what you know about the events at the monastery known as the Cradle of Solitude yesterday afternoon."

Annja had worked out what she wanted to say in advance, so she was prepared for the question. She told the inspector that she was at the monastery to try to find any records that might have been kept by Brother Markum, a former abbot who was also William Parker's distant cousin. She'd been getting ready to leave when armed gunmen burst through the front door. She and the rest of the occupants had run for their lives when the intruders started shooting. She managed to find her way to the roof, only to be cornered at the edge overlooking the river. With no other option, she'd jumped.

After surviving the fall, she'd returned to the monastery, discovered the bodies of the fallen and had immediately called emergency services. While waiting for their arrival, she'd become concerned that the intruders might still be about the grounds and so she'd escaped while she could.

She had no idea what the intruders were looking for, no more than she'd had with regard to the museum break-in. Perhaps it was something Bernard was involved in?

It was very close to the truth, which reduced the chances that she'd inadvertently give something away. Revealing what the intruders were really after might put Bernard's life at greater risk and that wasn't something Annja was willing to do. Since taking up the sword she'd discovered just how evil men could be and she'd lost what little faith she had that the authorities could handle problems like this. She and Garin had agreed that the best way to bring Bernard home safely was to keep the authorities as far away from the situation as possible.

Laroche took notes throughout her statement and when she was finished he began to use them in an effort to pick her story apart.

"You arrived at the monastery about what time?"

"Two-thirty."

"You went alone?"

"Yes?"

"Why?"

"Why did I go alone?"

"Yes."

"Who else would I have gone with?"

"I don't know. You tell me."

It went on like that for the better part of two hours, with Laroche asking the same questions several times in different ways, continually circling back to the reasons why she had been at the monastery in the first place and what she thought it was the assailants were after, and what it was that was worth killing over.

Annja stuck to her story.

Finally, as Laroche prepared to start in with another round of questions, Garin spoke up for the first time since they'd entered the room.

"Is Miss Creed under arrest, Commissaire?"

"No."

"Is she a suspect in the murder investigation?"

"No," he said, grudgingly.

"Then I think we're finished for today. You know where to reach her if necessary."

With that, Garin rose and led her out of the interview room. Laroche chose not to follow, which Annja took as a good sign.

By the time they reached the sidewalk, Garin's driver had the limousine waiting for them.

"Airport, James," Garin said as they pulled smoothly away from the curb.

"We can't go to the airport yet," Annja protested. "All of my things are still at the hotel and I'd like to—"

Garin cut her off. "I'll have someone collect your things or we'll simply buy new ones. But I think it would be best if we get out of France now, while we still can. That police inspector doesn't strike me as the stupid sort and he isn't going to be content with that bullshit you're feeding him for long. "We're leaving," Garin said, "while we still have the ability to do so."

19

They arrived at the airport thirty minutes later. Griggs was waiting for them, with Annja's backpack and luggage that he had collected from her hotel after Garin had a few words via telephone with the general manager. Her passport, which they needed to get out of the country, was in the backpack. Annja wasn't surprised Griggs had been able to retrieve her things so easily; Garin had connections everywhere, it seemed.

Inside the airport, they discovered that there was a flight leaving for Atlanta in just forty-five minutes that would get them there before sundown that day. Thanks to Garin's charm and money, they were able to secure two first-class seats and pass through security with a minimum of fuss. As evening approached, they were out over the Atlantic, winging their way toward the United States.

They were seated beside each other in the nearly empty first-class cabin, so Annja wasn't worried about being overheard when she turned to Garin and said,

"I think it's time you told me about the Friends of the South."

Garin was quiet for a moment, long enough in fact that Annja thought he was going to ignore the question, but then he began to speak.

"The Civil War was of great interest to many forces in Europe. Some for purely economic reasons. The trade with America had been booming before the war, and much of what was taken for granted among European society was considered the height of luxury in the States. The war had slowed profits considerably and many were looking for an end to the conflict and a return to the good old days."

As always, Annja listened with apt attention. Not because what Garin was saying was in and of itself news to her, but because when he mentioned historical events, it was always from a personal perspective rather than an analytical one. He'd witnessed some of history's most amazing moments and Annja envied that.

"A group of French businessmen with trade interests linked to the Confederate States, namely the importing of tobacco and cotton, banded together and formed a group known as the Friends of the South. They provided monetary and material support to President Davis's government throughout the conflict."

Annja was aware of some of the assistance that had filtered to the South from a few European nations, so Garin's information wasn't earth-shattering. But what he said next caught her attention.

"What most people don't realize is that the Friends of the South was actually just a puppet arm of a much more secretive group known as the Order of the Golden Phoenix. Membership was restricted to the richest and most ruthless French businessmen at the time and their ultimate goal was nothing short of French dominance worldwide. From exploiting the West Indies to bankrolling that megalomaniac Napoleon's return to power in 1815, they had their hands in just about everything."

Annja considered the implications of that for a few minutes. "Parker stated that the Friends of the South were 'more than they appeared to be' in his note to his subordinate, Sykes. Could that be what he was referring to? That the Friends of the South was really the Order of the Golden Phoenix?"

Garin shrugged. "It's certainly possible."

"But why should that matter?" Annja asked. "The South borrowed money from the French to help bankroll the last few years of the war. That's a well-documented historical fact—no one really disputes it. What difference would it have made if the money came from the Friends of the South or from the Order itself?"

"Perhaps it was a political issue."

Annja wasn't sure what he was getting at. "How so?" she asked.

"It was just a rumor, mind you, but at the time the Order was supposedly trying to instigate a British invasion of the United States. That might not have gone over well with the allies of President Davis."

Annja stared at him. "An invasion?"

"It wasn't such a bad idea actually. The Northern Army was exhausted, its supplies were dwindling and its manpower spread all to hell and back. The Southern Army was still going only through the generosity of its French backers. A sizable force could easily have landed in New York or Baltimore and threatened Washington in a matter of days."

Annja found the idea disturbing, probably because it would have had an excellent chance of succeeding.

"The Union Army would have been forced to march back north to deal with the intruders, leaving the Confederates to retake the territory it had lost," she said.

"True, but you're not taking it far enough yet. How would a strengthened British involvement in the U.S. have benefited France and, by extension, the Order?"

It took a few minutes of puzzling it through, but the answer finally came to her. "The Union wouldn't have gone down without a fight, which meant the British forces would have been tied up for some time. While they were otherwise occupied, the French could have taken advantage of the situation, by attacking British interests elsewhere."

Garin smiled and nodded as Annja continued to think out loud.

"Given the financial instability of the Confederacy at that point, it likely would have ended up a vassal state of France in all but name only, for it would have taken even larger infusions of French capital to help it recover on its own without the North's assistance. France wins on both sides of the war."

It was an audacious and cunning plan, one that would have required not only patience but skillful political maneuvering behind the scenes to put all the pieces in place at the proper time. The entire scheme could have been ruined with just a few words in the wrong man's ears.

The wrong man's ears...

Just like that, the whole tangled mess straightened itself out in her mind's eye and she could see the picture it formed clearly for the first time. She *knew* what had happened. William Parker had stumbled upon the Order's plans. Continuing the negotiations and returning the gold would have placed not just his president but his very country at stake. Unable to communicate quickly with those above him in the chain of command, Parker most likely acted on his own initiative, doing what he could to derail the process from the inside. Arranging to have the gold hidden in order to delay repaying the earlier loan would certainly have caused some waves.

She wondered what, exactly, had led to the fateful confrontation in the catacombs. Had he challenged his contact? Had he inadvertently let something slip? There seemed no way of knowing.

After laying out her thoughts to Garin, Annja asked, "So what happened to them? The Order, I mean?"

"The answer to that depends on who you want to believe. Some say there was a falling-out among the central members at the start of the twentieth century and the group eventually dissolved. Others suspect that the Order still exists and is still directing things behind the scenes in an effort to regain some of the glory that France has lost over the years."

"What do you think? Or better yet, what do you *know*?" Annja asked.

"As a long-standing member of the Order, I'm sworn to secrecy. Now, if you don't mind, I'm going to get some rest."

He leaned back and closed his eyes, leaving Annja gasping and wondering if he really had been a member of the Order.

He certainly seems to know a lot about them, she thought. She glared at his peaceful face knowing there was no point trying to get any further information out of him.

Since Garin had made the comment specifically to keep her wondering and to keep her attention on him, Annja resolved to do the exact opposite. She decided to find something else to occupy her attention. She wasn't particularly tired, not yet at least, so she pulled her laptop out of her backpack and fired it up.

She used the plane's Wi-Fi connection to log on to the internet and do some background research on the Chennault plantation.

The house had been built in 1853 by Dionysius Chennault, an elderly planter and Methodist minister, known to friends and family as Nish. He and his wife, his brother, John, and several other family members were present when Captain Parker arrived with his wagon train, seeking a place to shelter for the night. Chennault allowed them to use a nearby horse pasture but neither he nor his family members were aware of what Parker was transporting. At least, there was no mention of that in any of the records that Annja could find. Unfortunately for Chennault and his family, General Wilde, the Union officer in charge of the area, heard about the treasure and believed that the Chennaults knew more about it than they would admit. He arrived on site with soldiers and ordered them to torture the male family members, stringing them up by their thumbs until they talked. When they pleaded their innocence, he had them all arrested and transported to Washington, Georgia, for further questioning. Eventually, the Chennaults were declared innocent and released. The family returned to the plantation and remained there until the end of their days.

In the process of looking for information on the location, Annja discovered that the house was actually up for sale. The webpage listed the Realtor's name, Catherine Daley, as well as her cell phone number and email address, so Annja sent off a quick message stating she and a wealthy companion were flying into Atlanta that

afternoon and were looking to tour the property that
evening on extremely short notice. Could she accom-
modate them?

The Realtor returned her message within five minutes, stating she'd be happy to see them and provided
directions from the airport to the plantation.

Gotta love mobile technology, Annja thought as she
confirmed that they would be there and logged off. Satisfied she'd done what needed doing before landing, she
settled back to get some sleep.

20

They arrived in Atlanta just past four o'clock local time, thanks to the eight-hour flight and the six-hour time change. Having rested comfortably for most of the trip, they immediately collected the rental car Garin's people had arranged. In no time they were on the road.

Washington, Georgia, where the Chennault plantation was located, was about an hour and a half drive northeast of Atlanta. They managed to get out of the downtown area before the afternoon traffic became too heavy and made good time on the road, arriving just as the sun was beginning to set.

The directions given to them by the Realtor were excellent and they had no problems finding the antebellum mansion on the south side of town.

The house was surrounded on two sides by towering oaks and on the others by gently rolling hills that disappeared off into the distance. They pulled into the drive and parked behind the silver BMW that was already there. As they did so, the front door to the mansion opened and a woman came out to greet them.

Catherine Daley turned out to be a bleached blonde in her mid-fifties dressed in a cream-colored business suit. Annja's cargo pants, T-shirt and hiking shoes were a sharp contrast and the look on Catherine's face as Annja got out of the car told her all she needed to know about the woman's prejudices.

She didn't have to endure the Realtor's withering stare for long, however, because Garin stepped out of the passenger side at that point and the Realtor's gaze focused on him like a heat-seeking missile. Annja could have been dancing naked in the street with bells and whistles on and the other woman wouldn't have noticed.

"Mr. Boucher, I presume?" Catherine said in a thick Southern accent as she walked over on her three-inch heels and held out her hand.

Garin smiled and, without batting an eye, replied with a long stream of perfect French.

Catherine paused and said, "Oh."

Annja wanted to hit her already and they'd only been there two minutes. It was going to be a long appointment.

"Do you speak any English?" Catherine asked.

"Does you mother dress as badly as you?" he replied, again in French.

Thanks to his tone, it came out sounding mildly lascivious, making the Realtor flush. "Oh, my," she said.

Annja had had enough.

She stepped forward and extended her hand to the woman, saying, "Hi! I'm Annja. I emailed you."

"Um…yes, oh, yes, right. Miss Creed, correct?" Catherine's smile did its best not to falter.

"That's right. I'm Mr. Boucher's agent. I'd be happy to translate as you show us the property."

Catherine's smile grew tighter. "Of course. Shall we start with the ground floor, then?"

All Annja wanted to see was the wine cellar, but she knew that if she simply asked for them to be taken there directly it wouldn't look right. She wasn't worried so much about what Catherine might think, but she didn't want to give those coming after them any clues to where they had gone or what they had found. Best to just deal with the tour and the woman's prattling until they could conveniently ask to see the cellar.

Catherine led them through the house one room at a time, pointing out highlights and doing the usual schmoozing you'd expect from someone trying to sell an expensive estate.

The main level consisted of a formal parlor, a formal dining room, a music room, a guest wing with bedroom and bath, a keeping room, a butler's pantry, a detached country kitchen with Aga stove and a sitting porch overlooking raised garden beds. If you were into whitewashed walls and country antiques, it was quite beautiful.

Annja, however, was not. Neither was Garin; she could see him trying not to sneer at what he could only be thinking was clutter. Clean lines and modern minimalist styling were more to his taste. He hid it well, using the fact that the Realtor couldn't understand him to vent his distaste and frustration with the process in enthusiastic exclamations to Annja, all delivered in pleasant-sounding French.

The second floor contained four large bedrooms, each with its own fireplace, and two baths, one on either end of the central hall.

"Enough of this nonsense," Garin said to Annja in French, after sticking his nose into the final bathroom and pretending to examine it. "It's time we found that key."

Annja agreed. Turning to Catherine, she said, "Mr. Boucher wonders if it would be possible to see the wine cellar? He has an extensive collection and wants to understand what he'll need to do to bring the cellar up to his standards."

"Of course. This way, please."

The Realtor led them down to the first floor, out the back and around to the side of the house. A pair of doors were set into the side of the house, much like a storm cellar, and Catherine hauled them open, revealing a wooden staircase leading down into the ground.

"Please follow me, and watch your head. The ceiling on the steps is pretty low."

Annja pretended to translate for Garin.

Catherine led them down the steps into a large room hewn out of the bare earth. Wooden racks filled the center of the room and shelving lined the walls. Only one rack was being used and Annja could see a few dozen bottles of wine were stored on it.

"The room is naturally maintained at a temperature between sixty and sixty-five degrees Fahrenheit thanks to the thick Georgia clay in which it is dug. Even in the heat of the summer, it doesn't rise more than a degree or two down here. With some modern shelving and a decent lock on the door, Mr. Boucher's collection should be fine."

Garin was muttering something about how he'd never store a two-hundred-year-old bottle of wine in a dirty hole in the ground, but Annja ignored him and focused on the Realtor.

"Mr. Boucher is quite taken with the place. We'd like to spend a few minutes speaking privately, if we may."

Dollar signs dancing before her eyes, Catherine happily obliged. "Of course. I'll wait outside. Take as long as you need."

They waited until they couldn't hear her steps on the wooden stairs leading back outside and then moved to the center of the room where they could talk without being overheard. They continued speaking in French, just in case the Realtor returned unexpectedly.

"Remember, we're looking for a key without a lock," Annja said as she turned and surveyed the room.

"Right," Garin replied. He headed for the far side of the room to begin his search, leaving Annja to deal with the area closest to the door.

She'd given some thought to the riddle while on the drive but she still wasn't certain exactly what it was they were looking for. A key without a lock was pretty vague, as clues went. And the next one, the place where the two mouths meet, gave no hints to the meaning of the first. If it had mentioned a door or a lock or a container of some kind, Annja would know they were searching for an actual, physical key. Trouble was, it didn't.

And that left an awful lot of ground to cover.

She began scanning the wine racks and the bottles they held, looking for anything that might resemble a key. She knew the answer wouldn't be blatantly obvious; it wouldn't be an actual physical key. It might, however, be an image of a key, say on the label of a wine bottle, or maybe carved into the surface of one of the shelves before her. Parker would have had no way of knowing how long it would have taken Sykes to receive his message and then follow the clues to retrieve the treasure, so it made sense that he'd use something semipermanent for his clues. Something that was likely to have remained in the same place for a few weeks, maybe even a month or two.

I bet he never imagined it might take one hundred and forty years, Annja thought.

Between the two of them, the search didn't take very long.

They came up empty, however.

"Maybe we're taking it too literally," Garin suggested. "Maybe he wasn't referring to an actual key, but perhaps something with the word *key* in it? Could that be why it's a key without a lock? Because it's not really a key?"

He began rattling off every word he could think of that also had the word *key* in it.

"Key, keys, keyboard, key deer, key grip, keyhole, Key Largo, key lime, keynote, keystroke, Key West, keyword, keystone…"

Annja mentally dismissed each one as she heard it, until Garin came to the last.

Keystone, she thought, turning it over in her mind. *Keystone.*

She knew the word usually referred to the wedge-shaped stone that formed the top of an arch, so she began looking around the cellar, examining the doorways leading into the adjacent rooms.

There was no arch.

Garin was still rattling off suggestions but stopped when he saw her expression.

"What is it?" he asked, recognizing that particular look.

"Not sure yet…"

Annja walked over to the entrance to the wine cellar and called up the stairs.

"Catherine, Mr. Boucher would like to know if there are any arches on the property."

The swiftness of the response showed her suspicions had been right; the Realtor had been hanging about, hoping to overhear something useful.

"An arch? No, I don't believe so. Why?"

"No reason. Thank you."

Annja walked back to where Garin was standing, waiting for her.

"An arch?" he asked.

She explained how she thought Parker might have carved something into the surface of the keystone, providing the direction they needed to find the second clue.

"No arch, no keystone," she said. "Obviously I'm on the wrong track."

"Not necessarily," he replied, turning to pace the floor in short, sharp strides that seemed to punctuate what he was saying. "That's not the only definition of keystone, you know. It also refers to a central concept or idea, something that supports the whole by its very presence. So what would you consider to be *central* to the estate?"

The answer came to her as soon as he finished speaking.

"The cornerstone."

The first stone laid in a foundation, the one from which everything else extended. "The *key* to all the rest," she whispered.

They both knew she was right the moment she said it. Crossing the wine cellar, they climbed the stairs and found the Realtor standing nearby, debating the wisdom of going back down in the cellar to try and push for the sale.

"Oh," she said, startled by their sudden appearance. "Is everything all right?"

"We'd like to see the cornerstone, if we may," Annja said.

"The cornerstone?"

"Yes."

"Why?"

For a moment, Annja was flummoxed. She had no idea what to say. Why would anyone looking to purchase a house be interested in seeing the cornerstone?

Then it came to her. "Mr. Boucher would like to see the date for himself."

The Realtor stared at her oddly for a moment and Annja thought she was going to press for a deeper explanation, which would be a problem since she didn't have one, but apparently the woman chalked it up to eccentric behavior on the part of the wealthy client and shrugged it off.

"This way, please."

She led them around to the opposite side of the house and pointed to a stone set firmly in the foundation. Carved into its surface was the year 1853.

Next to that, someone had carved a crude compass.

The stone was weathered, so it was hard to say which one had come first, but to Annja's experienced eyes she thought the date looked older. It was deeper, for one thing, showing that whoever had done it had come prepared with the proper tools for the job. The compass, on the other hand, was more shallow, and the lines were thinner, too, making it seem like it was a rush job or that the creator had been forced to work with whatever tools had been on hand.

There was also the simple fact that the compass was pointing in the wrong direction.

The sun was setting off to Annja's right, directly in line with one arm of the compass. What was unusual was the fact that the arm in question was labeled as north, rather than west. Even more intriguing, the line was also a good two inches longer than the others.

That's got to be what we're looking for, Annja thought, and she could see by Garin's expression that he thought the same thing.

The trouble was, she wasn't certain how to interpret it. Did they follow the direction of the compass arrow and go west? Or did they assume the compass was telling them the proper direction, despite its being out of alignment, and go north?

Catherine, who had been quiet during their examination of the cornerstone, spoke up.

"As you can see, the house was indeed built in 1853, and I can assure you that the date has been verified by several sources, including the company that originally built the structure."

Annja interrupted her. "Is there anything around here, Catherine, that might be described as being a place where two mouths meet?"

The woman stared at her with such a strange expression that for a moment Annja feared she wouldn't answer. It was an odd question, she had to admit, but apparently Catherine had already decided that her potential client was truly an odd duck, for after a moment she answered as if it were the type of question she received every day.

"Well," Catherine said, with the kind of professional smile that was designed to hide her true thoughts, whatever they might be. "I'd think that such a phrase would probably refer to the conjunction of the Broad and Savannah rivers."

Annja's heart beat a little faster.

"And which direction would that be from here?"

The Realtor thought about it for a moment and then turned and pointed out across the hills toward the north.

"That way, about twenty miles I'd guess."

She turned to face Garin and, with another smile, went back to her pitch. "Now perhaps Mr. Boucher..."

That was as far as she got. Garin broke in with a long and unrelenting stream of French that grew louder and sounded more exasperated as it went on.

Annja pretended to listen to it, a grave expression on her face, and then turned to the Realtor.

"Thank you so much for your time, Catherine, but I'm afraid Mr. Boucher has decided to pass on the property. He's an eccentric sort, as you can imagine—most people with his level of money are, I've found—and he's just informed me that he can't possibly live in a home that was built in an odd-numbered year. I'm sure you understand."

Garin kept up the act, alternating waving his hands in the air and letting loose a fresh burst of French. The fact that he seemed to be spouting off his grocery list was completely lost on the poor woman, who looked confused and even a bit unsettled by her would-be client's sudden animation.

Annja took advantage of her hesitation to offer their excuses, blaming it all on herself and suggesting that she get Mr. Boucher away from the property before his anxiety levels grew too high and he had a fit or, heaven forbid, a heart attack.

As Catherine stood there and stared after them in stunned amazement, Annja dragged the ranting Garin back to the car and quickly drove away.

21

I bet they're sleeping together, Catherine Daley thought as she watched Mr. Boucher and his agent drive off down the street. There just wasn't any other explanation. After all, she'd given him the look more than once, and Lord knew that was all it usually took to reel them in like a catfish on a line. The fact that he'd basically ignored her in favor of that annoying woman was infuriating.

Look what she'd been wearing, for heaven's sake!

And that crazy fit he threw. Whoever heard of such a thing? What difference did it make if the house was built in an even-numbered year or an odd one? Such nonsense!

Yes, that would explain it. He had to be crazy. It certainly made much more sense to believe that he was nuts, than to entertain the thought that a man of Mr. Boucher's obvious sophistication and financial status wouldn't be interested in a woman of her caliber and breeding.

Feeling better about herself now that she understood

her worldview wasn't so drastically challenged, Catherine turned her attention to closing down the property.

As they were her last clients scheduled for the evening, she went through the house checking windows, turning off lights and locking up for the night. It took her some time and night had fully come by the time she was finished. She was walking out to her car when she saw the lights of a vehicle come down the road and pull into the drive.

For a moment she was hopeful that Mr. Boucher had reconsidered, but then she saw that the vehicle was an SUV and knew she couldn't be correct. Mr. Boucher had arrived in a Mercedes.

Another potential client? she thought, then quickly changed her mind. Not the way her week was going. People looking to spend just shy of a million dollars didn't just drop in off the street. It's probably just some tourist who got lost and needed directions.

She took a step toward the vehicle and then stopped as she saw the doors open and three men stepped out. She couldn't see them clearly, as the headlights created a glare, but that was solved a moment later as they moved toward where she was standing at the base of the wide veranda.

"Ms. Daley?" the lead man asked.

His accent was French, much like that of Mr. Boucher. As he came closer she could see that he was dressed similarly, too, in a sharply cut European suit. He was shorter than Mr. Boucher, and cut a less imposing figure, but there was the same assured confidence and expectation that others would do as they were asked.

He had money, that much was clear, and Catherine began to think her day might be looking up, after all.

She took a few steps closer to the newcomers, the

professional salesperson's smile already plastered across her face.

"Yes, I'm Catherine Daley. How can I help you? Have you come to see the plantation?"

Blaine Michaels smiled. "Indeed, I have, Ms. Daley. I'm particularly interested in the wine cellar."

Catherine frowned as the first inklings that all might not be well began to filter into her consciousness. The man's smile seemed off somehow, as if there was another expression lurking beneath it, one with decidedly less invitation. In fact, Catherine was starting to feel like a crippled deer in front of a hungry wolf and she wasn't sure what to do.

She caught a motion out of the corner of her eye and turned to find one of the other men standing close on her left. She started, taking a step away from him, only to bump into his companion, who had come out of the shadows on her right, effectively hemming her in between them.

Alarms began to sound in the depths of her mind and she spun, intent on locking herself in one of the back bedrooms and calling the sheriff on her cell phone, but her efforts were too little and far too late.

Almost languidly, the big man on her left reached out, sank his fingers into her carefully coiffed hair and yanked backward, pulling her off her feet.

He let go as her feet flew out from under her and the back of her head hit the wooden surface of the veranda with a loud *thunk*. Dazed, she could only struggle feebly as the man who'd grabbed her by the hair took some kind of restraint out of his pocket and quickly secured her hands and feet.

That was it. Just like that she was in their control

and Catherine Daley trembled in fear as she considered what these three men would do to her.

For the second time that evening, she simply didn't understand the dynamics of the situation in which she found herself. The three men who'd come to see her had far more on their minds than that which she feared.

As she stared up at them in horror, the leader of the group leaned in so that his face was only inches from hers.

"My name is Blaine Michaels, Ms. Daley, and if you want to get out of this alive, I suggest you answer all of my questions as truthfully as possible. Do you understand?"

Unable to find her voice due to the fear coursing through her body like a flood, she could only nod.

Michaels smiled again and this time there was no mistaking the malevolence beneath that expression. "Good. Now tell me everything you know about the key without a lock."

Unable to answer his question due to the fact that she didn't have the faintest idea what he was talking about, Catherine Daley finally understood the true depths of the trouble she was in.

22

Excited by their early success but exhausted from the long day's travel, Garin and Annja decided to make the short drive back into the town of Washington to find a place to get some dinner and a hotel to stay for the night.

Soon thereafter they were seated in a booth at Jenny's Barbecue Palace with racks of ribs in front of them, discussing what to do next.

"So what's the next stanza of the riddle?" Garin asked.

Annja recited it from memory. "'There you'll find the Lady, left alone and in distress. You must secure her when you're able, and take Ewell's Rifle from her crest.'"

"Which means what?"

Annja wasn't sure. She shared her thoughts aloud as she worked through it. "Captain Parker was fairly circumspect with the first clue, sort of talking around what he wanted to say, so I'd guess he did the same thing here. Which means the lady in question isn't really a lady, but something you might refer to in the feminine form."

"Like a boat," Garin said. "Since we're talking about the meeting place of two rivers, a boat's the obvious answer, I'd think."

Annja agreed. "And since the word *lady* was capitalized, I'd guess that's the name of the boat, or at least part of it. Lady something or other, maybe."

"Right," Garin replied, taking another bite of barbecued ribs in the process. He carefully chewed, swallowed and then said, "Left alone and in distress might indicate that it was abandoned, damaged in some way."

It seemed like they were on the right track to Annja. "So we're looking for a boat named *Lady* or with the word *lady* in the name that either ran aground or was damaged near the junction of the two rivers back in 1864."

"Right," Garin said, with more than a hint of sarcasm. "You make it sound so easy, Annja."

"Nothing wrong with being confident."

"Okay, so what about the rest? Who's this Ewell character and why is his rifle so special?"

That one Annja could answer easily enough. "Confederate Major General Richard Ewell. Took over command of Second Corps after the death of Stonewall Jackson. Perhaps most famously known for failing to take the heights at Gettysburg, which contributed significantly to the Confederate defeat there."

As for the rifle, Annja didn't know. "Perhaps the clue has been carved into the stock or hidden in the rifle barrel. We won't really know until we find it, now will we?"

They finished their meals and then made their way down the street to a family-owned hotel the owner of the restaurant had suggested. It turned out to be a decent, serviceable place and they got two rooms for the night, agreeing to meet for breakfast in the morning to continue their search.

That night, Annja used the hotel's internet connection to try and find any information on a Confederate-era boat or naval vessel that might have gone aground during the Civil War. She was able to log into the Atlanta public library and search through old issues of the *Columbus Enquirer, The Augusta Chronicle* and even *The Atlanta Constitution,* though that didn't begin publication until Georgia rejoined the Union in 1868. Unfortunately, none of them contained anything that was helpful to her search.

General searches through various publications and websites produced quite a few Confederate vessels that had run aground or been forced to do so in order to keep from sinking, including the CSS *Atlanta* and the CSS *Chattahoochee,* but none that were anywhere near the site of the two rivers.

Knowing she had to get some sleep if she was going to be at all useful in the morning, Annja decided to leave a question on her favorite newsgroups, hoping some Civil War buff out there in cyberspace might have the information she needed. She logged onto alt.archaeology and alt.archaeology.esoterica and left the same message on each.

I'm searching for information on a Confederate-era vessel that might have run aground near the junction of the Broad and Savannah rivers between 1863 and 1865. The ship's name might include the word *Lady* in some fashion. Any information would be helpful.

With that accomplished, she spent a few minutes looking into the issue of Ewell's Rifle. By the time she was finished, it was after midnight. Knowing she had a long day ahead of her, Annja shut down the laptop and tried to get some sleep.

Unfortunately, rest didn't come easy, as her thoughts kept wandering to Bernard and whether or not he was being treated properly by those who'd taken him. She fervently hoped Garin was right, that they needed Bernard in good health in order to help them find the treasure, which of course put more pressure on her to figure out the puzzle before they did.

Eventually, restless sleep finally came.

THE NEXT MORNING, when checking her accounts online, Annja found a response from someone with the screen name SouthernRising in the alt.archaeology newsgroup.

> The Lady in question is most likely the CSS *Marietta*, a Confederate ironclad that was nicknamed the "Old Lady" on account of her being one of the Confederacy's oldest vessels, built at Edwards Ferry, N.C., at the tail end of 1862. Ran aground at the junction of the Broad and Savannah rivers in 1864. The hulk was actually used as a temporary headquarters station during President Davis's flight south after the fall of Richmond.

I knew it! Annja thought.

It wasn't a big leap to think that Parker would have considered a grounded vessel as being in distress; he was a Navy man, after all. Depending upon how long the ship was used as a temporary headquarters, it also stood to reason that he would have set foot inside it at some point when the remains of the treasury were under his control, giving him the time he needed to leave a clue behind for those who were to come after him.

That was all well and good, except for the fact that expecting the remains of a Confederate ironclad, one of only thirty such ships ever built, to still be sitting on the side of the river after all this time was ridiculous, even to someone with her sense of optimism. She'd been witness to some strange miracles in the past few years, but that was asking too much. The historical value of the vessel alone would have resulted in its being salvaged in the modern era, if it had even lasted that long.

She wasn't willing to give up without looking into it, however. Bernard's life might depend on it.

Maybe it's in a museum somewhere, she thought.

A quick search in Google brought up some information on the subject.

The ship had, indeed, run aground in 1864, just as SouthernRising's message had indicated. After the war, the Union Navy made plans to free the *Marietta* from its inglorious beaching in mid-1894, intending to use what scrap iron they could salvage from the wreck on other reconstruction projects. The salvage crew managed to raise the hull from the clay it had been mired in over the years, but a lack of funding kept them from transporting it north until later that fall.

Once the money had been raised, the crew returned to the site, only to be delayed once more as a category-four hurricane came roaring out of the Atlantic and rushed across most of Georgia in early October.

After several days the hurricane eventually blew over, but the damage had been done. The hulk of the

Marietta had been carried away by the flooding waters of the Savannah River, never to be seen again.

"Damn it!" Annja said.

Without the ship, and Ewell's Rifle, they were dead in the water, no pun intended.

With no better idea of what to do next, Annja sent a message to SouthernRising via the email address he'd left at the end of his newsgroup posting.

Would you happen to know if any trace of the *Marietta* was uncovered after the hurricane?

To her surprise, his reply was almost immediate. She must have caught him at the computer.

Check this out, he suggested, including a link to an article from *The Atlanta Constitution* dated six months before. The article was in reference to a University of Atlanta–funded expedition to try and locate the *Diamond Jim,* a famous twin-wheeled paddleboat that had sunk in 1952 in the Savannah River. During the search, the university crew had chanced upon an area of the river bottom that had "an unusually high concentration of iron." There was some speculation in the article that the wreck might be that of a cargo barge that had gone down several years before during another period of flooding.

Annja looked at that article and in her gut she knew.

It wasn't a barge at all.

It was the missing *Marietta.*

But when she suggested as much to Garin at breakfast a half hour later, he laughed.

"You can't be serious, Annja!" he said. "A single reading of a mysterious metal anomaly in the middle of the river is your proof that the ship we're looking for, one that vanished over a hundred years ago, is sitting there waiting for us to come and get it?"

Annja nodded. "Yes, that's exactly what I'm saying." She caught his gaze with her own and stared back at him with complete confidence in her conviction. "Think about it, Garin. When have you known me to be wrong about this kind of thing?"

She'd been good at tracking down lost tombs and ancient civilizations before she'd taken up the sword and ever since she'd done so she'd only gotten better. It was as if the sword helped her focus in some strange way, made her better at those things at which she already excelled.

Grudgingly, he had to admit she could be right.

"Even if that is the *Marietta,*" he said, "how is that going to help us? It's been underwater for more than a century and that's not taking into account that it was put there by a hurricane. We'll be lucky if it isn't scattered into a thousand pieces across the river bottom."

"We won't know until we look and see, now will we?" she replied.

The question was, how were they going to manage that?

23

The plan, when it came to her, sounded reasonable, but she was going to need some help getting the equipment necessary to pull it off. That meant she needed to get in touch with Doug.

She put a call in to his office and, much to her surprise, got him on the first ring.

"Hi, Doug."

"Don't 'Hi, Doug' me. Why is some police inspector named Laroche calling me at all hours of the day and night looking for you, Annja?"

"You wouldn't believe me if I said I didn't have any idea, would you?"

"Not particularly," he replied.

"Well, then, he's probably a little ticked off that I left the country, given that I'm a witness in a murder investigation."

"Murder investigation? I thought the guy you found in the catacombs had been dead for decades?"

"He has. It wasn't Captain Parker that I—"

Doug cut in. "Good. We can't do a show about reanimated skeletons in the Paris catacombs if the guy's only been dead a few years. Who would believe that?"

Annja sighed.

"The show isn't about reanimated skeletons, Doug," she answered patiently.

"It will be when I'm done with it," he muttered.

"What was that?"

"Nothing, nothing. So why is this guy chasing after you?"

Annja explained as quickly as she could about her trip to the monastery, the riddle inside the puzzle box and the savage attack on the monastery's occupants that followed. She also told him about Professor Reinhardt's kidnapping.

As annoying as he might sometimes be, Doug was reasonably quick on the uptake in a crisis. "So you're trying to beat these guys to the missing treasure, in hope of bargaining with it for Reinhardt?"

"Got it in one, Doug."

He was quiet for a moment. "Where are you now?"

"A little town called Washington, Georgia. We deciphered the first clue, which led us here. But in order to get any further, I need some equipment that I can't get on my own."

"So you want me to use the show's cache, if you will, to get it for you?"

"Did you wake up on the smart side of the bed this morning, Doug?"

"That depends on who you think is going to pay for whatever it is you need."

Annja glanced across the table at Garin. "Oh, don't worry about that. I've got the payment issue handled. You just get me the gear."

She could hear him moving something around on his

desk, which she hoped meant he was going to write it down. It was going to be a long list.

"All right," he said, "I'm ready."

ON THE OTHER SIDE of town, Blaine Michaels climbed out of the back of the van in which he's been *discussing* the current status of their search for the missing treasure with Professor Reinhardt. He used his handkerchief to absently wipe the blood off the knuckles of his right hand as he considered what to do next.

He had not been pleased to arrive at the plantation last night only to discover that Annja Creed and a companion had arrived before him. The prattling idiot of a Realtor hadn't known much, but Blaine knew she was on to something, anyway. No one else would have had reason to ask about the phrase "where two mouths meet."

Clearly, the Creed woman had made a copy of the missive containing the clues to the treasure before his men had obtained it from her vehicle. Now she was using that information to try and find the treasure for herself.

The woman doesn't know when to quit, he thought.

Creed and Reinhardt had the same information available to them and, so far, Creed had been faster off the mark. As an American, her knowledge superseded Reinhardt's when it came to cultural and local references. If things continued in that fashion, he'd be runner-up for the treasure and that was something that was simply unacceptable. It could not, *would not,* happen.

It was time he was a bit more direct in his response to her interference.

He took his phone out of his pocket and made a

call. When it was answered, he asked, "Where are they now?"

The man sitting five tables away from Annja and Garin never looked in their direction as he replied, "The Good Day Diner on Main, between West and Stevens."

Michaels nodded to himself. That should work quite nicely.

"All right, here's what I want you to do."

THEY WERE GOING TO NEED a boat if Doug managed to secure the equipment they'd requested, so Annja flagged down their waitress and asked her if she knew where they might rent one. The waitress, Sue, wasn't certain, but she was willing to help, and inside of ten minutes she'd queried the regulars and come up with a name.

"Jimmy Mitchell," she said, handing Annja a napkin with an address and phone number written on it. "Hank says that he rents out his fishing trawler from time to time when money's getting low. Which, for Jimmy, is just about all the time."

Annja didn't know who Hank was, but she was happy enough to have a lead to work with and thanked the woman for her assistance.

"Anything for my favorite TV host!" Sue replied, winking at her. "I'm a big fan of the show."

In all the hubbub, neither Annja nor Garin saw the man a few tables away get up and slip out the back door.

As Garin watched with a bemused expression on his face, Annja signed one of the diner's T-shirts at Sue's insistence, then paid the bill, leaving a generous tip in the process.

"Not a word!" she said to Garin, once they were back outside on the street. The last thing she needed was to be ribbed by him all day for the notoriety the show gave her; she was having a hard enough time dealing with it already.

Jimmy Mitchell lived in the next town over, so they decided to drive there and see if they could speak to him in person. While Mitchell might be willing to rent out his boat, Annja had a feeling that he'd be less inclined to do so to strangers and she wanted to increase their chance of success as much as possible. It was easy to say no to someone over the phone; it was harder in person.

They'd parked at a meter several yards away from the diner and headed in that direction.

Behind them, a motorcycle turned onto the end of the street and headed toward them.

Annja saw the bike make the turn out of the corner of her eye and she registered its presence in the back of her mind, but she didn't pay any real attention to it at first. They were on a public street, after all, and vehicular traffic was to be expected, even in a quaint little town like this.

But when the driver kicked the bike into high gear, the roar of the engine cut through the mental fog like a siren, sending adrenaline pumping through her system. Time seemed to slow as she turned to her left, looking back up the street toward the oncoming traffic.

She caught sight of the biker right away, as he was now less than twenty feet away and coming on like the four horsemen of the apocalypse, the war cry of his steed a steady growl as the engine spurred the bike onward.

The biker's hand was coming up, something long and dark held securely in his grip.

Shotgun, Annja thought in the slow-motion reference of her hyperaware state, and knew instinctively that she and Garin were the target.

She had only seconds to act.

As the bike roared inexorably closer, Annja shoved backward with her left hand against Garin's chest, sending him off balance and stumbling out of the line of fire. At the same time she spun to her right, coming around in a semicircle that would put her a foot or two to the right of where she'd been standing the moment before.

She called her sword to hand.

The weapon responded as it always did, flashing into existence in a heartbeat, the hilt suddenly there in the palm of her hand, the blade quivering like a falcon eager to strike.

Annja didn't disappoint it.

The would-be killer had made an amateur mistake, closing the distance between himself and his targets in the hope of getting a tighter shot pattern rather than taking them out from farther away and then using a second shot to finish them off when they were no longer a threat. Annja made good use of his blunder.

As she completed her spin, she lashed up and out with the sword, the razor-sharp edge striking the barrel of the shotgun a split second before the killer pulled the weapon's trigger.

The sound of metal rang as her sword connected with the barrel of the shotgun. Half a second later the gun went off with a thunderous boom, but by then the killer's aim was off and the blast blew out the windshield of a nearby car rather than injuring either of its intended targets.

Annja found herself standing on the edge of the street, sword in hand, staring at the biker's back as he accelerated away from them at high speed. Garin stepped up beside her, a look of fury on his face as he reached inside his coat as if to draw a weapon, but he must have thought better of it at the last moment for his hand came out, empty.

"Are you all right?" he asked through clenched teeth.

"Peachy," was her reply as she watched the biker make the turn at the end of the road and disappear from sight.

With the threat now removed, Annja released her sword back into the otherwhere.

She was just in time, too, for a second later the doors to the diner burst open and Sue and several of the regulars charged out onto the street.

"Are you okay?" Sue asked, spying Annja and Garin standing near the edge of the sidewalk, next to the damaged car.

"We're fine," Annja said quickly. "A motorcycle just kicked up a rock unexpectedly and it shattered that windshield." She pointed at the vehicle ahead of them, as if that were explanation enough.

"But it sounded like a gunshot," Sue protested, glancing around as if she expected to see armed gunmen come running from around the corner of the building.

At this point Annja wouldn't have been surprised if they did.

Thankfully, Garin was thinking more quickly than she was. "It was just a truck backfiring. Coincidence, that's all." He flashed a smile, which helped ease Sue's anxiety and took her attention off the issue long enough for Annja to recover.

"Thanks again for your help," Annja told her, and then headed off toward their car as if nothing had happened.

Inside, however, she was seething. That was the

second time someone had tried to kill her since she'd agreed to help with the case. Three, if you counted the incident in the catacombs, which only an idiot would ignore at this point.

It only made her more determined than ever to be certain that whoever was after her never got their hands on the treasure.

The adrenaline dump had left her feeling worn out and tired, so Garin slid behind the wheel and let her take the passenger seat.

He started the car, paused and then said, "Thank you," in a tone far more reserved than usual.

Annja knew what the admission had cost him—he hated to be dependent on anyone for anything—so she simply nodded and let it go. She knew he'd have done the same if their positions had been reversed, so she didn't see what she'd done as extraordinary in any way, just necessary.

One thing was certain, that buckshot would have ripped him to shreds.

24

They decided it was prudent to get out of town as quickly as possible. If someone stumbled on the shell casing from the shotgun or noticed the pattern of holes in the hood of that car, they'd have a lot of explaining to do. As always, Annja didn't want to waste time answering questions at the police station.

They hadn't been on the road for more than ten minutes before Annja's cell phone rang. A glance at the caller ID showed an unknown number.

"Hello?"

"Miss Creed?"

"Yes," she answered. She didn't recognize the voice.

"You're intruding in something that's not your business, Miss Creed. I suggest you take recent events as a warning and stop while you're ahead."

"Who is this?"

Garin was looking at her curiously, so she mouthed "the Order" at him and put the phone on speaker.

"What you are searching for belongs to me. If you

continue to interfere, I'll be forced to take more radical measures."

Like trying to kill us isn't radical enough? she thought.

Annja decided she didn't have anything to gain by playing dumb so she went on the offensive instead.

"Yeah? Perhaps next time the Order will send a killer who can actually shoot straight. Tell you what, you give it your best shot. I'll be here waiting."

The caller, whoever he was, actually chuckled. "They said you were smart, Miss Creed, but I'm having a hard time seeing that. Perhaps this will raise your IQ a few points."

There was a pause and then another voice came on the line.

"Annja?"

It was Bernard. Or at least she thought it was. It sounded like he was speaking through swollen lips and possibly a broken nose.

"Do what they say, Annja. It isn't worth—"

The sound of something heavy hitting flesh interrupted whatever it was Bernard was trying to say. It came again, and again, and then there was silence.

"Bernard? Bernard!"

The other voice came back on the line. "I'm sorry, Miss Creed, but Professor Reinhardt isn't able to come to the phone at the moment."

Clenching her free hand into a fist, Annja fought to keep from screaming into the phone. "If you've hurt him, so help me I'm going to—"

"I don't think so, Miss Creed. You're not the one calling the shots here, I am. I'll say it one more time. Stay out of my business or both you and Professor Reinhardt are going to regret it."

The line went dead.

Into the silence, Annja said, "That is a dead man."

Garin, who had been quiet until now, finally spoke up. "I take it that means you have no intention of turning back now?"

"Hell, no!" she exclaimed. "It's more important than ever that we get possession of the treasure, and quickly, or we'll be too late to help Bernard."

"Just checking."

Annja opened her mouth to answer him when the phone in her hand rang again. Without thinking she stabbed the connect button and said, "You listen to me, you son of a—"

"Annja?"

It was Doug Morrell.

She blew the air out of her lungs in one hard push, trying to get her temper under control, and then said into the phone, "Sorry, Doug. I thought you were someone else."

"Glad I'm not him, that's all I can say. I've got what you need."

"Already?"

She was surprised; it hadn't taken him long at all.

"Turns out the archaeology department at the University of Atlanta was all too happy to help out the infamous Annja Creed. Especially when I told them you'd be happy to show up for the *Chasing History's Monsters* marathon weekend they're planning next month."

"You did what? No, never mind. Whatever they want, I'll do it. Tell me about the equipment."

Doug walked her through the entire list, confirming that he'd gotten it all, from the towed magnetometer to the scuba gear. "All I need to know is where to deliver it," he said.

Annja told him she'd call him back with that information once they'd had a chance to talk with their riverboat captain and then hung up.

They drove in silence for a while, until Garin said, "You're not really intending to give him the treasure, are you?"

"Not if I can help it," she replied.

And she'd do everything in her power to keep from having to. Provided she could keep Bernard safe in the process.

The trouble was, she was starting to doubt that she could.

Garin, however, seemed satisfied with her answer and let the matter drop.

Twenty-five minutes later they found themselves pulling into the driveway of a beat-up-looking house on the far side of a small town. A tall chain-link fence enclosed the entire property and the front yard was filled with various bits of equipment that partially obscured the single-level ranch behind it all.

A large dog, a rottweiler by the looks of it, barked at them from behind the fence.

As they got out of the car, Garin said, "It will be a miracle if the guy's boat actually floats."

"Quiet," Annja told him as the front door opened and a man dressed in grease-stained coveralls stepped out onto the porch. He was an inch or two shorter than Annja, but what he missed in height he made up for in the width of his brawny shoulders.

He seemed friendly enough.

"You folks lost?" he asked.

Annja smiled. "Depends. Are you Jimmy Mitchell?"

"Depends," came the quick reply, gently mocking

her at the same time. "You with the IRS or the Salvation Army?"

The Salvation Army? She wondered why he would say that.

"Nope. Neither. We're looking to hire us a riverboat captain."

"Preferably one with an actual boat," Garin added.

Mitchell squinted at him, then turned to look at Annja. "Does he think he's funny?" he asked, indicating Garin with a wave of his thumb.

"He does. We all have our crosses to bear."

Mitchell laughed. "Ain't that the truth, missy, ain't that the truth."

He came down off the porch and approached the fence, shooing the dog as he did. He unlatched the gate and invited them in.

"Jimmy Mitchell," he said, extending his hand to Annja.

"Annja Creed," she replied. "And the funny guy behind me is Garin Braden."

"What do you need the boat for?" he asked as he led them across the yard and up to the porch, where he indicated with a wave of his hand that they should grab one of several folding chairs stacked there and have a seat.

"We're trying to locate the wreck of a ship."

Mitchell squinted at them and Annja had the sense that he was trying to figure out if the city folk were pulling his leg.

"A shipwreck, huh?"

Annja explained about how the hurricane had pulled the CSS *Marietta* off the riverbank and sent it several miles downstream. She told him they had a general sense of where it might have ended up and that they needed him to run several passes up and down the river towing a magnetometer to help them pinpoint the actual location. At that point Annja and Garin would dive to the wreck and do what they could to confirm its identity.

"Sounds easy enough," Mitchell said. "Rentals in twenty-four-hour increments, but you'll have to pay the fuel charge, as well."

They dickered for a bit on price, but finally came to an agreement both parties could live with. Jimmy gave them the address of the wharf where his boat was docked and Annja relayed that to Doug, who informed them that the equipment could be delivered later that afternoon.

"About that price," Garin said to Annja as they made their way back to the car. "Just so you know, it's all coming off the top when we recover the treasure, anyway."

If we recover the treasure, Annja thought. She bit her tongue to keep from saying it aloud even as she reminded herself to have some confidence.

It's out there; you just have to get to it first, she told herself.

She had every intention of doing just that.

Unable to do anything more until the equipment arrived, the two of them decided to stay out of sight for the rest of the afternoon. The fact that the Order had not only tracked them to Washington but had also managed to get hold of Annja's cell phone number showed they had plenty of resources at their disposal, so Annja didn't want to take a chance of being exposed any more than necessary. They found a new hotel near the wharf where they would be meeting Mitchell in the morning and settled in, having both lunch and dinner delivered to them so they wouldn't have to go out.

Annja used the time to learn everything she could about the CSS *Marietta,* researching it on the internet and even speaking to one of the curators at the Museum of the Confederacy in Richmond, Virginia. By the time she finished several hours later, she thought she was reasonably well prepared for the difficult task ahead of them.

If they could find the boat, and if it was still intact, Annja was confident that she could locate what she was looking for.

That's a lot of *ifs…*

Early that evening she took another call from Doug.

"I received word that the equipment has been delivered as promised," he told her. "I'm going to be sending Richie down to meet you in the morning, to get all this on film for the episode."

"No!" Annja said sharply. There was no way she was going to put someone else in danger. "There's limited room on the boat, so I'll just use my handheld and capture the footage myself. We'll have enough to use. I promise."

Doug was a bit hesitant, but she finally convinced him that it was a bad idea and he reluctantly let it go.

"Just be sure that you get some decent footage. I don't know how we're going to use it in a show about reanimated Civil War soldiers in the Paris catacombs, but better safe than sorry."

"For the last time, Doug, it is not a show about re-animated—"

"Gotta go, Annja. Talk to you tomorrow."

And, with that, the son of a gun hung up.

25

The next day dawned cool and clear. Annja and Garin were up with the sunrise and waiting on the wharf when Jimmy Mitchell pulled up in a dilapidated Ford pickup truck.

He greeted them with enthusiasm and then led the way to the dockmaster's office where the equipment was delivered the night before. It took about two hours to sort through the boxes, unpack the equipment and confirm that it was all in good working order. One of the scuba tanks turned out to have a bad regulator so Annja switched that out for one of the spares she'd ordered. When they were finished, they loaded it all on a pair of dollies and moved it down to the wharf so they could load it onto the boat.

Their first look at the *Kelly May* wasn't encouraging.

She was a fiberglass fishing trawler with a small wheelhouse set two-thirds of the way back from the bow. A boom mast covered in flaking paint rose up behind the wheelhouse. Normally used to drag fishing nets, it would be used on this voyage to drag the magnetometer. The hull was faded, the name on the side of the boat barely legible, but Jimmy Mitchell stood there gazing at her proudly.

"Forty-two feet in length and fourteen feet abreast, with a six-foot draft. She'll do twelve knots while carrying fifteen tons of cargo," he said with a smile.

Yeah, but does it float? Annja felt like asking.

Garin seemed to have the same hesitation she had.

When Mitchell fired up the engines a few minutes later to warm them for the day's activity, much of Annja and Garin's anxiety was relieved. She might not look like much, but even a nongearhead like Annja could tell that engines were masterfully maintained. They purred with a throaty hum that spoke of power just waiting to be used.

That was good, as she intended to make use of every bit of it.

It took them another hour to load all the equipment and finish filling the tanks with fuel, but by nine that morning they were headed out onto the river to start their search.

Annja gathered her two companions together over the chart table in the wheelhouse and went through the plan she'd put together to find what they were looking for. Satisfied they all knew their assignments after twenty minutes of discussion, they sat back to enjoy the short trip downstream to the target area.

After they had arrived in the general location where the university team had recorded their earlier finding, it was time to get the search under way in earnest.

The magnetometer looked like a miniature rocket, with a blunt nose, long tube-shaped body and a set of fins in the rear. It was four feet long and weighed somewhere in the neighborhood of twelve pounds. After assembling it, Garin launched the magnetometer over the side while Annja played out the line until it was being towed roughly fifty feet behind the boat at a depth of about one hundred and fifty feet. The device was designed to pick up variations in the earth's natural magnetic field. Large quantities of iron, like that used in the construction of the CSS *Marietta,* would alter that field and show up on the device's screen. The accompanying GPS would allow them to note the exact coordinates and reveal the width and length of the debris field, as well.

As they began the long, slow process of trawling up and down the river, searching for an anomaly with the magnetometer, Jimmy spoke up.

"So tell me about this boat we're looking for."

Annja glanced up at him and then back down to the dials on the magnetometer's control box. "The CSS *Marietta.* She's an old Confederate ironclad built back in 1862."

"Cool," Mitchell said, and then, completely unselfconsciously, asked in the same breath, "What's an ironclad?"

Annja laughed good-naturedly. "Basically, it's a steam-propelled wooden warship that's fitted with iron plates for protection."

Mitchell thought about that for a minute. "So they took a steamboat and stuck it in a suit of armor?"

It wasn't exactly the way Annja would have explained it, but it worked just the same. "Yes," she told him, "that's pretty much it."

She went on. "There were several different types built during the Civil War, but the most common was the casemate ironclad. Think of it as an armored box, with slanting sides, built to protect the guns and crew from enemy shot. They often had a reinforced bow that was used to ram enemy vessels, as well. The *Marietta,* the ship we're looking for, was a casemate ironclad."

"That means it should light up the magnetometer like a Christmas tree," Garin put in.

Annja nodded. "That's the hope, anyway."

As if on cue the magnetometer began beeping and a section of the screen suddenly bloomed with color. Hearing it, Mitchell slowed the boat to a crawl, letting the magnetometer get a good long look.

The men turned expectant gazes in her direction, but after studying the readings for a moment, Annja had to shake her head. The object, while certainly iron, was too small to be the *Marietta.*

More like somebody's old hot-water heater, she thought to herself, and quelled the sense of disappointment that threatened. She guessed there had been plenty of junk dumped into the river over the years and they were likely to get a lot of false positives before they found the real target.

To try and limit that as much as possible, Annja moved the gamma setting from three to nine, ensuring that they would only pick up larger concentrations of iron, and signaled to Mitchell to get the boat moving again.

By midafternoon they'd stopped four more times. Each time Annja had suited up in wetsuit and scuba gear and, with the help of a diving sled outfitted with high-powered spotlights, had gone down into the murky water to take a look. Each time she'd been filled with anticipation, her heart pounding as her diving fins pushed her through the dark toward the unknown. Each time she'd been disappointed. So far she discovered an abandoned station wagon, an industrial-size boiler, a pile of cast-iron sinks and, much to her surprise, a steam locomotive. The train had just been sitting there on the river bottom, the round bulb of its front light looking like an eye gazing back at her out of the gloom. Seeing it sent her imagination into overdrive and she found herself wondering what train it was from and how it had come to be here, at the bottom of the Savannah River. When she surfaced, she made a note on the charts, indicating the find, and made a mental note as well to return to the spot one day to learn more.

For now, though, they still had an ironclad to find.

They were on the very edge of the target area, just finishing off their complete pass, when the magnetometer's alarm went off for the fifth time that day. The display showed a good-size target, so Annja zipped up her wetsuit and prepared to dive again.

"Want me to take it this time?" Garin asked.

Annja was tempted but, after a moment's consideration, shook her head. She wanted to be the first to see the *Marietta*'s final resting place; call her selfish, she didn't care.

"Thanks, but I've got it," she told him.

"Suit yourself. Remember to use one of the strobes if you get into trouble—white for marking the wreck and red for an emergency."

"Right. Wish me luck," she said as she put her mouthpiece between her teeth and went over the side for the fifth time that day. When she surfaced, Garin handed the light sled down to her, waited until she'd turned it on to check how much battery power was left and then played out her dive rope behind her as she sunk beneath the surface.

The weights on her belt helped her resist the river's

current and took her to the bottom fairly quickly. They'd loaded the exact location into the GPS unit she wore on her wrist, so it was a simple matter of following the signal to the site.

Except there was nothing there.

Or rather, nothing that looked to her like the wreckage of a Civil War ironclad.

She began swimming in a wide circle, moving through the target area methodically. At this point in the river a wide ridge rose up about ten feet along the bottom, just large enough that she couldn't see over it and long enough that she couldn't see past it in the gloom. She kept it close on her left, keeping it as a reference point so she wouldn't get confused in the murky water.

Damn, it's dark down here, she thought.

She'd almost reached the end of the ridgeline when she saw something sticking out of the muck at the point where the ridge rose up from the river bottom.

Something that looked far too symmetrical and round to be natural.

Annja shone the light directly at it.

The open mouth of a Civil War–era cannon gaped at her.

With a grunt of surprise, she understood what had been eluding her for the past several minutes.

The hurricane must have pushed the wreckage deep into the silt of the river bottom, where it had become lodged against the current. Over time, spring floods and the occasional high-water storm had deposited more and more debris atop the wreck, until it was essentially entombed in the earth, forming the underwater ridge she'd been swimming beside.

Better yet, based on the size and shape of the ridge,

it appeared that the *Marietta* might have remained reasonably intact, despite the force of the water.

Annja felt her excitement grow at the realization.

If the ship was intact and she could find a way inside, they might still be able to recover Ewell's Rifle and continue the search for the treasure!

She gave a powerful kick and began swimming along the length of the ridge, looking for some way inside the hull she knew was hidden beneath.

It didn't take long.

A shelf jutted out from the rounded side of the ridge and a school of fish shot out from beneath when her light washed across it. When she moved in for a closer look, pointing her light like a beacon into the darkness, she found herself staring at the algae-encrusted edges of a wide hole that led farther into darkness.

At some point in the distant past, a hole had been gouged through the casemate armor that surrounded the hull. Annja didn't know if it happened when the ship ran aground or prior to that, during the battle itself that had forced the CSS *Marietta* to heave to or risk sinking with all hands on board, but it didn't really matter. The hole provided a way inside the vessel and that's what she needed to allow her to search inside the ship for what they come here for.

But first, she had to tell the others....

She pulled one of the white emergency flare lights off her belt and clipped it to the edge of the hull. She gave the top a twist, activating the strobe inside it, and then pushed off for the surface, rising through water suddenly lit up with the pulsing white light of the flare.

26

The wide smile on her face must have given her news away, for her two companions took one look at her and began whooping and hollering like a couple of two-year-olds. Annja swam over to the boat, passed the light sled up to Mitchell and then accepted Garin's hand to help pull her aboard.

"Talk to me," he said to her, grinning like a baboon.

Glad I'm not the only one, she thought.

"She's down there all right, almost completely buried in the mud at the river bottom. Thankfully, she appears to be mostly intact!"

"So what do you think? Can we get inside?" Garin asked.

Annja nodded. "I found a hole about three-quarters of the way along the hull that's wide enough for us to swim through."

"Did you try to get inside?"

"Not yet, but it doesn't look like it will be a problem. I could see down to the lower deck from where I stood outside the gap and it looks like there is room enough to move around inside. That doesn't mean a bulkhead somewhere hasn't been crushed or the captain's cabin, where what we need was stored, is still accessible, but at least it gives us a chance."

Garin nodded. "All right. Take half an hour to rest and then we'll go down together."

She didn't want to wait. She wanted to simply switch tanks and dive immediately, but she knew he was right. The ship had been there this long and it wasn't going anywhere anytime soon, so there was no reason to take a chance with safety. Tired divers made stupid mistakes and mistakes were something they couldn't afford.

She used the downtime to grab some water and a quick snack out of the cooler they'd brought along. Rehydrated and feeling energized after the quick sugar rush, Annja prepped the underwater camera she'd be using to take pictures of their incursion inside the vessel and then changed out her previous breathing tank for a new one. When Garin was finished going over his own gear, they decided they'd been cautious enough and got ready to dive.

Annja explained their intentions to Mitchell.

"We're going to use the dive line to get us back to the wreck, but after that we're going off of it. I don't want to take the chance of having the line get held up on something inside the wreck and end up with one of us trapped down there."

Mitchell nodded. "Got it."

"We shouldn't be down there for more than an hour. If we run into any trouble we'll signal with a red strobe. You're not to leave the boat, though. Call for help if you think we're having difficulty."

"Roger that. Stay out of trouble and we won't have to worry about any of that," he replied, not knowing that trouble had a tendency to find Annja and not the other way around.

She smiled, gave him a thumbs-up and disappeared over the side of the boat.

Garin was waiting for her just beneath the surface. She swam by him, knowing he'd follow her down as planned. The strobe light she'd placed near the wreck had started to dim but was still strong enough for her to focus as she descended. Minutes later she was hovering just outside the opening, Garin at her side.

The dive line was attached to her belt with a carabiner. She unclipped it and then hunted around for a moment until she found a spot on the wreck where she could attach it. That way they would maintain a link to the boat above, but still be free to move around inside the wreckage without worrying about the line getting snagged on a piece of equipment or preventing them from getting through a tough spot.

Garin flipped on the handheld spotlight he carried, then signaled that he was ready. Annja did the same with her own light, then slipped through the opening and led the way inside the wreckage.

Most of the Confederate ironclads had nearly identical interior layouts, with three decks running throughout the structure. The first deck, known as the gun deck, was the portion of the main deck that was located inside the protective casemate armor. The guns were located there and, as one would expect, it was also where the crew spent most of their time. Meals were taken on foldaway, tables and hammocks were slung between the guns for sleeping.

The berthing deck, just below the gun deck, was a mezzanine-style deck, with its aft compartment fitted around the engine and its accompanying boiler. The forward compartment was divided into several areas, including additional crew quarters, the galley, paymaster's office, wardroom, sick bay and the captain's cabin.

The third and final deck, the orlop deck, housed all the stores. Dry provisions were near the bow, the magazine at midships and the wardroom stores usually near the rear. Just aft of this deck were the water tanks, boiler room and engine room, with all the machinery you would expect in such an area.

Shining their lights around the interior, it was clear that the ship was resting on her side. The "floor" they were hovering over was actually the port side of the vessel and anything that had not been bolted down at the time of the hurricane had been strewn about the chamber in a tangled mess. Most of it appeared to be the smashed remains of wooden furniture, which puzzled her for a moment until she remembered that the ship had been used as a regional headquarters in the months before the hurricane.

She glanced around, orienting herself with her mental understanding of the expected layout and then pointed to her left, indicating they were to move in that direction.

Garin nodded to show he understood.

Parker's second clue instructed them to find the Lady in distress, which they had determined was the CSS *Marietta,* and to then "take Ewell's Rifle from her crest." A ship's crest, also known as a coat of arms, was usually located in the captain's cabin so it made sense to start there given they didn't have any indication that it would be found elsewhere. That meant they had to go down one more deck and then move forward, toward the bow of the vessel, until they located the right cabin.

They moved through the open space of the gun deck

until they came to a square opening in the "wall" on their right that Annja recognized as a ventilation shaft. Once covered by a metal grate, the shaft would have allowed cool air from above to filter down belowdecks where it was desperately needed.

It was wide enough to allow them to pass through without difficulty and they used it now like a doorway to swim from the gun deck to the berthing deck just beyond.

They found themselves staring at a large metal tank that filled most of the space from the floor to the ceiling.

Boiler room, Annja thought to herself.

She shone her light beyond it, where she could see a convoluted series of metal shafts, pipes and gears, marking that space as the engine room. Garin had already turned his back on the equipment and was moving toward the open doorway at the other end of the room, so Annja had no choice but to follow, despite her desire to poke about and examine the engine. If she started, she knew she'd be there all day.

They passed through the wardroom, with its officers' bunks, and the galley with its tangled heap of cookware, before coming to a narrow corridor with open doors on either side. The second room they checked turned out to be the captain's cabin.

It was bigger than the others they'd seen, with a bunk bed built against the bulkhead and a narrow desk nailed to the floor just beyond.

The ship's crest, a large wooden plaque cut into the shape of a shield, hung above the desk.

Her excitement growing, Annja swam over to it.

Up close, it was unlike any crest she'd seen before. Most crests were carved from a single block of wood, so that each of the items that made up the crest were actually part of the whole. In this case, however, the flat surface of the shield was one piece of wood, with each of the adorning items making up the coat of arms having been carved separately and added one at a time.

At the top of the crest were two crossed rifles, in this case a pair of Enfield muskets, one of the most common weapons carried by Confederate soldiers throughout the war. A cavalry saber ran vertically through the space behind the center of the crossed rifles, the tip of its blade pointing at the object beneath them, which happened to be the statue of a horse rearing up on its hind legs. Underneath that, at the bottom of the crest, was a ship's wheel. A linked chain, perhaps representing a ship's anchor chain, ran around the edge of the entire device.

Garin followed her over, waited patiently for Annja to finish her examination, and then reached up to remove one of the rifles from the top of the crest, only to have Annja put out a hand to stop him.

Even through his face mask she could see him giving her an impatient look.

We came for the rifle, so that's what I'm taking with us, his eyes seemed to say.

But Annja knew better.

Motioning for him to wait a moment, Annja turned her attention back to the crest and ran her fingers over the statue of the horse.

Take Ewell's Rifle from her crest...

Richard S. Ewell had been a Confederate general who fought well under Stonewall Jackson and had taken command of Second Corps when the former fell in battle. He'd made a fateful mistake at Gettysburg, failing to push for the heights of Cemetery Hill despite the discretionary orders he'd received from Robert E. Lee telling him to engage if he found it to be "practicable." The second day of fighting at Gettysburg might have been radically different if he'd done so.

Ewell's Rifle hadn't been a firearm, Annja remembered, but rather the trusted horse on which he rode into battle.

A horse like the one in front of her now.

Unable to find a switch or a lever that might release the horse from its position on the crest, Annja grasped it with one hand and tried to turn it. She felt something click beneath the pressure she was exerting and the statue came free in her hand.

Garin had been hanging back, watching her, but when the horse came free in her hand he crowded close, wanting a look for himself. She passed it over to him and let him examine it for a moment, before taking it back. When doing so, she noted that it felt heavier than something that size would normally weigh, signaling to Annja that there was more there than met the eye. She'd have to examine it more closely once they got it up to the surface.

Opening the dive bag at her waist, Annja dropped the statue inside. A glance at the dive computer on her wrist told her they'd been down for twenty minutes at this point. At their current depth, that meant they were now at the halfway mark.

Plenty of time to get back to the top, she thought.

She signaled to Garin that they were ready and followed him back through the wreckage the same way they'd come in until they reached the gun deck and the opening in the hull through which they'd entered the ship.

27

With a nod to her, Garin slipped out of the opening, located the dive line and, using it as a guide, headed for the surface. Annja moved as if to follow but then stopped for a moment before leaving the wreck, wanting to be certain that the bag containing the artifact was tied securely to her dive belt. She didn't want the river current to tear it free while she was surfacing.

Satisfied, she turned to follow Garin, only to hesitate at the exit, a sense of unease stealing over her. She couldn't put her finger on precisely what it was, but she had that sinking feeling in her gut, that tingling at the edge of her spine that sometimes warned her when something was about to go very wrong.

She'd learned to trust her instincts and listen to that feeling.

She extended her arm outside the wreck and waved her spotlight about, looking for she didn't know what.

The beam of light could only cut through the water for a short distance before the murk swallowed it up.

Still, she thought she saw something swimming through the dark waters at the edge of the light's reach.

That's just Garin, she tried to reassure herself.

She pulled the spotlight back inside, turned it up to its most powerful setting and flashed it back in the same direction.

This time there was nothing there.

Satisfied, she clipped the light to her belt and leaned out of the opening, her hand groping for the dive line that she intended to follow to the surface. A dark shape rushed forward out of the murky water to her left. She saw it and flinched backward, her body reacting to the threat before her conscious mind had processed exactly what it was. She caught sight of a scaly hide and a flash of teeth before the alligator's powerful jaws slammed shut just inches from her face.

Half a second later the creature was gone, lost once more in the murk.

Heart pounding, Annja backed away from the opening. She knew that contrary to popular belief, alligators actually had excellent eyesight and, being natural predators, were attracted to movement. She was hoping that the creature would just continue on and leave her alone if she didn't give it any reason to come after her.

She called forth her sword and felt a little less anxious when her hand closed around the hilt. Unlike a firearm, a melee weapon like her sword would work pretty effectively underwater, provided she stuck with actions that didn't generate a lot of resistance. Great slashing strokes were out of the question, but she could stab with it easily enough. Armed, her chances improved almost a hundredfold. Most alligators avoided human contact as much as possible, and the larger the creatures, the more shy they were. The average alligator was about twelve feet in length, she knew, which put the one she'd just seen well in the upper percentile.

That's one big lizard, she thought.

She checked her dive computer again and saw that she had another five minutes of air, plus a ten-minute safety margin. Hopefully the alligator would grow bored and wander off long before that.

But that wasn't to be.

Even as she thought about it being gone, the gator swam back into view. It cut through the water like a torpedo, approaching her hiding place but not intent on attacking, at least as far as she could tell. It seemed to be just swimming about, waiting for her to emerge from her little cave.

She held her breath, as if breathing might alert it to her presence somehow and continued backing up.

As she did so, she bumped into one of the cannons that had been tossed about by the hurricane. It wasn't a hard blow, by any means, but it hit her side at just the right angle to set off one of the emergency strobe lights she had hanging on her belt.

The water around her was suddenly filled with a blazing red light that pulsed outward into the darkness. It flashed over the alligator, catching its attention and causing the beast to turn back toward her.

It was facing her direction when the next pulse of light went out and the alligator reacted to it instantly, charging directly toward her.

BELIEVING ANNJA TO BE right behind him, Garin headed for the surface without a backward glance. He was on limited air at this point and didn't want to stay under any longer than necessary.

The sun cut down through the murky water, and as he drew closer to the surface he could make out the dark shadow of the *Kelly May*'s hull in the water above him.

To his surprise, however, he saw that she was no longer alone. Another, larger shadow loomed next to her. The second vessel was a good deal larger than the *Kelly May* and, from below it, looked as if there were only a few feet separating the two boats. Garin hesitated, hanging in the water a few feet below the surface. Warning bells were going off in the back of his mind, the other vessel's presence making him uncomfortable. He didn't know if it was the position of the boat or the fact that it was there at all, but hundreds of years of trusting his instincts told him that he needed to be careful.

He glanced down into the water below him, looking for Annja. She should have been here by now, he thought.

But there was no sign of her in the murky water beneath him.

For a moment he considered diving back down toward the wreck, but a glance at his dive computer told him that would be a bad idea. He had only a few minutes of air left; descending would leave him stranded at the bottom without enough oxygen to get back to the surface. Even if he did find Annja, he'd only be putting them both into increased danger.

His lack of air also meant he didn't have a lot of time to decide what he was going to do about the mysterious vessel above him.

He might be worried for nothing, he knew. After all, there were probably half a dozen legitimate reasons for the presence of the second vessel, from a quick coast guard inspection to a chance visit from one of Mitchell's fellow trawler captains. He really didn't have access to enough information yet to come to a useful conclusion.

His best bet was to see about getting some.

Kicking himself into motion, he swam beneath the hulls of both boats until he was on the far side of the larger vessel. Once in position, he gently surfaced, trying to make as little noise as possible as his head and shoulders came up above the waterline. His new location gave him a good look at the other boat.

Unlike the *Kelly May,* this one would never be confused as anything but a pleasure craft. Where the *Kelly May* looked weathered and used, the newcomer practically gleamed, from its showroom-bright white paint to its newly polished brass sparkling in the sunlight. Garin could see it had at least two decks above the waterline and those were topped by a floating bridge for fly-fishing. From the size of her, Garin guessed she ran on a crew of four, minimum.

Thankfully, none of them were in sight.

He could hear voices coming from the far side of the boat where the *Kelly May* was anchored, but he couldn't make out what they were saying. The voices sounded angry, however, which only served to reinforce his sense of caution.

Garin swam over to the side of the boat where an aluminum ladder descended from the deck down to the waterline. Grasping the nearest rung in both hands, he quickly climbed to the deck above. He didn't want the scuba tank he wore to hinder his movements as he skulked about the boat, so he unbuckled his harness and quietly lowered the tank to the deck. He removed his flippers, too.

A quick glance told him he was still alone. Satisfied

that he could move with stealth, he set out to discover just what was going on.

He crept forward, keeping his back to the wall and his head below the level of the windows. He could see a staircase ahead of him, leading to the decks above, so he made his way over to it and ascended as quickly and as quietly as he could. He passed the door to the second deck without stopping, headed for the sun deck above. At the top he peeked over the edge, looking for signs of the crew.

The deck appeared to be empty.

The voices were louder now and a few short sharp sentences were followed by the unmistakable sound of a fist striking bare flesh. Whoever they were, they weren't there to make friends, it seemed.

Still not having seen anyone, Garin took a chance to swiftly cross the deck, threading his way through the lounge chairs until he reached the far side.

Crouched down next to the railing, he cautiously raised his head to get a look at what was happening on board the *Kelly May* below him.

He could see Jimmy Mitchell kneeling in the middle of the deck with his hands in the air, his face battered and swollen. A large thug in a dark jacket and jeans stood looming over him, no doubt the source of the bruises. Two other thugs, similarly dressed, stood a few feet behind the pair. Both of them held automatic rifles in their hands.

A fourth man stood near the stern of the boat, watching the proceedings with a bored look on his face. He was better dressed than the other three and was clearly the man in charge. He glanced away from his captive, toward the dive line that stretched down into the water, and Garin got a good look at his face.

To his surprise, he recognized the man. He'd seen his face staring back at him from the photo in the file Griggs had handed him just a few days before.

Blaine Michaels, the man who currently headed the Order of the Golden Phoenix.

Garin was suddenly glad he'd opted for the cautious approach. By the way Michaels was watching the dive line, it was clear that Mitchell had told him that his two companions were in the water below.

Where was Annja? Garin had yet to see any indication that she'd surfaced after him and that concerned him even more than the newcomers aboard the *Kelly May.* She should have done so by now. Her air supply had to be running dangerously low at this point.

It seemed Michaels knew that, as well, for he kept glancing toward the dive line, watching for movement that might signal Annja's ascendance. Garin didn't spare a second thought for Jimmy Mitchell; the man was an uncultured bore who more than likely deserved what he had coming to him.

But Annja was another story. Michaels's men had already tried to kill Annja once and Garin had no doubt that things wouldn't end well if she fell into his clutches at this point.

He had to find a way to warn her off before she surfaced.

Garin turned away from the rail with some vague plan of hustling back across the deck and returning to the water half formed in his mind. He walked right into a punch thrown by the man standing behind him.

If he'd been standing, the blow would have hit him in the stomach, but because he was crouched over, it caught him on the chin. The force of the blow knocked him off his feet and sent him sprawling to the deck.

Even with his head spinning from the unexpected blow, Garin kept enough of his wits about him to sense the other man moving in to finish the job. As he drew closer, Garin spun around in a half circle and lashed out with his legs, striking his assailant behind the ankles and sweeping him off his feet.

No sooner had the other man hit the deck than Garin swarmed atop him, covering him with his body to keep the other man from getting back up and locking his hands around his throat to prevent him from shouting a warning.

The newcomer wasn't going to go down without a fight, though. He grabbed Garin's hands in his own, trying to pull them off his throat. Rather than wasting more of his energy and air when that didn't immediately work, he switched tactics, pounding at the sides of Garin's body with his big fists, alternating those strikes with attempts to land a good solid cross on Garin's face.

Garin, however, was in excellent physical condition and he simply ignored the body strikes, knowing it would be a while before the other man did enough damage to trouble him. He tucked his head between his outstretched arms to keep it from being hit by a wayward blow and tightened his grip on the other's man's neck, hoping to choke his assailant into unconsciousness as quickly as possible.

As the seconds ticked past, and the other man refused to weaken, Garin's frustration grew. He had no choice but to end this as quickly as possible.

When the solution occurred to him, he cursed himself for not thinking of it immediately.

As his attacker's flailing continued, Garin reared back and then thrust his head forward, slamming the crown of his skull into the other man's forehead with an audible crack.

It was like turning off a light switch. One moment the man was bucking and struggling away beneath him, the next he lay still, knocked into unconsciousness by the force of the blow.

Garin climbed off the other man, intent on making his escape, only to be brought up short by the cold touch of a gun barrel against the side of his head.

"Ne se déplacent pas."

Don't move.

Garin put his hands in the air, surrendering.

28

Annja fumbled at her belt with her free hand, trying to free the device, but it was no use. It had gotten stuck somehow and wouldn't come free. She gave it one more tug as the alligator closed the distance between them and then she had no choice but to take hold of her sword in both hands as the beast was upon her.

It thrust its snout forward, jaws open wide, ready to snap them shut on her tender flesh, but Annja was no longer where she had been a second before. At the last moment she turned to her left, evading the snap of the gator's massive jaws and stabbing with her sword.

She felt the tip of her blade bite into the creature's flesh as it rushed past, blood spilling into the water.

While she might have drawn first blood, the alligator didn't come out completely behind in the exchange. As it swept past, one of its legs lashed out, clawing Annja across the ribs and adding some of her blood to the mix.

She didn't have time to worry about it, because if she didn't do something quickly she'd be gator lunch.

Everything flashed around her in a strange liquid

dance, the gator's motions seeming oddly disjointed in the flashing light of the strobe. The creature rushed past her, slamming into the opposite bulkhead thanks to the momentum of its charge. As it righted itself it lashed out with its powerful tail, sending a stack of three cannons tumbling downward to the floor. For a moment, it was trapped behind a debris pile of its own making.

Annja saw her chance. While the alligator was thrashing about, trying to right itself in the narrow space, she turned and threw herself toward the opening, trying to get clear of the wreckage while ignoring the pain in her side at the same time.

For a split second she thought about making a run for the surface. If she could get up to the boat before it freed itself...

But then reason reasserted itself.

If the alligator caught her in the open water, she'd be dead.

And chances were, injured and exhausted as she was, it *would* catch her.

So rather than trying to make a run for it, she turned around as soon as she was clear of the opening and positioned herself atop the overhang that covered it, legs braced shoulder-width apart and the sword held point downward in her two hands.

I'm only going to get one shot....

Having already tasted the sharpness of her blade, the alligator was more cautious leaving the wreck than it had been when entering, which was exactly what Annja was counting on.

It stuck its snout out of the opening first, testing the water.

That was the target Annja had been waiting for. The moment the alligator's snout came into view, Annja stepped off the ledge, thrusting her sword downward with all her might as she fell.

The resistance of the water delayed her blow slightly, but she'd anticipated that and planned for it. Thanks to the delay, rather than passing through the top of the creature's snout, which only would have enraged it more, her sword pierced the beast's skull a few inches behind its eyes as her weight settled fully atop the beast.

It reacted instantly, throwing itself around like a bucking bronco, but Annja wrapped her legs around the creature's neck and held on to the sword with all her might, still pushing downward.

Blood spilled into the water, obscuring them both, but Annja didn't care. She was too focused on driving that sword deeper and was holding on with her legs for dear life.

There was a moment of resistance and then the blade slid all the way home, the guard on the hilt coming to rest against the reptile's bony hide.

Beneath her, the alligator finally went still.

Annja held on, waiting, wanting to be sure before she let go, but when it hadn't moved for several long moments she finally released her death grip on both the sword and the alligator.

The sword vanished back into the otherwhere, as if it had never been, leaving only Annja's blood-covered form and the sinking body of a dead alligator as evidence that it had existed at all.

Annja tried to draw in a deep breath from her regulator and got only a thin mouthful of air.

Uh-oh.

A glance at her air gauge told her she was well into the red. She had only moments of air left.

Trying to keep from panicking, Annja hung in the

water for a moment, watching her air bubbles. All the gator's thrashing had disoriented her and she needed to determine which way was up before she started swimming. She didn't want to head off in the wrong direction and make things worse.

When she saw the direction the air bubbles were rising, she began swimming frantically in the same direction.

She almost made it, too.

She was only ten feet from the surface when her air tank ran completely dry.

Annja didn't let that stop her, though. She spit the regulator from her mouth and kicked harder, pushing herself up toward the light shining down from above.

She broke the surface of the water and sucked in a great, life-giving breath of fresh air.

That was when she noticed the man standing on the stern of the *Kelly May,* pointing the muzzle of the automatic rifle at her.

29

"You don't listen too good, do you, Miss Creed?"

Annja stared up at the speaker, a dark-haired man in his mid-forties standing next to the gunman, and resisted the urge to correct his grammar. No sense in antagonizing him, at least not yet.

Behind him she could see Jimmy Mitchell and Garin kneeling on the deck, a second gunman standing far enough away that he could keep his weapon trained on them without worrying about being jumped. Three other thugs stood nearby, guns in hand but not pointed at anyone. All around it was a good, tactical position and, seeing it, Annja knew they were dealing with professionals.

That was going to make things more difficult.

She turned her head slightly, taking in the large yacht that was tied up next to the smaller *Kelly May*. That explained where the men had come from. She could see several other men on board the other vessel, which told her they were vastly outnumbered.

It didn't look like there was an easy way out of this one.

"I thought I was quite clear," the speaker said. "Or is there some other way of interpreting 'stay out of my business'?"

Annja focused her attention back on him. "Who are you and what do you want?" she asked.

The man laughed. "Who am I? Oh, that's rich, Miss Creed. Truly. You're being held at gunpoint and the first thing you care about is being sure we're properly introduced." He shook his head, as if in disbelief. "Reinhardt told me you were a little spitfire, but I must admit I didn't quite believe him. Now I know better."

Annja's eyes narrowed at the mention of Bernard, but she didn't say anything, not yet. There would be time enough to deal with that. Right now she wanted to prevent them all from being killed.

"Let me introduce myself, then." The man affected a little bow. "Blaine Michaels, at your service. As for what I want? I think we both know the answer to that."

"You're after the treasure," Annja said, stalling for time while trying to come up with a plan. With the gun pointed at her head, she didn't have many options. Diving back down beneath the surface was out of the question. She'd never make it deep enough quickly enough to avoid the gunfire that was sure to follow, and besides, that would leave Garin and Mitchell in their hands along with Bernard. Nor could she hope to climb aboard and free them before being cut down by gunfire.

"Out of the water, please."

Somehow, Michaels made the word *please* sound anything but polite.

Annja swam the last few feet to the side of the boat. When no one moved to help her up, she pulled herself up and over the stern. After fighting off an alligator and running out of air, that final effort nearly exhausted her. She sat with her back against the gunwale and panted to catch her breath.

"The rifle. Where is it?" Michaels said.

She looked up at him, feigning confusion. "The what? I'm sorry, I don't know what you're talking about."

In hindsight, she realized she should have expected it. After all, nothing Michaels had done so far gave her any reason to think he was anything but deadly serious.

Michaels didn't bother arguing with her. He didn't say anything at all, in fact. He just gave a little wave of his hand—nothing to it really, just a flick of the fingers—and the man holding the gun on Annja's companions pulled the trigger.

There was the crack of a gunshot and Jimmy Mitchell dropped to the deck, his sightless eyes staring in her direction as blood leaked from the hole in his forehead to mingle with the flow pouring out of what was left of the back of his skull after the bullet burst through it.

Annja came halfway off the deck, her hands clenched, adrenaline surging through her system. It took incredible force of will to keep from drawing her sword, but somehow she managed it. Michaels and his men were too far away for it to do her any good and drawing it now would only give away her one real advantage.

"You bastard," she snarled.

"Tsk, tsk, Miss Creed. Such language. There's no need for it, really." He took a couple of steps forward and stared down at her with contempt.

"I'll only ask you once more. Where is the rifle?"

She didn't see any option but to tell him. If she'd been

on her own, she might have taken a chance in drawing her sword and trying to get her hands on Michaels before his henchman could line up a shot, but with Garin still under gunpoint she didn't have that choice. Michaels had already shown he wouldn't hesitate to fire and she didn't want any more blood on her hands.

"It's in my dive bag," she said.

He glared at her for a long moment and she could see in his expression that he was trying to work out how that was possible.

Not as smart as you think, are you? she thought.

Michaels turned and looked at one of the thugs watching from the sidelines. The man got the message without being told and moved swiftly to Annja's side.

For just a second she thought about grabbing him, using his body as a shield to keep from getting shot as she tried to maneuver into a better position, but something in Michaels's eyes told her it wouldn't matter. He'd simply shoot through his underling in order to get to her.

So she sat quietly instead, not doing anything as Michaels's henchman came over, knelt beside her and, producing a knife from somewhere inside his jacket, cut the dive bag from her belt. He carried it over to Michaels.

Annja watched as Michaels drew open the drawstrings and peered inside.

"What the hell is this?" he asked, looking back up at her.

"Ewell's Rifle," she replied wearily.

If I can get them to think I've given up, they might make a mistake. And one mistake will be all I'll need, she thought.

Turning the bag over, Michaels poured the statue into his hand. He held it up for her to see.

"Does this look like a rifle to you?" he asked, and this time she could hear the anger in his voice.

"It does when you understand that the horse General Ewell rode into battle more than any other was named Rifle."

He opened his mouth and then shut it again without saying anything. Clearly, he hadn't known. Annja watched as he processed that piece of information, imagining that she could almost see the information firing through the various synapses in his brain as he tried to make sense of all the angles that information generated.

"I see," he said slowly.

"You've got the statue, now let us go!" Garin said angrily, speaking up for the first time.

Michaels didn't even bother looking in his direction, just inclined his head toward his man with the gun standing nearby.

"No!" Annja shouted, fearing the worse.

The gunman stepped forward and cracked Garin across the face with the stock of the automatic rifle in his hands.

Garin went down, hard, blood spraying from his mouth.

"If he says another word, kill him," Michaels said matter-of-factly. Annja knew he meant it.

Across the deck, Garin shook his head, as if to clear it, spat blood on the deck and then pushed himself back up to his knees, glaring at the man who'd struck him.

The other man smirked and raised the stock of his weapon again, trying unsuccessfully to make his captive flinch, never noticing that the man he thought was helpless before him was now several feet closer than he'd been before.

Not yet, Garin, not yet, Annja thought, and prayed he wouldn't make a move before she was ready.

Unfortunately for them both, Blaine Michaels had just made several mental connections that would radically alter his plans for moving forward and rob the two of them of their opportunity to escape.

He hefted the horse, perhaps noticing the weight of it for the first time, and then looked at Annja.

"Let me guess. There's something inside it, isn't there?"

Annja shrugged.

That was apparently answer enough, though, for Michaels suddenly raised the statue and then dashed it against the hard surface of the deck between his feet, shattering it into several pieces.

From where she sat on the deck nearby, Annja could see a small metallic object lying amid the shattered porcelain.

In that second, everyone's attention was on the remains of the statue and nowhere else.

Now, Annja thought, and she tensed, ready to move, but before she could do so things took another turn.

A pair of figures stepped out onto the deck of the other boat and Annja's gaze automatically flicked over in that direction. Bernard stood there, his hands tied in front of him, and a blindfold on his face. Beside him was another of Michaels's thugs, a gun stuck in Bernard's side.

As if reading her intentions, Michaels looked up from the debris at his feet and asked, "Going somewhere, Miss Creed?"

Annja bit back her reply and released the tension in her limbs. Whatever she'd hoped to do, it was too late now.

Over Michaels's shoulder, Annja could see Garin come to the same conclusion.

Michaels bent down, brushed aside the broken porcelain and picked up the object that had been hidden inside the statue.

"Bring me the professor," he called out, and waited while Bernard was led across the deck and then helped across the gap between the boats.

When the professor was standing in front of him, Michaels ripped off the blindfold and held up the object he'd taken from inside the statue. "What is this?" he asked.

From where she sat on the deck, Annja could see that Michaels was holding a metal disk about twice the size of a half-dollar. Another piece of metal had been inserted in the center of the disk, this one in the shape of an eight-pointed star. As she watched, he spun the star so that it rotated within the confines of the disk, making an odd clicking sound as it did so.

Bernard was much closer to the object than she was, and therefore could get a better look at it, but it was clear from the expression on his face that he didn't recognize it.

Annja wasn't the only one who noticed, either.

"I'm getting the feeling you don't have any idea what this is, do you, Professor?"

"Of course I do," Bernard said indignantly, his professional pride stung from the accusation. Or maybe it was just the muzzle of the pistol the guard jabbed him with when he seemed hesitant to answer. "It's a…well… I think…"

Michaels sighed and there was something downright menacing in the exaggerated way he did so. "Perhaps it hasn't occurred to you yet, Professor Reinhardt, but your usefulness to me is severely limited if you can't give me the information I need."

Bernard held up his hands in a placating gesture. "Just give me a minute… It's coming to me…."

"It's a Jeffersonian Key," Annja said, coming to his rescue.

Michaels turned and looked at her. "Go on."

"They were invented by Thomas Jefferson near the close of the American Revolution. The star on the disk acts as a primitive combination lock, releasing successive layers of the corresponding locking mechanism when inserted into the lock and turned in the proper direction."

Michaels stared at her for a long moment without saying anything. "It would seem, Miss Creed, that you are better prepared to find the treasure than your colleague."

Annja didn't say anything. She didn't know where Michaels was going with this and didn't want to do anything to tip the scales in the wrong direction. If Bernard was no longer seen as useful, then Michaels might be tempted to get rid of him. Permanently.

"In fact, I don't see any reason to keep floundering around, following the professor's instructions, while you beat us to the jackpot each time. I think it would be much better if you did the dirty work, found the treasure and then just turned it over to me."

"Like hell I will," Annja said quietly.

Michaels laughed. "That's precisely what I'd expect you to say, Miss Creed, which is why I'm glad I don't have to depend on your good-natured cooperation."

Without looking away from her, he said, "Kill one of them. I don't care which one."

"Wait! " Annja shouted, cursing inwardly. "Just wait a moment. I'm sure we can work this out."

Michaels cocked his head to one side. "Work this out?" he asked. "What is there to work out? You'll either find the treasure for me or I'll shoot your friends. It's pretty simple."

Annja's hand ached from her efforts to keep from calling the sword and charging forward. She wanted to wipe that annoying smile off the smug bastard's face, but knew the moment she made her move someone else would wind up dead and the chances that it would be herself or one of her friends was pretty damn high.

Patience, Grasshopper, patience, she told herself.

"Fine," she said. "I'll do it."

Michaels's grin widened. "See? That wasn't so difficult, now was it?"

He waited for her to shake her head, the very act acknowledging his control over her, and then, over his shoulder, he said to his henchman, "What are you waiting for? I told you to kill one of them."

At first she thought she'd misheard him, but then the air was filled with the terrible sound of a gunshot and Annja watched in horror as Bernard's body slumped over on the deck in front of her.

"You son of a bitch!" she cried, surging to her feet, the blood pounding in her ears as she mentally reached for her sword…

…only to be struck in the face with the butt end of the assault rifle held in her guard's hands.

The blow was hard enough to knock her unconscious. As she tumbled backward, she thought she heard someone call her name and, over that, the sound of the madman in front of her cackling like a particularly vicious little child, and then the darkness had her and she knew no more.

30

When Annja regained consciousness, she found herself lying on the deck of the *Kelly May* with the dead for company.

The bodies of Jimmy Mitchell and Bernard Reinhardt lay where they had fallen, their blood staining the wood beneath their still forms, their sightless eyes staring out at the world from which they'd been taken too soon.

Of the others, there was no sign.

Blaine Michaels and his henchmen were gone.

The boat that they had arrived in was gone, as well.

Garin was missing, too.

Annja pushed herself up into a sitting position and was nearly overwhelmed by a wave of dizziness that washed over her. She held still, waiting for it to pass. Her face hurt and her nose throbbed, but a gentle exploration of both with her fingertips told her that nothing seemed to be broken. Swollen, yes, but not broken.

When the dizziness had passed and she was reasonably sure she wouldn't vomit, she climbed to her feet.

"Hello?" she called, or tried to, at least. Her voice came out as more of a croak and she could taste the blood from her damaged nose at the back of her throat.

No one answered her.

Well, who did you expect? she asked herself. The Ghost of Christmas Past? You can see there's no one here.

She could, too. There really wasn't all that much more to the boat than she could see. Foredeck. Aft deck. And the wheelhouse. From where she stood she could observe both decks and everything above waist height in the wheelhouse, so unless someone was crouching on the floor of the latter, she was on her own.

An image of a wounded Garin lying bruised and bloody on the wheelhouse floor came to her, and though she didn't think it likely, she knew she wouldn't be able to put it out of her mind until she checked, just to be sure. She wobbled forward on unsteady legs, her equilibrium still out of whack from the blow to the head, and peered inside the wheelhouse.

There was no one there.

That didn't mean there wasn't anything of interest inside, however.

A black cell phone stood on the control panel right next to the throttle, plainly visible from the wheelhouse door. It was one of those disposable models that you could buy in just about any corner store these days. She didn't remember seeing Jimmy with a phone like that and she knew it wasn't hers or Garin's. It seemed it had been left there specifically for her.

Next to it was the Jeffersonian Key that had been secreted inside the porcelain horse.

She crossed over to the phone and picked it up. A quick examination showed her that there was a single number stored in the device's memory. She called the number, listening to the line ring for a few moments before it was answered by Michaels.

"Welcome back, Miss Creed."

Her fury rose at the sound of his voice. "I'm going to kill you for what you've done," she told him, and meant every word of it.

"You can certainly try," he replied, and then laughed at the very idea of it.

For a long moment all Annja could see was red. When she came back to herself she was clutching her sword in her hand, her fingers wrapped so tightly around the hilt that they were turning white. Michaels was speaking.

"Wait, what?" she asked, shaking her head to clear it while releasing her sword back into the otherwhere with a flick of her hand. She hadn't unconsciously called her sword before, and its appearance was a bit surprising, but she didn't have time then to puzzle it out.

"Pay attention, Miss Creed! Your friend's life depends on it."

"What did you do with him?"

"Do? Why, nothing. I simply invited him to accompany us for a bit while you finished the task ahead of you."

"If you harm him—"

"You'll do what, Miss Creed?" He laughed again, setting her teeth on edge. "You're not in a position to do anything but what I tell you to do. And I'm telling you to find the missing treasury if you want to see your friend again."

Annja knew when she'd been backed into a corner. She'd have to figure out a way to get both herself and

Garin out of this mess, once she had the treasure in hand.

"Fine."

His voice was practically dripping with satisfaction as he said, "Excellent. Take the phone with you. I'll expect a call from you inside of seventy-two hours at which point I'll tell you where to rendezvous with me to turn over the treasure."

"Seventy-two hours? Are you crazy? I can't possibly find it in that kind of time frame."

Michaels's tone was firm and brooked no disagreement. "You can and you will. Or you can say goodbye to your friend. Seventy-two hours, Miss Creed. That's all you get."

There was a click and the line went dead.

Seventy-two hours? How the hell was she supposed to accomplish that?

By moving your ass, girl, she told herself. Stop whining and get to work!

She grabbed the key and the phone. Her gaze flicked across the pair of bodies on the aft deck. They were lying right out in the open, visible to anyone who happened to pass by, and Annja knew she couldn't leave them that way.

Something had to be done.

Routing around in the storage compartments at the rear of the boat, Annja found several large tarps and she used those as a temporary solution to cover the bodies of her friends. She weighed the edges of the tarps down in several places so that the wind wouldn't pick them up and blow them aside once they got under way.

Because that's exactly what she was going to have to do. Get under way. She couldn't just leave the boat here, in the middle of the river, no matter how badly she might want to in order to avoid having to deal with the mess Michaels had dumped in her lap. Bernard deserved better than being left behind like some discarded piece of trash. Jimmy Mitchell did, too.

She was going to have to bring the boat back to the marina, put it in its proper slip and hope no one observed her when she made her departure.

The dive line and magnetometer were still being towed behind them, so she had to bring those aboard first and stow them. Despite not having seen another boat other than Michaels's the entire time they been on the river, she was still filled with anxiety as she worked, afraid another vessel was going to come along at any moment and notice something irregular.

Like the two corpses on the aft deck, she thought with a shudder.

Getting caught seemingly red-handed with the dead bodies of her friends with the deck beneath them covered in their congealing blood was not something she thought she had a chance of walking away from. She'd be locked up quicker than she could blink. If that happened, Garin would be left at the mercy of that psycho, Michaels.

So make sure it doesn't happen, she told herself. Get off the main river and out of sight for a bit while you figure out what to do.

With that in mind, she went into the wheelhouse and examined the controls after the dive line and magnetometer had been brought aboard and stowed away. The controls seemed fairly intuitive and the time she'd spent watching Mitchell maneuver the boat earlier that morning would likely be helpful, as well. With only a little trouble, she got the engines started and the boat turned

around, heading back in the direction from which
they'd come.

She encountered only one other vessel while out on
the open river, a small fishing boat with an outboard
motor. As they passed by on the port side she was filled
with a sense of impending doom. They were going to
see the bundle and know exactly what was underneath
it! Annja was sure of it.

Of course, nothing of the sort happened. The other
boat was far too low in the water to allow its passengers to see her deck, never mind figure out what was
under the weighted tarp. They passed with a friendly
nod and a quick wave, allowing Annja to get back to
worrying needlessly.

Twenty minutes farther along, she spotted the mouth
of a tributary large enough to handle the boat and turned
in that direction. About a dozen yards down its length,
the channel curved sharply to one side. Anything
around the bend would be out of sight of the main wa-
terway. It was just what she needed.

Once in position, she brought the boat to a stop and
shut down the engine. She listened for the sound of another engine nearby, but all that came back to her was
the gentle lapping of the water on the hull and the occasional cry of a hunting bird of prey.

She couldn't bring the boat into dock with two
corpses under a tarp on the back deck, she reminded
herself. They might not be noticed for a day, maybe
two, but the minute they started smelling someone was
bound to come aboard and investigate.

She needed somewhere that she could store them
until this entire mess was sorted out. She felt terrible
about it, but what choice did she have? If she called the
police now they'd hold her for questioning, perhaps even

decide that she was the prime suspect and lock her up. She'd be condemning Garin to certain death.

As it turned out, the answer was right there behind her.

A pair of doors was set in the center of the aft deck a few feet forward of the stern gunwale. Opening them, Annja discovered the refrigerated fish hold. On a working trawler, the fish would be rinsed with high-powered hoses that would push them over the lip of the hatch into the hold below. The refrigeration unit built into the walls of the hold would then keep the fish fresh until the boat returned to dock and the catch was sorted, boxed and then iced for its journey to the preparation plant.

If she could get the bodies into the fish hold, they'd be out of sight and chilled enough to stop major decomposition for the time being.

The trouble was, she didn't want to handle them. Not because she was squeamish, she was a far cry from that, but because she didn't want to leave any trace evidence on them if she could help it. She was already going to have a hard enough time explaining things when she got the chance. She'd be a suspect in their deaths, for sure. Add that to the recent killings she'd been involved in overseas and she knew she'd be answering police questions for weeks, if not months. Giving the police evidence that she'd been in physical contact with the victims was not going to help her case, not at all.

The problem was partially alleviated, she realized, by the fact that she was still in her neoprene wetsuit. With the hood up and her neoprene dive gloves on, the only part of her body that wasn't completely covered was her face. Even her hair was secured beneath the tight-fitting hood. The fabric of the suit would help repel any blood that got on her, and since she had other clothes to change into, she could always spray herself down with the high-powered hose and then dispose of the suit when she was finished.

Satisfied with her plan, or at least as much of a plan as she had, she got to work rigging the rest of the equipment she needed to pull this off.

She moved one of the booms into position over the doors to the fish hold and then attached a rope pulley to it. She dug around in the storage lockers until she found a medium-size net that would be large enough to hold both Jimmy's and Bernard's bodies and laid it out flat beside the hatch.

Then, donning her gloves, she took off the tarps and put them aside. She'd deal with them in a bit. Right now she needed to get the bodies into the net and then maneuver the net over the hatch so she could gently lower the whole contraption to the deck below.

She supposed it might have been easier to just roll them over the edge and into the hold, but she just couldn't bring herself to do that. Not so much earlier both men were laughing and joking with her and the idea of treating their earthly remains like, well, sacks of meat just wasn't going to cut it. She'd spend the extra time to lower them into the hold gently, and if someone came along while she was doing it she'd worry about it then.

She shifted the bodies one at a time and put them in the net. She then attached the hooks on the sides of the net to a sling and tied the sling off to the rope she'd threaded through the pulley earlier. She gave all the connections a few tugs, and found that they were secure.

Satisfied, she moved over to the other end of the rope, sat down on the deck with her back to the gunwale and, taking the rope between, began to heave it backward. It went easily at first, for all they were doing was taking up the slack. But after that, when the weight of the two bodies was pulling against her, she was thankful that she had the pulley or it would have been all over before it began.

Annja managed to lift the net a few inches off the ground, then used the tip of her foot to maneuver it out over the open doors to the hold. The moment it was she let the rope slip through her hands and the bodies of the two men disappeared into the hold with nary a sound.

After that all the equipment, including the tarps and the pulley itself, were tossed down beside the bodies. She used the high-pressure hose to spray down the deck, flushing the bloodstains out as best she could and sending the water over the side into the river. She then turned the hose on herself. She changed the setting to low and rinsed every inch of herself. Satisfied that there was no blood on her, she flushed the deck of the boat a final time. She stripped out of her gloves and wetsuit, tossing them into the fish locker with everything else. Last but not least, she closed the hatch and locked it up tight with a padlock she found in the toolbox.

If somebody wanted into the fish locker, they were going to have to work at it.

Having already dug a change of clothing out of her backpack, Annja got dressed. Just being back in her jeans and sweatshirt made her feel better, made her feel more ready to take on the challenge ahead of her.

With the clock ticking down, she didn't have time to waste. She fired up *Kelly May*'s engines and maneuvered her back into the main river channel. Once there, Annja opened up the throttle and headed for the marina as fast as she dared.

By the time she drove the boat into the narrow tributary that marked the only entrance to the marina where Mitchell had a slip, she was feeling fairly competent with the controls.

That was a good thing, because there was a lot more activity around the marina than there had been on the way out that morning.

Or you're just paying more attention to it, she told herself.

Either way, she was thankful that the wheelhouse was enclosed. Several folks recognized the boat and waved as she went past and their inability to see her clearly meant she didn't have to explain why she was at the controls instead of Jimmy.

Or where Jimmy was, for that matter.

She carefully maneuvered the boat into its slip and then shut down the engine. She watched the activity going on around her through the darkened wheelhouse windows, waited for her chance and then made a break for it, leaving the boat tied up behind her.

31

Blaine Michaels had given Annja just seventy-two hours to solve the final clues and find the treasure. That wasn't a lot of time to begin with and she'd wasted several hours of it getting the boat back to dock. Annja was feeling the pressure as she got inside the rental car and pulled out of the marina.

She recited the third clue again to herself as she drove.

"'Take the rifle to the place of Lee's greatest failure, where the Peacock freely roamed. Find the spot where my doppelgänger rests eternal, deep beneath the loam.'"

Now that she'd gotten a sense for how Parker had constructed the verses, she was fairly confident that she knew how to decipher this one.

The Lee in "Lee's greatest failure" was most likely Robert E. Lee. No other Lee held greater significance for the South. Parker would have known that his executive officer, Sykes, would understand who he was referring to immediately. That meant in order to locate her next destination, she had to figure out the place and time where Lee had failed more spectacularly than at any other.

That it was most likely a battlefield went without saying. While Lee had his share of troubles as a young man, none of his personal failures would have meant as much to Captain Parker as the events that unfurled in the closing days of the war. Lee's actions and choices had significance at that point that went far beyond his own person. He was the symbol of a nation, the iconic presence who could rally the Rebels just by passing through camp, and his greatest failure, she reasoned, would have had national significance, as well.

Annja considered the major battles where Lee had been defeated. There was Cheat Mountain. He'd earned the nickname "Granny Lee" when his vastly superior Confederate force of fifteen thousand men had been unable to defeat two thousand Union soldiers. Seven Days, South Mountain and Antietam in 1862. Gettysburg in 1863, of course, followed by the tactical draws of the Wilderness, Spotsylvania and Cold Harbor. The final defeat of the Army of Northern Virginia, the backbone of the Confederate armed forces, at Appomattox in 1865.

While the obvious choice might be Appomattox, something about it just didn't feel right to Annja. It hadn't been a failure in the sense that Lee had done something tactically wrong; he'd simply run out of the food, ammunition and the men he needed to keep the war effort going. That wasn't so much Lee's failure, she knew, as a failure of the nation.

Scratch off Appomattox, she thought.

Likewise, she could forget about the battles in the early part of the war, as well. Cheat Mountain, South Mountain, the Seven Days—none of them had any major impact on the success or failure of the war overall. Both sides had been feeling each other out, getting a sense of this thing called civil war.

That left her with two choices.

Antietam and Gettysburg.

Gettysburg might be better known to the average American, she thought, but it was Antietam that held the most significance for the war effort. Lee had chosen to ignore his advisers and push north, into Union territory, rather than try to defend Vicksburg. His immediate goal had been to secure desperately needed supplies from the rich farm country of Pennsylvania, but his decision proved to be a monumental error. Antietam proved to be the bloodiest single-day battle in the entire Civil War, with more than twenty-five thousand casualties. It was the first major battle fought on Union soil, but it did not turn out the way Lee had hoped. The Confederacy lost control of its western region and Lee himself nearly lost his army. He'd been forced to fight his way clear at Gettysburg and the Antietam campaign had been the last time Lee invaded northern territory. From that point on, it had all been downhill.

There wouldn't have even been a Gettysburg if Lee hadn't lost the fight at Antietam.

Lee's greatest failure, Annja reasoned, was therefore Antietam.

That was where she had to go next.

It was all well and good, except for the fact that Sharpsburg, Maryland, was more than four hundred miles from her current location in northern Georgia. She was looking at seven, maybe eight hours of driving time and that was without any major stops.

There had to be an easier way.

Annja drove a bit farther until she saw a fast-food

restaurant ahead of her. She pulled into the lot and found a place to park. Taking her laptop out of her backpack, she fired it up and connected to the restaurant's free Wi-Fi service. Just a few moments later she connected to an online travel site and was looking to find the fastest and easiest way to get to Pennsylvania.

As it turned out, Antietam was only fifty miles or so away from Washington, DC. If she could catch a flight into Washington from either Atlanta or Savannah and rent a car on the other end, she could save herself several hours.

And if you rest on the plane, you might actually start to feel like a human being again, she told herself.

She checked the flight schedules. Atlanta sounded like the more logical choice, as it was the bigger airport, but as it turned out, a flight leaving Savannah at 5:20 p.m. not only got her into Washington sooner, but it saved her additional driving time as she was closer to that airport.

She booked the flight and then took a moment to check her email. There were several messages from Commissaire Laroche, first asking and then demanding that she get in touch. She didn't have time to deal with him, so she simply deleted the messages, telling herself she'd get in touch when this was all said and done. Right now, she needed to focus on finding the treasure and freeing Garin.

Realizing it had been hours since she'd eaten, Annja went to the drive-through, picking up a soda and a few cheeseburgers for the ride. As she was waiting for her order, three police cars went roaring past the restaurant, sirens blaring, heading in the direction of the marina.

The police could have been going anywhere, responding to a hundred different calls, but upon seeing

them Annja was convinced that the bodies aboard the
Kelly May had been found and that any minute now
they'd realize where she was and come looking for her.

The sooner she got out of there, the better.

The food server handed over her order and Annja
drove off, getting on the highway and heading south
toward Savannah as quickly as she dared.

32

The Savannah airport was larger than she'd expected, but not by much. She found the car rental return, dropped the keys and the rental agreement, unsigned since it was in Garin's name, into the slot and headed into the terminal. She checked in at one of the self-service kiosks and then quickly made her way toward security.

While she was standing in line at the security checkpoint, she noticed a man in a dark windbreaker and jeans a few lines over. Something about him looked familiar, but she couldn't place where she had seen him before. He glanced in her direction, his gaze sliding over her without showing any sign of recognition, and Annja decided that he was just another traveler waiting to get through security.

No big deal.

She handed her ID and boarding pass to the security agent, waiting a moment for him to review it, and then moved on and dealt with the X-ray machine. After collecting her things on the other side, she headed for her gate.

She saw the man again a few minutes later, walking along behind her as part of a crowd of other passengers. He didn't have any luggage with him, which she thought was odd, though in and of itself it didn't prove anything, for he could have easily checked it at the ticket counter. But he seemed to be doing everything he could not to look in her direction and that sent warning signs flashing through her brain.

Something just wasn't right.

She'd seen a ladies' room down a short side hallway a few minutes earlier and decided it was time to see if she was imagining things or not. Without looking at him, Annja slowed, pretended to change her mind and headed back in the direction that she had come. She kept her head down and angled to the side so that she could see him out of the corner of her eye as she moved away.

Just as she'd suspected, he waited a moment for her to move ahead and then quickly broke ranks with the other passengers and headed back in the same direction she was going.

Now convinced that she was being followed, she began to be curious just who it was and what he wanted.

Her decision to come to Savannah had been impulsive, as well. If someone had been expecting her to go through an airport, the logical choice would have been Atlanta. After all, that's where she had been headed until she'd double-checked the times of the flights she'd needed.

There wasn't any reason for Savannah to be on anyone's radar.

She considered the possibility that he might be a fan

of the show and was simply too shy to approach her directly, but dismissed the notion as soon as it occurred to her. A fan would be openly staring. Even a shy fan would be trying to get closer, rather than hanging back and attempting to blend into the peoplescape.

No, whoever he was, he was up to no good. She could feel it in her bones. And she fully intended to confront him and to teach him the error of his ways.

The bathroom she was headed toward was at the end of a corridor that made two quick dogleg turns. She passed the first and kept walking, her ears straining to pick up the sounds of his feet on the tile as he followed behind her.

For a minute she thought he'd decided against leaving the protection of the crowd, but then she caught the sound of the soles of his shoes catching on the freshly mopped tile floor and knew he was still with her.

When she got around the second dogleg she flattened herself against the wall and waited. She'd had enough playing the mouse; it was time to be the cat, and this cat, at least, had sharp claws.

She could hear him coming toward her and she set her feet firmly where she wanted them, prepping them for the test of balance that was about to come.

As he came around the corner she grabbed him by the front of the coat and shoved him into the door of the ladies' room just beyond. It bounced open, sending him sprawling to the floor.

She followed him in and when he moved to get back to his feet she stuck the point of her sword against his throat and waited to see if he could take a hint.

He froze in place, his hands held out in a defensive posture.

"What do you want?" she demanded in a low voice,

not wanting to attract undue attention by yelling, but needing to release the anger she felt building inside her.

"Easy now," he said. "No need for trouble."

"You got trouble the minute you decided to muck about in my business," she told him, pushing the tip of her sword forward slightly to prove her point. A tiny drop of blood spilled out where her sword met the skin of his throat.

He swallowed hard and Annja could see the pulse in his neck start to beat harder.

"Who sent you?"

His reply was immediate. Clearly, he wanted to be seen as cooperating. "Mr. Michaels."

No surprise, that.

"How did you know where to find me? Have you been following me since the river?"

He shook his head. "I don't know what you are talking about. Mr. Michaels told me that you were on your way here and that I was to keep an eye on you."

What? How did Michaels know where she was headed? She hadn't called anyone, hadn't told anyone what she was up to.

Her gaze fell on the cell phone sticking out of the man's pocket and the pieces suddenly fell into place.

How could she have been so stupid?

"When you see Michaels, you tell him to stay the hell away from me until I get in touch. You got that?"

He nodded.

She pulled the point away from his throat and took a step back.

A look of relief crossed his face.

Annja quickly knocked it off his face when she brought the hand holding the sword down sharply, hitting him on the head with the blunt end of the pommel.

Her would-be tracker fell over unconscious.

Releasing her sword to vanish back into the other-where, Annja quickly frisked him, removing his wallet and cell phone. She then grabbed him by the ankles and dragged him into a nearby stall, leaving him propped up next to the toilet with his back to the wall.

Annja stepped out of the bathroom and retraced her steps, headed back toward her gate.

Behind her, a woman began screaming and Annja knew the thug had just been discovered.

He was going to have a hard time explaining what he was doing in the ladies' room and his lack of iden-tification wasn't going to make things easier.

Too bad, Annja thought as she tossed his wallet into a nearby trash can.

When she reached her gate, she took a seat away from the rest of the crowd and took out the cell phone she'd been given by Michaels. Accessing the call his-tory, she wrote down the last number called, knowing she was going to need it later. Once she had done that, she carefully pried open the phone's battery compart-ment.

She didn't know all that much about how cell phones operated, but she was savvy enough to recognize that the small black chip that was taped to the front of the battery shouldn't be there.

Michaels had been following her every move from the moment she left the *Kelly May.* He must have been afraid she'd just take the money and run when she found it, rather than going back for Garin.

Oh, ye of little faith.

Unwilling to let Michaels keep tabs on her every move, Annja was preparing to smash the phone beneath the heel of her hiking boots when another idea occurred to her. She replaced the top of the battery compartment and turned the phone back on. A nearby snack cart selling ice-cream cones had a small crowd standing in front of it so Annja headed in that direction. She got close to a woman carrying three bags while at the same time trying to deal with two squalling children under the age of five.

When the woman's attention was elsewhere, Annja dropped the cell phone into the opening of her handbag.

With any luck, the woman would be headed for Argentina.

She checked the battery compartment of the phone she'd taken from her would-be pursuer, saw that it was clean and then programmed the number she'd memorized into that phone instead.

Fifteen minutes later, Annja boarded her own plane, content that she now held the upper hand.

33

Night had fallen by the time she deplaned in Washington, which meant the Antietam Battlefield Park would be closed. In one sense it was a blessing; Annja was exhausted. In the past twenty-four hours she'd faced off against a hungry alligator, gun-wielding psychopaths and overenthusiastic henchmen, never mind running from the police and expecting to be arrested for murder at any moment. It was too much for anyone, sword-bearer or not. She needed to get some sleep if she was going to be any use to herself or to Garin in the morning.

She decided against picking up her rental car and instead strode across the street from the terminal and walked to the hotel just beyond. She got a room for the night, arranged for an early wake-up call and was asleep within thirty seconds of her head hitting the pillow.

The alarm woke her early the next morning and she didn't waste any time. She showered, dressed and was out the door inside of ten minutes. She walked back across the street to the airport and took the shuttle bus over to the rental car facility, where she picked up the car she'd neglected to get the night before.

She got on the highway and headed south. Antietam was less than seventy miles away and, with the traffic headed into the city instead of out, she made good time on the road. It was just after eight-thirty when she drove into the town of Sharpsburg, population 692. The battle had been fought near Antietam Creek, hence the name, and the majority of the land on which the battle had taken place was now part of Antietam National Battlefield.

She drove around town for a few minutes, wanting the park to be open for a while before she arrived so she wouldn't appear too eager to any of the employees. The last thing she wanted was to arouse suspicion. If her hunch was correct, she was going to need her anonymity later, so it was better to be overprotective now than risk not having it when she needed it.

She parked in the parking lot outside the visitor center and then spent a few minutes just standing outside, staring off into the distance. It was hard to look out on these grassy fields and rolling hills and realize that one of the bloodiest battles ever fought on U.S. soil took place here. Annja closed her eyes, listening, and slowly the sounds of the conflict fell over her—the neighing of the horses, the cries of the men, the crack of the muskets and the boom of the cannons. The shouts of the Yankees in those hard Northern accents were eclipsed by the ululating cry that was the famed Rebel yell.

A hand gripped her shoulder, pulling her out of her reverie.

"You all right, miss?" a kindly voice asked, and Annja opened her eyes to find an elderly park ranger standing at her elbow. "You seemed to be lost there for a moment."

"Oh, yes," she replied, smiling genuinely for the first time in days. "I was just trying to imagine what it would have been like."

He glanced out over the field and the same wistful look that Annja was certain was in her own eyes crept into his. She realized she had found a kindred spirit. The ranger knew what she was talking about; she didn't need to specify that she'd been trying to imagine what it would have been like on the day of the battle.

"Hell on earth, I suspect, miss—hell on earth."

That was as good a description as any, she supposed.

He shook himself, as if clearing away the vision, and turned back to her with a smile. "Charlie Connolly," he said, extending his hand.

She shook. "Annja Creed."

"I thought I recognized you. Planning on doing a show on the ghosts of Antietam?"

The question caught her off guard and the only thing she could think to say in response was to ask, "You've got ghosts?"

"Even if we didn't, would that stop that show of yours?" he asked, and then laughed aloud at his wittiness.

Annja had to admit that he had her there.

After laughing with him for a moment, Annja asked, "Can you tell me where I can find a listing of all the graves in the park?"

"Looking for someone in particular or just doing research?" he wanted to know, once he stopped chuckling and had wiped the tears of merriment out of his eyes.

"Does it make a difference?"

He shrugged. "If you're looking for general information, I can probably help you out myself, but if you're looking for a certain grave, you'll have to use the computers in the main wing of the visitor's center.

He took a map out of his back pocket, opened it so Annja could see the small jumble of buildings at the west entrance and then circled one of them with a felt-tip pen he took out of his pocket.

"That there's the visitor's center and it should have what you need."

Annja thanked him for his kindness and headed in that direction.

The visitor's center was a granite-fronted single-story steel-and-glass building. Inside were historical exhibits, a theater, a series of public computers for learning more about the site and a park store. Annja paid for a half hour of time on the computer and went right to work.

The records system was straightforward and easy to use. All she had to do was put the soldier's name into the system and it would tell her if, indeed, he was buried at the park and what section and row his marker could be found in if he were.

Eager to get on with finding the treasure, Annja typed *William Parker, Captain* into the search field.

The machine clanked and whirred for a second and then spit out a reply.

No information found.

That's strange, she thought.

She tried again, this time typing slowly and being certain she'd spelled things correctly.

Still nothing.

She tried without the captain. And finally another time with the last name first, followed by the first name.

The computer just didn't want to take it.

"That doesn't make any sense," she said to herself.

The clue instructed her to find Parker's doppelgänger's grave. That seemed straightforward enough. A doppelgänger was a German word that meant, literally, body double. A mystical creature that looked precisely like the original and had a tendency to try and take over the other's life.

Obviously mystical creatures didn't exist, which meant the word needed to be read in a more realistic sense. To Annja's way of thought, that meant someone with the same name.

But she'd been through the database a couple of times and there wasn't anyone buried in Antietam National Cemetery with the name William Parker. There was a Corey Parker, and a Parker Blue, but no William Parker.

She didn't understand. The grave should be here!

Unless you're in the wrong place.

The thought loomed up suddenly from the depths of her mind, but once it had surfaced she couldn't dismiss it as easily as it had arrived.

Was that it? Had she chosen the wrong place?

Annja sat back and mentally reviewed the choices she'd made to arrive at this particular place over some other. She felt like her reasoning was sound. Antietam had been a major turning point for Lee and for the South, as well. Some historians even called it the beginning of the end. Never again would Lee's precious Army of Northern Virginia invade Union soil. Never again would Lee have the chance to disrupt the organization of the North on such a grand scale. By failing at Antietam, Lee had determined the final course of the war. It had just taken a few more years for that course to play out.

So what had she missed?

She took a moment and wrote out the clue on the piece of scrap paper she had in front of her.

The minute she did so, she saw her mistake.

In deciding that Antietam was the right place, she'd skipped an entire line of the verse.

"'Where the Peacock freely roamed...'" she said softly.

What the hell does that mean?

It had to be significant; it wouldn't be there otherwise.

She got up from her seat and wandered over to the information desk, where the fussy secretary had been replaced by the kind old park ranger who'd asked over her welfare earlier.

Seeing her, he asked, "Find what you was lookin' for, miss?"

"Not quite. Does the name 'the Peacock' mean anything to you?"

He laughed, "You mean other than the name of the bar I used to frequent in Bangkok during the war?"

Annja smiled. "While I'd love to hear your reminiscences, and it sounds like a fascinating place, I was thinking more in direct relation to the Civil War."

He nodded. "I reckon you're talking about General Stuart, then."

"Stuart?" She was familiar with most of the war's central figures, and while she recognized the name, she couldn't put a finger on who he was or why he might have been called the Peacock.

"General James Ewell Brown Stuart. Commander of the cavalry under Robert E. Lee. Known as 'the eyes of the Army' as well as 'the Peacock.'"

Now she could place him. Here at Antietam he'd ridden completely around General George McClellan's

Union Army undetected, not a small feat for a force of that size on horseback.

"I understand the 'eyes of the Army' reference, but why 'the Peacock'?"

"Stuart had a habit of dressing, shall we say, a bit flamboyantly. One of his favorite outfits consisted of a bright red cape, a yellow sash and a jaunty little cap with a peacock feather stuffed in the hatband. Because of that feather, and his tendency to puff up over his accomplishments whenever he had the opportunity to talk about them, his many detractors labeled him the Peacock."

The Peacock. How funny, she thought, and how fitting.

Stuart had been here. "The Peacock" had roamed free at Antietam. It seemed as if her decision to come here had been correct. So what was she missing?

"One more question for you. What battle would you label General Lee's greatest error?"

He didn't hesitate. "Gettysburg."

"Gettysburg? Really?" She was surprised. She'd fully expected him to say Antietam. "Why, if I may ask?"

It was as if Annja had just said the magic words. Charlie's face lit up, like a junior scholar who'd just been asked by the king for his opinion on an important matter of state.

"Lee shouldn't have lost at Gettysburg. He had the Union Army in retreat to the north and west of town on the first day of battle. He understood the tactical advantage of taking the high ground and, had he done so, the Rebels most certainly would have won the day."

"So why didn't he?" Annja asked.

"Well, that's where folks' opinions tend to differ a bit. Lee did order General Ewell and Second Corps to take Cemetery Hill that first day, but he did so in the form of a discretionary order. Take the hill if its practical, you see. Lee was used to relaying orders like that to Stonewall Jackson, Second Corps prior commander. The discretionary nature of the orders allowed Jackson great flexibility, increasing his usefulness in the overall command. Lee always knew he could count on Jackson to attack, so even if an order was discretionary, more often than not it was carried out with aplomb."

Charlie sighed. "Unfortunately, while a good general, Ewell was no Stonewall Jackson. The heights looked difficult to take and the orders had given him leeway not to risk his men if he didn't have to, so he made the decision to stay put, never realizing that he was dooming his men to a suicidal attack the next day, long after the Union troops had dug in."

"Where was General Stuart during all this?"

Charlie grimaced. "Now there's the true culprit of the battle, if you ask me. The Peacock was out and about with his three cavalry brigades, "roaming around the Rebels," as he called it. He didn't arrive at Gettysburg until midafternoon of the second day and his men didn't even see action until day three. It was a travesty."

Charlie's turn of phrase echoed in her ear. Stuart had been roaming around.

Where the Peacock freely roamed...

She was in the wrong place.

A glance at her watch told her it was almost eleven. She'd been there for almost two hours.

Two hours wasted.

Two hours closer to Garin's execution.

She had to hurry.

"You've been very helpful. Thanks, Charlie!" she said as she turned and headed for the door, leaving the park ranger standing there, shaking his head and wondering just what it was that he had said.

Ten minutes later Annja was back behind the wheel headed toward Pennsylvania and Gettysburg National Military Park. Thankfully, the two battlefields were less than an hour away from each other. She could be in Gettysburg just after lunch. That should give her time to locate the doppelgänger's grave and figure out what to do from there.

She wondered how Garin was doing and if he was all right. He was tough—of that there wasn't any doubt—so she wasn't as concerned as she'd been when Bernard was in the hands of that madman Michaels.

When she first realized that Garin had been taken, she'd thought about calling in Griggs and the rest of the Dragontech Security team. No doubt there was some rapid-response system worked out if Garin ever went missing, but she'd ultimately rejected the idea because she realized she didn't know how to get in touch with Griggs directly. She'd never had reason to, until now.

Sure, she could call the company and ask for him, but if Dragontech was run anything like the other security firms she'd had the dubious pleasure of dealing with in the past, they wouldn't even acknowledge that he worked there, never mind connect her call to him. By the time she patiently worked her way through the various layers of security that isolated frontline men like Griggs, her deadline would be up and it would be too late to try and rescue Garin, anyway.

She was going to have to handle this one on her own.

34

Just as was the case at Antietam, the visitor's center at Gettysburg National Military Park had a room containing a series of public computers that could be used to learn more information about the battlefield and the monuments that now marked it. Annja immediately called up the catalog of the more than six thousand souls interred in Gettysburg National Cemetery.

This time, the name came up on the first try.

Captain William Parker, Thirteenth Massachusetts.

She printed out directions to the grave marker and drove over to the site. The cemetery had started atop Cemetery Hill, the site of the Union's fierce resistance against Pickett's Charge, and slowly spread down the slopes of the hill until it almost reached the road that wound its way slowly through the rest of the park.

Annja parked in the designated area and then climbed the hill, wandering amid the markers until she found the section she wanted. The graves had been grouped by units, so that made it easier to find the individual grave marker she was searching for.

It was set off slightly from the others, resting in the shade of a nearby maple tree on the downward slope of Cemetery Hill. It was a simple granite marker, like many of the others, but where so many of those were rectangular with rounded tops, this one was in the shape of a cross.

The words *William Parker, Captain* were etched into its surface, but that was all. No birth or death dates. No epitaph.

It was almost as if someone wanted to be certain that it wasn't confused with any of the other gravestones.

She looked closely at the marker, but did not see anywhere that the metal "key" from the *Marietta* could be inserted or used in any fashion. Not that she expected some hidden trigger to reveal a secret passage as in the movie *National Treasure,* but it would have been nice to have some indication as to what it was used for.

I'm going to have to do it the hard way, as usual, she thought.

The final verse of the puzzle Parker had left told her to "Disburb him in his slumber, wake him from his rest; To find that which you are seeking, use the key to unlock the chest."

Unless she was recalling it incorrectly, it was telling her to disinter the grave and open the casket. She didn't see any other way of interpreting the need to "disturb him in his slumber."

So she got to add grave robbing to the list of things she'd had to do to try and unravel this mystery and save Garin's life. Her critics would have a field day with that one if it ever got out.

Even worse, Doug would probably want to have an episode revolve around it.

Annja turned in a slow circle, making note of the surrounding landmarks and firmly setting the location of the marker in her mind. She was going to have to find it again later in the dark and didn't want to be stumbling about, which would increase her chances of being caught.

From the map she'd seen in the visitor's center, she knew that the cemetery wasn't far from the edge of the park. Since she couldn't just waltz in the front gates with a shovel over her shoulder, she was going to have to find an alternate means of entry. Looking down from the top of the hill at the trees marking the park's perimeter, Annja thought she might have found her solution.

She looked around, making certain that no one was particularly interested in what she was doing, and then slipped off down the back of the hill toward the trees. She kept her attention focused ahead of her, as if she had every reason to be there, and when she reached the tree line she didn't stop but strode right in among the trunks. Only then, when she was out of sight from the hilltop, did she stop and look back.

There was no one there.

Satisfied her little side trip hadn't been noticed, Annja turned around and moved deeper into the woods. Less than ten minutes later she emerged from the trees and found herself looking at a chain-link fence that stretched in both directions. Just beyond that was a single-lane road that looked like it hadn't seen much use lately; weeds were growing through cracks in the pavement and there were a few fallen tree branches visible from where she stood.

It was exactly what she was looking for.

In order to make it easier to find the proper position from the other side, Annja broke a leafy branch from a nearby tree and jammed it through one of the holes in the fence so that it stuck there. When she returned later that night, she'd just have to look for the branch in order to know she was adjacent to the cemetery.

Satisfied with her arrangements, Annja turned around and worked her way back through the woods to the base of Cemetery Hill. She was halfway up its slope when a horse and rider came around the side of the hill, startling her.

"Everything all right, miss?" the rider asked. As he was dressed in a gray shirt, dark green pants and a tan Smokey the Bear hat, Annja felt fairly confident labeling him as a park ranger.

"Just fine, thanks," she said, smiling at him.

He looked at her and then down the slope of the hill in the direction she'd come from, a puzzled expression on his face.

He knows, she thought, and waited for him to ask what she'd been doing down there in the woods. She already knew what she would say; she just had to make the excuse about an urgent call of nature sound genuine and was trying to come up with a way to do just that when a smile broke out across his face.

"Will ya look at that?" he said, and pointed over her shoulder back down the hill.

Annja turned around and saw a doe and her fawn standing very close to the spot where she'd exited the trees. They stepped hesitantly out on the grassy slope, eyeing the clovers mixed into the grass nearby, no doubt, and Annja felt a smile of her own cross her face.

Thank you, Bambi.

"Beautiful, aren't they?" the ranger asked.

Annja agreed that they were.

"You don't usually see them out this late in the day.

During the early-morning patrol, sure, but by the time the park opens they're usually long gone," he told her.

She saw a chance to extract a little information. "Is that what you do all day, patrol the grounds? That's an awful lot of space to cover, isn't it?"

"Over eight hundred acres," he said, with not a little pride in his voice. "But they don't make us patrol all day long. Just a few hours here and there. Really just an excuse to give Chestnut here—" he patted the horse's flank "—some exercise."

"That's all? I'd have thought they'd make you patrol more often."

He shook his head. "No real need for it, I guess. Nothing much to steal out here except some old gravestones and a flag or two. We do a few rounds at night, checking the place out, but for the most part it's peaceful. If you can stand the ghosts, that is."

He winked at her when he said it and then added a grin for good measure, making it quite clear what his intentions were. If she'd had the time, she probably would have taken him up on the challenge; he looked pretty damn good in that uniform, she had to admit.

But time was not something she had an abundance of at the moment and she was already calculating how to get rid of him without arousing his suspicions even as she flirted back with him.

"Ghosts? You're just pulling my leg," she said, while glancing casually around for something to use as a distraction.

The ranger's radio went off at that point, calling him back to the visitor's center, and she was saved the effort of coming up with a story to get rid of him. He rode off with a wave, a smile and an offer to show her the ghosts of Gettysburg any night she wanted.

Annja had to give him credit; it was one of the more original pickup lines she'd heard.

Too bad she had more important things to do.

She made her way back to the visitor's center and from there to the parking lot. Once in her rental car, she set out to locate the road that was going to provide her access to the park after dark. Letting her instincts, and the fact that she'd been blessed with a pretty decent sense of direction, be her guide, she meandered down country road after country road until at last she found the right one.

The entrance was at the very end of a long country lane, past a pair of dairy farms. Two posts had been set up on either side of the road and a chain ran between then, blocking access. When Annja got out of the car to investigate, though, she found that the chain had simply been hooked to each side. Without a lock on it, there was nothing preventing her from unhooking it, driving her vehicle to the other side and then rehooking the chain back in place, except for the Private Property—Do Not Enter sign.

Ten more minutes of driving, and two trips out of the car to clear debris from the road, brought her directly opposite the location she'd marked on the fence.

Satisfied that she could find it again, even in the dark, she turned the car around, retraced her route to the main road and then headed back into Gettysburg to do some shopping and find a place to hole up for a few hours. Once the sun went down she'd pay Parker's doppelgänger a visit and hopefully get to the bottom of this thing once and for all.

35

While Annja was wandering around Cemetery Hill looking for the grave of a man who couldn't possibly be buried in it, Garin Braden was busy plotting his escape from captivity.

He'd watched dispassionately as Blaine Michaels ordered Reinhardt's execution. Garin had known Michaels was a ruthless bastard and the decision to have the professor killed after Annja had agreed to help them hadn't surprised him at all. Garin might have done the same thing himself, if the situation had been reversed. With that one move Michaels had shown his enemy— in this particular case, Annja—that he was not a man to be trifled with.

Knowing exactly how she'd react to the death of an innocent man, especially one she called a friend, Garin had tried to come to her aid when she rushed forward, but the quick blow of a rifle butt to the back of his head had ended his feeble attempt.

When he'd regained consciousness some unknown number of hours later, he'd discovered he was locked in a wardroom, with nothing to do but stare at the ceiling tiles and hope to be rescued.

Or so his captors thought.

Garin, of course, had other plans.

He'd been aboard enough luxury yachts to realize that he was being held captive on one now. He suspected that it was the same boat he'd snuck aboard earlier after diving from the *Marietta*. The low rumble of the engines, discernible to him through the floor beneath his feet, told him he was belowdecks and likely in the aft section of the craft. Breaking out would therefore mean making his way up through at least one, possibly two decks, without being seen, just to get above the waterline. Since the engines were running, he knew they weren't sitting idle at the dock, so from there he'd have to figure out a way to get off the boat without ending up stranded in the middle of the river or, worse yet, the Atlantic Ocean.

It was certainly doable, but Garin thought he knew an easier way.

He moved to the wardroom door and tried the handle. It was locked, as he'd expected. He stood and listened carefully for a moment, only to be rewarded with the sound of a low cough coming from the other side of the door. Garin nodded in satisfaction.

He reached out and began pounding on the door with his heavy fist.

"Hey!" he shouted. "I want to talk to your boss. Tell him it's about the Order's plans for the treasure."

He kept it up for several minutes, pounding on the door and generally making as much noise as he could. He was all but certain his message was already on its way to Michaels's ear. The guards might not know what he was talking about, but whatever he said was sure to be reported and his comment about the Order would definitely grab his captor's attention.

Garin had just decided he'd made his point and sat back down on the small bunk when he heard the sound of the key in the lock. The door opened, revealing his escort. All four men were close to Garin's height and build. That did little to faze him, however, for he knew sheer size often meant little in a fight against a skilled opponent. It was the firearms each of them carried that interested him more than anything else. If he could get hold of one of them at the right moment...

After sizing them up, Garin was confident he could take them if it became necessary. He filed that information away for later, in case an opportunity presented itself. For now, though, he intended to stick with his plan.

The thug in the lead held up a thick, law-enforcement-style zip tie and said, "Turn around."

Garin complied, surreptitiously clenching and unclenching his fists several times in the process. He kept his hands clenched as they used the zip tie to secure his hands behind his back as well, the two actions momentarily filling the tissues of his wrists with blood and making them slightly larger than they normally were. It was a tactic he'd learned years before that kept the tie looser than his captors intended for it to be. He had no idea if he was going to need to get out of his bonds in a hurry, but felt it was better to be prepared just in case.

Once he was secured they led him out of the room, down the length of the hull and up two decks to a closed door at the end of the hall. The guard knocked, waited for a muffled reply from within and then led Garin inside.

Michaels was waiting for him in an elegantly appointed dining room, a large meal spread out on the table before him. The guards marched Garin halfway across the room, but refused to let him approach Michaels. Garin felt his stomach clench as the smell of the filet mignon on the plate hit him full force; it had been hours since he'd eaten. He knew the scene was intentional, just more of the mind games Michaels apparently liked to play, so Garin steeled his features and kept the hunger from showing on his face.

After a moment, Michaels looked up from his meal and waved impatiently for the guards to bring the prisoner forward.

"This had better be good," Michaels said. "I'm a busy man and don't appreciate those who waste my time."

You're a thug and a boor, Garin thought, but managed to refrain from saying so to the man's face. It wasn't so much the actions that Michaels took that troubled Garin—for, after all, he'd certainly done worse things himself. It was just the man's innate lack of style or finesse that galled him to no end.

Time to take him down a notch or two.

"Your name is Blaine Michaels," Garin began. "You're the current head of an organization that stretches back to the sixteenth century. An organization known as the Order of the Golden Phoenix."

Michaels stared at him for a moment and then slowly lowered his fork down to the plate in front of him.

"I believe you have me at a disadvantage," Michaels said finally.

"I'm Garin Braden, of Dragontech Security."

Michaels gave that a few moments of thought and Garin was happy to give him the time, knowing he'd eventually begin to put things together. Michaels wasn't a fool and, if he was anything like the men who'd held his particular position before him, he'd be well versed on the various organizations that had clashed with his own during the course of his leadership. He was bound to have heard the name of Garin's private security firm, both for its public activities and for those it was rumored to carry out in the shadows.

It was a reputation that Garin had carefully cultivated over the years and one designed to serve him well in situations just like this one.

"Indeed?" Michaels replied, the surprise evident on his face. "Why should I believe you?"

Garin laughed. "Do you honestly think I would claim to be someone I am not in this day and age? When a simple Google search can give you a photograph of most individuals over the age of fifteen?"

Michaels quickly glanced over Garin's shoulder and he gave a subtle nod to the guard standing behind him. Garin tensed, waiting for the blow, but none came. Instead, the guard lifted his hands and cut the zip tie binding them. Another glance from Michaels sent the guard scurrying to produce a chair for Garin's benefit.

When they were comfortably seated on opposite sides of the table, Michaels looked at him intently. "You said something about the treasure?"

Garin leaned back in his chair. "You know as well as I do that Annja Creed is not going to hand over even a single Mexican half-dollar to you."

To his credit, Michaels didn't react with anything more than a shrug. "That remains to be seen."

"If you believe that, then you haven't done your due diligence with regard to the woman you are dealing with. Trust me, Annja Creed would no more cooperate with a man she considers a cold-blooded murderer than she would wake up tomorrow and declare that the world was flat. Whatever she's doing, you can rest assured that she's planning a way to get back at you for what you've done."

Michaels scoffed. "She's one woman. I doubt she has the resources or the determination to stand up to the Order."

You have no idea, Garin thought, recalling the number of times she'd foiled his own carefully laid plans.

"Are you willing to bet the treasure on that? Or would you rather take action now, while you still can, and ensure that the gold winds up in the proper hands?"

Michaels eyed him with a curious expression. "You have obviously given this some thought. I'm curious to hear what you have in mind."

Garin smiled. "I thought you'd never ask…."

36

It was four hours after sunset.

Annja drove carefully down the narrow, weed-infested road until she could see the branch she'd stuck through the fence as a marker earlier that afternoon. She pulled over, parked and got out of the car as quickly and quietly as possible.

Opening the trunk, she removed a pickax and shovel, then closed the lid carefully so as not to attract any attention. She was still a few hundred yards on the other side of the woods from Cemetery Hill, but she knew she should be extracautious.

Getting caught grave robbing in a national cemetery was not something that would be easily explained or overlooked.

When her eyes had adjusted fully to the darkness, she stepped up to the fence and threw her pick and shovel over one at a time. They landed in the grass on the other side with soft thuds, barely audible above the sound of the light wind that was blowing.

She grabbed the fence with both hands and quickly scaled it.

She paused to look around, confirmed she was alone and then headed through the woods to the edge of the park. She stood in the trees for several long moments, watching the grassy field and the hill that rose up just beyond that. She was going to have to cross that open space and climb the hill in order to reach the grave. That would leave her exposed to view for several minutes. Her conversation with the park ranger had revealed that the park was patrolled, but not very regularly. If she could get amid the graves without being seen and keep the noise to a minimum, she had a chance of pulling this off.

Okay Annja, it's now or never, she told herself.

She picked up her tools and headed across the open field at a light jog. Despite her desire to cross the open space as quickly as possible, she avoided picking up speed. The high grass could hide any number of hazards and she didn't want to end up turning an ankle in an unseen rabbit hole that might require medical assistance just to get out of the park. The jog would get her there quickly without endangering her mission.

It only took her a few minutes to reach the top of the hill, but to Annja it felt like hours. She kept waiting for a light to snap on in the darkness, pinning her in place, to hear a guard yelling at her to stop what she was doing or he'd be forced to fire. But none of that happened.

A lone tree stood on the summit and Annja used the shadows at its base to conceal herself as she looked down into the cemetery spread out below.

In the days after the Battle of Gettysburg, the dead had been buried in hastily dug graves across the battlefield itself. Later, with the support of the governor of

Pennsylvania, the dead were moved to a more permanent cemetery close to Cemetery Hill. How Parker had discovered that there was a Union soldier with the same name as himself buried there, Annja had no idea. Perhaps no one was buried there at all and the grave had just been dug to support Parker's machinations behind the scenes. She couldn't know for sure, though she had her suspicions given the very different appearance of the headstone.

You'll find out soon enough, she told herself.

She stepped out into the open, making her way down the slope with the help of the red-lensed flashlight that she'd picked up earlier that day at an Army-Navy surplus store. The colored light would be difficult for an observer to see at night but provided enough illumination for her to locate the grave she was looking for. The unique shape of the gravestone allowed her to find it easily.

Parker's instructions echoed in her mind.

"Disturb him in his slumber, wake him from his rest."

She set the flashlight down on the top of the gravestone, illuminating the well-manicured grass that covered the grave site.

Here goes nothing, she thought as she took a deep breath.

Laying the pick aside, she used the edge of the shovel to mark a rectangular shape in the grass along the direction that she thought the coffin would have been placed. She carefully cut the turf free in large pieces and then moved them to one side, doing what she could to preserve the sod intact. If she had the time, she intended to replace the grass before leaving, which might help keep the evidence of her activity from being discovered right away.

Once she had cleared the sod from her target area, she began rotating back and forth between the two tools, using the pick to break up the earth and then scooping the loose dirt out with the shovel. The work was made harder by her effort to keep the noise down and the fact that she stopped regularly to listen to avoid having anyone sneak up on her in the darkness.

Annja had been working for about an hour and had uniformly gone down about three feet across the entire surface of the grave, when her shovel hit something solid. The sound of metal striking metal was partially muted by the earth, but to her it sounded unnaturally loud. She winced and held the shovel still, listening.

All was quiet for a moment and Annja was about to breathe a sigh of relief when a horse whinnied somewhere off to her left.

She reached for the flashlight and shut it off as quickly as she dared.

The only horses in the park that she knew of were those ridden by the park rangers like the one she'd run into earlier that afternoon. Unless they let them out to roam the grounds at night, something she thought unlikely, there had to be a mounted patrol headed in her direction.

The question was how far away were they?

Her mind was racing. Was it already too late? Were they even now calling in backup? Could she possibly escape?

She didn't know what to do and that worried her more than if sirens and flashing lights had suddenly split the night air in response.

A minute passed, then two, as Annja strained her

eyes to see who might be out there in the darkness. Finally the gleam of a cigarette caught her eye, flaring red in the darkness for a moment and then dimming again. It was down the hill and off to her left, a few hundred yards away. She couldn't be sure, but it looked like the light was moving toward her.

She had a decision to make.

If she left now, the open grave would most likely be discovered. If that happened, she'd never get another chance at it; they'd probably post armed guards around the grave site and she'd lose access to whatever it was that Parker had hidden there.

And she'd lose her shot at finding the treasure and using it, in turn, to rescue Garin.

If she stayed and finished the work, she risked getting caught in the act and charged with several different crimes. Criminal trespass. Desecration of a grave. Destruction of federal property. And who knew what else.

Clearly there was only one logical choice.

With her heart beating faster over the possibility of discovery, Annja picked up the flashlight and put it in the bottom of the hole she was digging before turning it back on, knowing the high walls of the grave would keep it from being seen right away. If she worked quickly, she might be able to get out of there before the rider got close enough to know she was even there.

She went back to work with the shovel, breaking up the dirt around the metal object and scooping as much of it out of the way as possible. After a moment a small, rectangular-shaped object became visible in the red light.

The horse neighed again and this time she clearly heard a male voice saying something in response to the animal. They were too far away for her to make out the specifics of what was said, but there was no doubt that they were headed her way.

She was running out of time.

Annja got down on her hands and knees, shielding the light with her body. Clearing the last of the dirt away from the top of the object with her hands, she revealed a small metal chest about the size of a bread box.

But when she tried to tug it free, she found that the earth didn't want to let go of its prize so easily.

She was going to have to keep digging.

She raised her head slightly so she could see over the lip of the hole where she crouched and was just in time to see the beam of a flashlight arc out over the gravestones at the base of the hill.

Hell! she thought.

Now she was in trouble.

As the rider swept the light around, she could see that it was the park ranger she'd encountered earlier that afternoon, astride the same dark-colored mount, no doubt in the midst of his occasional nightly rounds. He was looking around a bit too earnestly for it to be just a coincidence that he was in this area; he must have heard her.

There was nothing she could do about it.

Now it was a race to see if she could finish unearthing the chest before he discovered where she was hiding.

Annja ducked back down and began scraping furiously at the dirt alongside the edges of the chest, no longer caring if she was making noise. If she didn't get the chest free in time, all her efforts would be for naught.

"Hello?" the ranger called. "Anyone out there?"

No one but us ghosts, Annja thought, remembering

his earlier remark, and she had to bite her tongue to keep from laughing at the insanity of it all.

She cleared one side of the chest and moved on to the other, her fingers scratching at the earth, shoving it aside as quickly as she loosened it.

She stole another glance over the edge of the grave.

As she watched, the ranger dismounted and took a few steps forward, his hand on the butt of his holstered revolver. "I can hear you out there," he called. "Identify yourself!"

He wasn't looking in her direction, so she felt safe ignoring his command. All she needed was a few more seconds, anyway....

"I'm warning you! Show yourself now and save us both a lot of grief."

She grabbed the handle on the edge of the chest and pulled.

The chest shifted a little but it didn't come free.

"Last time!" the ranger called out.

She planted her feet against the wall of the grave and used them as leverage, pulling harder. She could feel her shoulder muscles straining, could feel the earth's grip loosening...and with a sudden release the chest came free of the earth that had imprisoned it for so long.

Annja fell over backward as the resistance was released. As if fate was determined to prevent her from succeeding in her task, the metal side of the chest struck the blade of her shovel as she toppled over. The sound of metal striking metal rang out over the cemetery in the crisp night air.

The ranger had had enough. He drew his revolver and waved it back and forth in front of him, uncertain precisely where to point it but certain now that he wasn't alone. The light from his flashlight arced out in her direction.

Annja pulled the chest close to her side and kept her head down for the moment, waiting for the light to move on. When it swept away in the other direction, she boosted herself out of the hole and rolled over flat on her stomach so she was facing toward the ranger, covering the chest with her body.

The light came back toward her a moment later, just as she expected. She tucked her face into the crook of her arm to keep the light from reflecting off her skin and then held as still as possible. The urge to get the heck out of there while she still could was strong, especially when the light danced across the place where she was hiding, but she fought it off, mentally ordering herself not to move. That would only attract attention; if she stayed where she was, chances were good that her dark clothing would help her blend into the landscape and she'd go unnoticed.

The light stopped a few inches to her left and stayed there so long that Annja began to think that her foot was sticking out, in plain sight, and that the ranger was just playing with her. Her heart began to pound in her chest and a thin trickle of sweat rolled down the side of her face despite the cool night air. She tensed, preparing to face off against the ranger should that prove necessary, knowing she couldn't let herself be caught at this stage of the game.

A rustling sound came from her left, about halfway between her position and that of the ranger. It was easily loud enough for him to hear it as well and Annja watched as his light shifted directly toward it.

Is someone else out here? she wondered.

The sound came again and she could see the ranger

growing more agitated by the moment. The muzzle of the gun jerked back and forth, seeking a target.

Then two things happened simultaneously.

The ranger's light fell on the white-tailed deer that had come down into the cemetery to graze. It was standing just a headstone or two away from where Annja was doing her best to squeeze herself down into the earth to keep from being seen. The ranger's light caused the creature to bolt, and the ranger, seeing the deer's big eyes staring back at him out of the darkness, pulled the trigger of his revolver in surprise.

The deer leaped over the grave Annja had spent the past few hours digging and disappeared into the darkness.

The bullet bounced off a nearby headstone and embedded itself in the earth near Annja's face.

It happened so fast she didn't even have time to flinch.

"Stupid deer!" the ranger shouted after the already departed animal. "You're lucky you didn't get shot!"

That, at least, was a sentiment that Annja could heartily agree with.

She remained where she was as the ranger flung a few more choice words in the direction the deer had run and then got himself under control. Once he had calmed down, he climbed back astride his horse and rode off, leaving Annja alone with the dead.

She waited a few minutes to be certain, but when the ranger didn't return she climbed slowly to her feet, picked up the chest and fled as quickly as caution allowed.

37

Annja drove straight back to her motel. She parked her car out of sight between a pair of oversize pickup trucks at the back of the lot and then carried the chest up to her room.

The light in the bathroom was brighter than that in the bedroom, so she took the chest in there and set it on the counter next to the sink. There was still a thin patina of dirt covering the outside of the chest so she grabbed a washcloth from the towel rack and used it to clear as much of it off as possible.

It wasn't anything to look at, really. It was just a simple metal box with a circular indentation in the lid. Aside from that there weren't any other markings or decorations of any kind.

Functional was the word that came to mind.

After all the time it had spent in the earth, she hoped it still remained that way, as well.

She took the Jeffersonian Key out of her pocket and, with more than a bit of trepidation, placed it into the indentation on the lid.

With a deep breath and a silent prayer to whoever might be listening, Annja placed a finger against the center of the star and pushed down on the disk.

There was an audible *click* and a previously unseen seam opened up along the outline of the disk. Then she heard the whir and ticking of a clockwork mechanism and the disk sank half an inch into the top of the chest.

Taking hold of the eight-pointed star that sat atop the disk, Annja put her ear next to the box and slowly began to turn the star to the right, like a safecracker listening for the correct number on the dial. She was afraid she would miss it and there was no telling what would happen if she did. She'd encountered her fair share of reliquaries and other storage devices in the past that had been rigged to cause damage to their contents should the opening sequence not be performed correctly. She'd seen them all—everything from acid baths to sudden bursts of flame. It wouldn't do Garin any good for her to have come this far only to screw it up at the last minute.

She needn't have worried, however. The minute the dial had been turned the right distance, it clicked loudly into place. Annja pulled back at the sound and watched as the top third of the box extended outward in all directions, the pieces twisting and turning in individual squares like the parts of a Rubik's Cube. The ticking came again and then the parts rapidly reassembled themselves until the top of a cylinder with the same circumference as the key jutted out of the upper third of the device.

Annja's pulse was pounding in her ears as she reached out and turned the key back in the other direction, just as she would if dialing the combination on her locker at the gym.

The star spun in the other direction, all the way around past the first location once, twice, and then, as the main point of the star came around to true north for the third time, there was another *click*. Just as before, the box underwent a strange mechanical transformation, rearranging itself into the center section of the cylinder. One more turn of the dial, this time back in the original direction, another surge of activity, and Annja was left with a vertical cylinder about the size of a cookie jar, with the eight-pointed star as a lid. The letters *CSA* stretched down the front of the cylinder in faded red paint.

"All right, Parker," she said to the container. "You've led me on a merry chase, now it's time to give up the ghost and tell me what you did with that treasure."

She tugged the lid free and looked inside.

There was nothing there.

She put the lid down on the counter and frantically ran her right hand around inside the cylinder, looking for a hidden catch or something that might reveal a final secret not quite visible to the naked eye.

The second time around she told herself to go slower, to take her time and be as thorough as possible. These kinds of things could be delicate, she knew, and she might miss something in her excited state. She took a few deep breaths to calm her anxious heart and then tried again.

After the third attempt she had no choice but to admit the obvious.

The cylinder was empty.

She stared at her reflection in the mirror over the sink. Was that accusation in her eyes? All that effort and nothing to show for any of it. Where had she gone wrong?

And, more importantly, what now? How was she going to rescue Garin without the treasure?

Her head sagged forward in resignation and as it did her gaze fell on the reflection of the interior surface of the cylinder lid in the mirror in front of her.

There was something written there!

She snatched up the lid and turned it around. What was written made little sense until she realized that not only was she holding the lid upside down, but that it had been written backward, as well. Flipping it over and holding it up to the mirror allowed her to read it.

34 44 23.1
83 23 42.8

Grabbing the bar of soap from the dispenser next to her, Annja used it to scrawl the numbers on the mirror in front of her.

Despite the absence of the symbols noting degrees and minutes, the numbers were easily recognizable as latitude and longitude notations and could be nothing less than the location of the treasure.

All she had to do now was determine where, exactly, those notations indicated.

She didn't have her computer with her, so she couldn't just look it up. The motel she was staying in didn't have public internet access, either.

She thought about her options.

She knew it was a risk. The bodies aboard the *Kelly May* had probably been found by now. That would have led to a thorough examination of Jimmy Mitchell's contacts over the past few days, which would have turned up the delivery of the equipment Doug had arranged to borrow from the university. Her name, and possibly Garin's, too, were no doubt known to the police at this point. Right about now the authorities were either dredging the river looking for her corpse or, more likely, were looking for her as the prime suspect in the deaths of Jimmy and Bernard.

If that was the case, they might even have Doug under surveillance and any attempt to reach out to him could put the police right on her tail.

She thought it was worth the risk, though. She needed to find the location of these coordinates and Doug was the fastest means of getting it done. If Doug was under surveillance, the worst the police could do was trace the call to her motel. It would take time for the New York authorities to inform the local Pennsylvania authorities. By the time the locals arrived at the motel, she should be well on her way somewhere else.

Decision made, Annja picked up the phone. She dialed Doug's office number but then changed her mind and disconnected before it rang through. His cell would be harder for the police to trace and so she tried that instead.

The very fact that you know that shows what kind of life you've been living lately, she mused.

Ignoring the voice of her conscience, Annja punched in the number, keeping her eyes on the clock as she did so.

It rang quite a few times before being answered.

"Doug Morrell."

He sounded tired, as if she'd woken him up. Given that it was four o'clock in the morning, she wasn't surprised. She knew he would recognize her voice so she didn't bother with the usual niceties. "It's me. Can you talk?"

There was a slight pause and then Doug replied, "I'm sorry you must have the wrong number."

Damn!

"Have the police been to see you?"

"Uh-huh. Well, have you tried his office number?"

It took her a second and then Annja understood. She grabbed the pen and paper off the motel nightstand and said, "Go ahead."

"I'd give him a half hour or so, but after that you should be able to reach him at…" Doug replied, and rattled off a different telephone number.

Annja wrote it down and hung up.

The call had lasted less than two minutes. It always took at least three minutes for the cops to trace a number on *Law and Order,* and while network television dramas weren't always the most accurate, it was the only gauge Annja had to go by. She hoped they'd gotten it right.

She sat down on the edge of the bed to wait.

The thirty minutes Doug had suggested she wait felt like forever and she spent most of the time pacing across her tiny motel room floor. When the half hour was up she snatched the receiver and dialed the number he'd given her.

He answered on the first ring. "Jeez! Give me a heart attack, why don't you?" Doug said. "Where have you been? Are you all right? Do you realize how many people are looking for you?"

Annja didn't have time to explain everything that had happened, so she said, "I'm fine but I need some help."

She could hear street noise in the background and realized that he must have given her the number for the pay phone on the corner near his apartment. Why he had that number in the first place, she didn't know, but she was thankful that he did.

"We'll get you the best lawyer we can, Annja. Right now I think it…"

"Doug?"

"…best if you just turn yourself in to the nearest police—"

"Doug!"

"What?"

"I'm not turning myself in. I didn't do whatever it is they're saying I did."

She could hear the hesitation in his voice as he responded. "I'm not sure that's such a good idea, Annja. The police are looking for you and I think it'd be better if—"

"Listen to me!" she yelled, the stress of the past few days finally getting the better of her. "Lives are in danger here, Doug! I need your help!"

That shut him up. Into the silence, she said, "The men who killed Jimmy Mitchell and Bernard Reinhardt are holding others captive. I've got to find a specific location in order to help them and all I have are latitude and longitude numbers."

"Why don't you just plug them into a GPS?"

She gritted her teeth. "I don't have a GPS unit, Doug. That's why I'm calling you."

"Oh, okay, hang on. I've got one right here on my cell phone." There was a moment's pause and then he said, "Give me the coordinates."

She read the degrees and minutes off the mirror where she had written them earlier.

It took him less than thirty seconds to come back with the information she needed.

"The Genoa Mine in Tallulah Gorge."

Annja scrawled it on the paper in front of her. "Tallulah Gorge? Where the heck is that?"

"Hang on... Would you believe Georgia?"

Yes, she thought wearily, yes, she would believe Georgia. This had all started in Georgia so it made sense that it would end there, as well.

"Where in Georgia?" she asked.

Doug gave her the details. Tallulah Gorge was located in a state park of the same name at the very northeastern edge of Georgia, about ten miles north of the town of Tallulah Falls and roughly eight hundred miles south of where she now stood.

Annja had another decision to make.

She could call Michaels, give him the coordinates as agreed and hope he'd live up to his word to release Garin once she had located the treasure.

It was the easiest thing to do and would also ensure that she accomplished the goal before the deadline.

She knew that doing so, however, would be an act of sheer stupidity.

Both she and Garin had seen Michaels have his men execute Reinhardt and Mitchell. There was no way that Michaels would let them go free as a result. There was a chance that Garin was already dead, but Annja doubted Michaels would throw away his ace in the hole easily. With Garin alive he could force her cooperation. With him dead, there was nothing stopping Annja from going to the police with everything she knew.

No, she suspected that Michaels would live up to his end of the agreement, at least until he had the whereabouts of the treasure guaranteed.

When that happened, all bets were off. There was nothing stopping Michaels from putting a bullet in both of them at that point except Annja's own ingenuity. She had to find a way to get Garin out into the open before turning over the coordinates. That way she'd have a chance of getting them both out of this mess alive.

Perhaps Tallulah Gorge was the answer she'd been looking for in more ways than one.

With the police actively seeking her, there was no way she could risk getting on a flight. She was going to have to make the trip from Pennsylvania to Georgia by car, a drive of about twelve hours, if she did it without stopping.

She glanced at the clock and did some quick mental arithmetic. If all went well, she'd arrive at the Gorge with barely an hour to spare before the end of Michaels's deadline.

Theoretically speaking, it was doable, but that didn't take into account the events of the past few days. The constant travel combined with her need to be up all night in order to recover the chest from the cemetery had left her dead on her feet. There was no way she was going to be able to make a twelve-hour drive without getting some sleep first. But doing so meant she would fail to meet Michaels's deadline.

In order to pull it off, she was going to need some help.

"...it'll be the best episode we've ever had!"

She realized with a start that Doug had been speaking to her the whole time. She hadn't heard a word he'd said nor did she have time to deal with whatever cockamamie plan he'd come up with, so she did what she always did when Doug went off on one of his rabbit trails; she ignored him.

"I'm going to need you to arrange for a car and driver for me, Doug."

"I know I can get the network's approval and…wait a minute! What?"

"I need a car and a driver. There's no way I can make the drive to Tallulah Gorge on my own. You're going to have to arrange to have someone meet me somewhere. Maybe Richmond?"

Doug tried to catch up with her line of thought. "Tallulah Gorge? Why are you going there?"

"I don't have time to explain, Doug. Can you get me a car and driver or not?"

He hesitated. "I don't know, Annja. The cops are already crawling all over me because of that diving equipment I arranged for you. I spent half the day at the police station answering questions and for all I know they're bugging my telephone!"

That explained the pay phone.

Still, time was ticking and she didn't have any to waste. Michaels's deadline was looming closer with every minute.

"A man's life is at stake, Doug. I need that car!"

"All right, all right. Give me a minute," he said.

The street sounds got louder as he took the pay phone receiver away from his ear and then she could hear the beeping of his cell phone as he clicked through different screens. She could hear him start speaking to someone on the other line and she tapped her foot impatiently.

There was a rustle as he picked up the phone again and said, "You said Richmond, right?"

"Yes."

"That's, uh, in Virginia, right?"

Annja sighed. "Yes, Doug, that's in Virginia."

"Cool. Hang on…"

It took him another couple of minutes, and a few more questions, but in the end the arrangements were made. She would meet her driver in the parking lot of the Marriott Hotel just after seven that morning, as the drive to Richmond would take Annja about two hours. A phone call to the rental car company would inform them of the location of their vehicle and the driver would then chauffeur Annja the rest of the way to Georgia. Once in Tallulah Falls, the driver would leave the vehicle with Annja and she could use it for as long as she needed.

"Thank you, Doug," she told him, when he'd finished relaying the details. "You're a lifesaver. Literally."

"Yeah, sure. Just get this squared away quickly, will ya? Once you do we can get started on the fugitive episode. I can't wait!"

Alarm bells began ringing in the back of her mind. Just what had she missed earlier when she hadn't been listening?

"What are you talking about? What fugitive episode?"

Apparently she wasn't the only one with selective hearing. "Good luck! Call me once you catch up with the driver," he said, and then hung up.

That was twice now that he'd gotten the better of her. Clearly she was slipping.

38

Two hours later Annja found herself driving through downtown Richmond, right past the very house Jefferson Davis had used to run his presidency. The White House of the Confederacy, as it was now called, was the centerpiece of a museum devoted to the era and Annja found herself wishing she had the time to wander through the halls, to see with her own eyes the artifacts and exhibits on display there, to try and better understand the man who had ordered the treasury moved in the first place.

But she wasn't here as a tourist and she drove past, telling herself that she'd return some other time, when her life was less hectic.

Whenever that might be.

She found the Marriott Hotel without difficulty, parked her car and went inside. She was thinking of approaching the concierge and asking for assistance in locating her driver when she spotted two young guys in their early twenties, dressed in dark suits, one of them carrying a hand-lettered sign that read *Chasing History's Monsters*.

So much for keeping a low profile, she thought. She hoped she could get out of there quickly before anyone noticed her.

Annja strode over to the pair and introduced herself. The two men, David and Andrew, were complete professionals and it wasn't long before Annja was resting comfortably in the back of a Cadillac, David behind the wheel, while Andrew drove her rental car back to his apartment. He would hold on to it for twenty-four hours before returning it to the Richmond airport in her name. By then things would have unfolded one way or another with Michaels, and she'd no longer be worried about the local authorities getting a fix on her location.

Good or bad, it would all be over by then.

She intended to use the time to get some sleep, but first she had to set the stage for Garin's eventual rescue.

She pulled out the phone she'd taken from Michaels's henchman in the airport—what felt like a lifetime ago—and dialed the number she'd memorized.

It rang several times before being answered. "Yes?" said a gruff French voice.

"Get me Michaels."

The man in question must have been sitting right there, for the pause was only a few seconds.

"Do you have what I need, Miss Creed?"

Damn right I do, she thought as an image of her sword loomed large in her mind, but she answered with a simple, "Yes."

"Excellent. I have lived up to my part of the bargain, as well. Your friend, Mr. Braden, is alive and well."

Mr. Braden? Garin had given his real name. She wondered what that meant and what other surprises

Michaels might have in store for her, but knew she'd find out soon enough.

"How do I know you're telling the truth?" she asked, putting everything else out of her mind for the time being. One thing at a time, Annja, she thought, calming her anger.

There was silence on the line for a moment and Annja was just about to repeat her question when she heard a muffled sound as the phone changed hands.

"Annja?"

It was Garin; she knew it as surely as she knew how to draw her sword.

"Are you all right?"

"Fine. I've survived far worse in my day."

Given the length of "his day," she thought it was probably the understatement of the year. She was about to answer him, only to hear the menacing voice of Michaels come back on the line.

"As I said, Miss Creed, your Mr. Braden is just fine."

"Good. See that he stays that way. Meet me in the parking lot of the Tallulah Gorge State Park in Tallulah Falls, Georgia, in two hours. Have Garin with you."

"I hardly think you're in a position to dictate terms to me," Michaels said.

"Who asked you to think?" Annja replied, and then broke the connection.

Michaels wanted the treasure; Annja had no doubt that he would follow her orders.

39

Annja found herself standing beside the Cadillac in the all-but-empty parking lot at the Tallulah Gorge State Park just over an hour and a half later. After speaking to Michaels, she had passed the rest of the journey in contemplative silence until her driver had indicated that they had reached the outskirts of Clayton, which was just north of Tallulah Falls. He drove to the local Greyhound station, where he got out, turned the car over to Annja and then purchased a bus ticket back to Richmond.

Annja made the rest of the journey on her own.

When she came up with her plan earlier that morning, she'd expected the parking lot at the Gorge to be full of eager tourists. Unfortunately, Mother Nature had other ideas. The blue skies had given way to stone gray and a light drizzle had begun to fall in the early afternoon. By the time Annja arrived, the park was mostly deserted.

So much for making the exchange in public.

Nothing in the past day had changed her view that

Michaels would kill both her and Garin once he had the coordinates. Her only chance to pull this off was to get Garin out in the open where they had a possibility of getting away from Michaels and his men before she was forced to give up the location of the treasure.

How she was going to do that, she still wasn't certain.

Great time not to have a plan, the nagging little voice in the back of her mind told her as she saw Michaels and his entourage approach.

Three black SUVs drove into the parking lot and parked a short distance away from her car. Four men got out of each of the two lead vehicles and took up positions around the third, though what they thought they were guarding against, Annja had no idea. Once the team leader was apparently satisfied with the situation, he knocked on the glass of the final vehicle with the knuckles of one hand.

The doors opened. Blaine Michaels emerged from the front passenger seat, while Garin and two more thugs got out of the rear.

Eleven against two. Not the best odds, but she'd deal with it.

Leaving the vast majority of his men behind him with the vehicles, Michaels strode toward her. Garin came along, as well, escorted on either side by two guards. She could see from the way he held himself that Garin's arms were secured behind his back. She knew the guards, and perhaps even Michaels, would be armed, but none of their firearms were in evidence at the moment, which was a point in her favor.

It wasn't much but at least it was something.

Now if she could just get Garin into the proper position.

She'd chosen her current location with care. The car was parked lengthwise across several parking spaces at the back of the lot. Just beyond it, hidden by the bulk of the vehicle, at least at a distance, was a trailhead leading into the dense Georgia forest at her back. If she and Garin could get into the thick of the trees, they stood a chance of getting away from their pursuers before any serious damage could be done.

Michaels stopped within arm's reach, facing her, his long trench coat hiding any weapons he might be carrying.

"I believe you have something for me," he said.

Annja ignored him, looking over his shoulder at Garin instead. "Are you all right?"

"Peachy," he replied, and then, ever so slightly, nodded his head.

It was a signal and one that didn't take a lot of brain-power to understand.

Garin was ready for whatever she had planned for getting them out of this mess.

His faith in her was reassuring.

Her lack of a specific plan was not.

Michaels was tired of waiting. "The treasure, Miss Creed."

She shook her head. "Not until you release him."

Expecting him to argue, she was surprised when he turned, studied Garin for a moment and then nodded at the guard standing beside his captive.

The guard drew a clasp knife out of his pocket, opened it and stepped up behind Garin.

"Don't even think about it…" Annja warned, the tone of her voice dark and deadly. Her concern was misplaced, however. The guard simply used the knife to slash Garin's bonds.

Garin brought his arms up in front of his chest, using his hands to rub each of his wrists in turn where the zip tie had dug into the skin. While the movement looked perfectly natural, Annja knew better. Garin was preparing for action.

"I won't ask again," Michaels said in an icy tone, one hand reaching inside his coat.

Annja held up her hands in front of her in a gesture of surrender. "No need for anger. I have what you need," she told him, smiling at the same time to help reinforce the idea that she wasn't a threat.

When she saw Michaels relax slightly as a result, she made her move.

She lashed out with a savage front kick, catching Michaels square between the legs with one booted foot. As the pain slammed into him a half second after the strike he dropped to his knees and toppled to the ground, groaning in agony.

Annja wasn't waiting around to see the results, however. She was already in motion, driving forward toward the guard on Garin's left. The man was just reaching inside his coat for his weapon when Annja called her sword to hand and ran him through. He looked down at the length of steel sticking out of his gut, tried to say something through the blood that was suddenly filling his throat and then collapsed.

Garin moved in the same instant as Annja. He smashed his elbow into the face of the guard on the other side of him and followed it up with several short, sharp punches that sent the man reeling to the ground.

"Follow me!" Annja shouted as she slid over the hood of the Cadillac, glancing back at the rest of Michaels's men as she did so.

It was not a pretty sight. The guards were charging

toward them, guns in hand, and even as Garin bent over to grab the pistol out of the hand of the guard he'd knocked over, the bullets started flying.

"Come on, Garin! Move!" she roared.

She felt useless standing there with her sword in hand, but there wasn't anything she could do. They had to get under cover of the trees before the rest of the guards caught up with them or they would be killed.

Garin threw himself over the hood of the car, rolled to his feet and spun back around. He snapped off three quick shots, sending the gunmen diving for cover, then grinned at her.

"What are you waiting for?" he asked.

She turned and ran for the trailhead, Garin at her heels.

They were almost within the trees when the gunfire started again. She could hear bullets striking the Cadillac behind them and was grateful for her foresight in setting it up as a barrier. She was just about convinced they could make a clean getaway when she heard a grunt of pain and felt Garin stumble into her.

She caught him before he could fall and helped him stumble forward into the dense protection of the trees. His right hand was clasped to his left shoulder, blood seeping through his fingers, and the gun he'd risked himself to retrieve was nowhere to be seen.

"How bad?" she asked as he righted himself and continued under his own power.

"It's nothing," he said. "Went clean through."

The pain in his voice told her differently, though.

Their chances of escape had just been cut in half.

Without any idea where the trail actually went, they were stuck just following it, hoping it would lead them somewhere safe. Annja could hear Michaels shouting at his men to find them and knew their pursuers wouldn't be slow in doing as instructed.

Suddenly they burst free of the tree line and found themselves standing on a promontory that jutted out into the canyon. In front of them, a sagging old bridge connected their side of the canyon to the other.

The bridge was essentially just two parallel strains of braided steel cable to which slats of wood had been secured at six-inch intervals. The cables were less than an inch in diameter and painted red with rust. The slats weren't in much better shape. In more than a handful of places they had been eaten clear through by the elements. Only the rope railings that stretched the length of the bridge's span appeared to be in decent shape.

Annja did not want to cross that bridge. She looked frantically about, searching for some other way out of their predicament. About a quarter of a mile up the canyon from where they stood she could see the modern bridge, a graceful span of iron and steel, but there was no way for them to get to it. They'd have to backtrack the way they'd come to get off the promontory and somehow manage to elude their pursuers while doing so.

A glance behind let her know that wasn't possible; she could see forms approaching through the trees and knew it was Michaels's thugs closing in on them. It would only be a matter of moments before they were within shooting distance.

No choice, then.

"Come on!" she shouted, grabbing Garin's arm and literally dragging him out onto the bridge in her wake.

The sagging old structure jerked and swayed with their every step but Annja didn't care. All she wanted to do was make it to the other side. She kept her doubts to herself.

Garin, on the other hand, wasn't shy about voicing his concerns.

"Are you nuts, Annja? We're sitting ducks out here!" he shouted as he made his way along as best he could with only one arm to steady himself. "The minute they reach the clearing, it will be like shooting fish in a barrel."

Annja shook her head. "They won't shoot," she told him as she carefully stepped across an opening where a pair of slats had rotted through. She could see the river rushing past a hundred feet beneath them, the water churned into a white froth from the boulders strewn about its path. She helped Garin across and then continued forward.

"Says who?" he asked, already out of breath from the exertion of keeping his balance on the shifting platform beneath his feet.

"I'm telling you, they won't shoot. Michaels wants the location of the gold. If they shoot us, they won't have any way of getting it."

They were halfway across when they felt the bridge suddenly lurch violently. Annja wrapped her arm around the rope railing next to her to steady her balance and to keep from sliding off, then chanced a look back.

Two of their pursuers had stepped out onto the bridge behind them. They were slowly making their way forward, but each step they took made the bridge sway dangerously to either side, creaking and groaning like an old rocking chair as it did. Annja had a sudden vision of the bridge giving way, plunging them all into the gorge below.

Apparently their pursuers must have imagined the same thing, for after another few steps they decided discretion was the better part of valor and retreated back the way they had come.

Garin suddenly swore beneath his breath.

Annja turned forward only to find the source of his distress. Michaels and several more of his henchmen were standing on the far side of the chasm. They must have found another trail and circled around ahead of them.

We're done, she thought.

As if he'd heard her, Michaels shouted, "Now what, Miss Creed? Intending to sprout wings and fly away like a little bird?"

Several choice replies sprang to mind, but she managed to keep her temper and not let them free. She was getting so tired of this, though. Why couldn't something go their way for a change?

"I want that location, Creed!" Michaels shouted.

"So come and get it!" she shouted back.

Beside her, she felt Garin stiffen. "What are you doing, Annja?" he asked.

"If the bastard wants the treasure, he can come out here and get the location. If he's dumb enough to do so, we'll use him as a hostage to force them to let us go."

It was a crazy plan, but she was all out of ideas. They couldn't go forward, they couldn't go back, and she had little hope that the bridge would support them indefinitely. Something was going to have to change if they were going to get out of this alive.

"How about I just shoot you instead?" Michaels threatened, raising his arm and pointing the pistol he held in his hand directly at them.

Annja tapped her head with one finger. "Go ahead

and shoot! Be awfully damn hard to get the coordinates at that point, since they're all up here!"

Michaels frowned, then lowered his weapon. He seemed undecided about his next course of action.

In the space of a few seconds the game had turned and she now held the upper hand. Annja was as surprised as Michaels that it had turned out this way, but she wasn't about to look a gift horse in the mouth.

If Michaels shot the two of them where they stood, he'd lose out on the coordinates and, in turn, the treasure. If he sent a group of his men across the bridge after them, from this side or from the other, the decaying structure was likely to come apart and plunge the whole lot of them into the rapids below, with the end result being the same. He couldn't even wait them out; the fact that they were on the bridge in the first place was sure to bring the park rangers running sooner or later. Someone had to have heard the gunshots and maybe have seen them by now, and even hikers carried cell phones these days.

If he wanted the treasure, he really didn't have much choice, she thought.

Michaels turned his back on her and began issuing instructions to the men with him. Since he was no longer shouting, the distance was too great for Annja to hear any of what he said, but she had little doubt it couldn't be good.

The bridge swayed as Garin tried to find some relief for his tiring limbs.

"You all right?" she asked, not daring to take her gaze off Michaels.

"For now," he replied. He was quiet for a moment and then asked, "Do you really know where it is?"

She answered without thinking. "It's right here in the gorge somewhere. Inside the old Genoa Mine."

Garin laughed. "I told him you'd find it."

Before she could ask what he meant, she was distracted by the sight of Michaels walking to the bridge and then striding out onto it, heading in their direction. She watched him approach until there was only about ten feet between them.

Rather than addressing her, however, Michaels looked past her to Garin instead.

"Time to live up to your side of the bargain," Michaels said, gesturing at Annja.

"What's he talking about, Garin?" she asked, without taking her gaze off Michaels. He still had a gun in his right hand and it would only take a moment's distraction for him to shoot.

"I don't have any idea," Garin replied.

Even as he said it, though, she felt the bridge sway slightly beneath his weight and heard the sound of a gun's slide being worked.

Her blood ran cold at the sound. Garin hadn't dropped the gun somewhere, after all, he'd just hidden it in his coat. Why would he do that? Could he have really cut a deal with Michaels? It wouldn't be the first time he'd disappointed her, but then again, why go through the charade of trying to escape if he only intended to double-cross her in the end? That was just too low, even for Garin. It didn't make sense.

Michaels, however, was more than happy to explain it to her. "Your friend Mr. Braden has a decided interest in the treasure, Miss Creed," he said, over his shark-tooth smile. "And I'm afraid it doesn't involve giving a share to you."

Annja felt the hairs on the back of her neck stand

at attention as she heard the truth in Michaels's voice. Behind her, Garin shifted positions, causing the bridge to rock a bit more wildly than before.

What the hell was he doing?

Still, she didn't dare turn around.

"The treasure's in the old Genoa Mine," Garin said. "She told me herself not two minutes ago."

Annja couldn't believe her ears. Garin had just given up their one bargaining chip, the one piece of information she'd been risking her life to protect!

Her dismay must have shown on her face for Michaels suddenly threw back his head and laughed. "Did you think I was just going to let you walk away?" he asked.

As Annja groped for an answer, Michaels looked at Garin over her shoulder. "Get rid of her," he said.

There was no way she could summon her sword, turn and deal with Garin before he shot her. She knew him, knew how fast he was with a handgun. He'd be watching for the sword and wouldn't hesitate to fire the second she moved.

He had her dead to rights.

She was trapped.

She wasn't the type to go down without a fight, however, and even though she thought it was futile she was still going to do her best to survive to fight another day.

With a shout she called her sword from the otherwhere, the cold steel blade flashing into existence in the space of a heartbeat. Time seemed to slow as she felt her fingers close tightly around the well-worn hilt, felt the bridge reacting to her sudden motion, shifting and rolling beneath her feet, watched as Michaels's eyes went wide at the sudden appearance of the weapon.

She had barely started her turn when she felt, and then heard, the gun going off behind her.

The bullet, the one she thought was destined to put an end to her time as the bearer of Joan's mystical sword, shot past her shoulder so closely that she felt the heat of its passage.

She watched in amazement as a bright red flower blossomed on the front of Michaels's shirt. She realized at the same moment that Michaels's expression of surprise didn't have anything to do with the appearance of her sword at all, but was rather a reaction to the sight of the muzzle of the gun held in Garin's hand being pointed in his direction.

Garin hadn't betrayed her at all!

The shot knocked Michaels backward a few feet into the rope railing and for a moment Annja thought he was going to tip right over it. But he managed to grab hold of the rope with his free hand and arrest his fall.

The gun in his other hand began to come up.

Behind her, she heard Garin give a wordless grunt of victory as he pulled the trigger a second time, intending to end this once and for all.

The hammer gave a dry click as it fell on an empty chamber.

In the space of a heartbeat Annja realized that she was too far away to reach Michaels, even with her sword, and they had only a split second in which to react before he fired his own weapon.

This close, the bullet was sure to hit one or the other of them.

Annja didn't stop to think, she just reacted, stepping backward into Garin and covering him with her body.

The muzzle of Michaels's gun loomed large before her.

A shot rang out, echoing through the gorge, and it took Annja a moment to realize she wasn't injured.

She hadn't, in fact, been shot as she'd fully expected to be.

Her gaze flicked to Michaels and she was just in time to see him drop to his knees on the bridge, his hands covering the eruption of blood that was now spilling from the hole in his throat.

He turned to face her, perhaps to plead for help, perhaps to curse her name with his dying breath, but never got the chance for either.

The wood he was kneeling on chose that moment to decide it had had enough and gave way with a loud crack.

One moment Michaels was kneeling before her, the next he was plunging into the seething waters below.

If he screamed as he fell, Annja didn't hear it, for the gorge was suddenly filled with the rhythmic sound of a helicopter's rotors. As she and Garin looked on, the black fuselage of a Dragontech Security helicopter came swooping down from above, armed gunmen leaning out the open doors on either side. The hail of bullets the gunmen sent slamming into the ground on either side of the bridge forced Michaels's thugs to run for their lives.

A glance upstream showed a dark-suited figure standing on the new bridge with what looked like a long-barreled rifle in his hands. He lifted a hand in greeting and a relieved Annja waved back.

For now at least, the threat was over.

40

"No, not that camera, you idiot! The other one!"

Annja watched Doug Morrell as he stalked over to the intern he'd been addressing and made short work of swapping out the video camera the young man had been holding with another one from the pile of equipment in the back of the van *Chasing History's Monsters* had rented to transport their gear. Normally it was Annja who got exasperated from Doug's undying eagerness and it was nice to see the tables turned for a change.

It had been two months since her rescue from the bridge over Tallulah Gorge by the operatives of Dragontech Security. Of course, they would probably still be searching aimlessly for their boss, Garin Braden, if they hadn't put two and two together after their systems alerted them to Annja's phone call with Doug and realizing she was trying to save Garin by finding the location of the treasure. Since Annja had given Doug the coordinates she'd discovered marking the location of the missing Confederate treasury, Dragontech's senior commander, Matthew Griggs, had quickly put a plan in motion and help had been on the way.

Of course, Annja hadn't known that at the time, so she'd been convinced that it was all going to end on that lonely windswept bridge.

Several times during the past two weeks she'd almost wished it had. The police investigation into the death of Blaine Michaels had been nothing short of grueling. Annja had spent hours being interviewed by law enforcement personnel from both sides of the Atlantic. Fortunately, her story was backed up not only by Garin himself, but also by several of Michaels's former henchmen, all eager to avoid harsher sentences by giving up their comrades in plea bargain after plea bargain. The deaths of Jimmy Mitchell, Bernard Reinhardt and Catherine Daley were laid at the feet of Blaine Michaels. In France, his former empire was reeling from revelation after revelation of the activities Michaels and his associates had been involved in. It wasn't a pretty picture.

In the United States, Annja's own illegal activities, including the desecration of a federal cemetery, not to mention failure to report a crime and fleeing across state lines, were all determined to be either self-defense or carried out under duress and with the intent of saving lives. Despite some pressure from various police agencies, and with the help of Garin's considerable influence, Annja was eventually cleared of any wrongdoing.

At last, they had returned to Tallulah Gorge in an effort to locate the final resting place of the missing Confederate treasury. And they were going to film it, as part of a special segment of the *Chasing History's Monsters* episode that Annja had started all those weeks before. She had tried to talk Doug out of it but he reminded her that she owed him so she went along with it.

Doug finally got the intern straightened out and wandered back to where Annja was waiting. With her was Steve Southwood, the park guide they had hired to help them with the day's shoot. It would be Southwood's job to lead them into the depths of the Genoa Mine to the coordinates that Captain Parker had indicated in his final message to his partner-in-crime, Jonathan Sykes.

It was a beautiful spring day. Annja was curious to see what it would bring. Southwood had informed them that the Genoa Mine had been sealed up by the parks commission more than fifty years earlier and he thought the chances were good that Parker's hiding place remained untouched, all these years later.

"Are we ready, Annja?" Doug asked.

She glanced at Southwood, got a nod of agreement and said, "Ready as we'll ever be."

"All right, then, let's get the show on the road."

Annja winked at Southwood, then stepped over to where the cameraman was waiting. She took the microphone from his hand, and set herself up in the spot they had chosen, with the mountains rising in the distance behind her. The cameraman counted down and gave her the signal to begin. Annja looked directly at the camera, smiled and began talking.

"Welcome once again to *Chasing History's Monsters*. Today we're in search of a monster of a different kind, a treasure of legendary proportions and, if all goes well, we hope to share the rediscovery of this important historical find with you as it happens."

Annja let the familiar rhythms of the show wash over her and gradually the smile she'd put on her face for theatrical purposes shifted into something more genuine. She'd worked hard to follow the clues Captain Parker had left behind and even though she knew they wouldn't find anything, with the fruition of her quest close at hand, she couldn't help but be excited to see it through to the end.

Annja thought about the note she'd received from Garin Braden after he'd flown back to Europe.

Thanks for the adventure! I'll consider the gold as payment for the expense I went to in order to rescue you. Until next time.

G.

She'd been angry at first but then she realized she'd never cared about the treasure for its monetary value, only for its historical value. And she had been able to find it, even if she didn't get to keep it or share her discovery with the rest of the world. She'd just have to add it to the list of secrets she tried to keep about herself, Roux and Garin.

But even as she struck out on the trail following Southwood toward the hidden location of the Genoa Mine, Annja couldn't help but wonder where her next adventure might take her and what dangerous activities might be lying in wait for her there, as well.

* * * * *

The Don Pendleton's
Executioner®
DAMAGE RADIUS

The Big Easy becomes a playground of destruction

A criminal kingpin has taken over the streets of New Orleans, and is not just dealing in guns, drugs and fixed fights—he's handing out death warrants. Before any more people disappear, Washington decides it's time to shut this operation down, and Mack Bolan is just the man for the job.

James Axler
Outlanders®

PLANET HATE

A self-styled new god hijacks humanity in his quest for ultimate vengeance…

With their greatest asset, archivist Brigid Baptiste, lost to the enemy, Kane and the Cerberus rebels are losing the battle—but not yet the war. As Kane succumbs to incapacitating hallucinations, Brigid's dark avatar lays siege to a special child who is the link to a ghastly pantheon of despotic rule.

Available February wherever books are sold.